MW00575730

BENEATH

THE JACK-O-LANTERN SKY

TALES OF SWEET HOLLOW

By
TYLOR JAMES

IS LIMITED TO 100 SIGNED AND NUMBERED TRADE PAPERBACKS

This is number ___43___

TYLOR JAMES

BENEATH
THE JACK-O-LANTERN SKY
TALES OF SWEET HOLLOW

BENEATH THE JACK-O-LANTERN SKY

TALES OF SWEET HOLLOW

TYLOR JAMES

WEIRD HOUSE

Introduction and text © 2022 Tylor James

ISBN: 978-1-957121-24-6

Edited by Curtis M. Lawson

Editor and Publisher, Joe Morey

Cover and interior design © by Cyrus Wraith Walker

Weird House Press
Central Point, OR 97502
www.weirdhousepress.com

THE DREAMS

Anyone could see that the wind was a special wind this night, and the darkness took on a special feel because it was All Hallows' Eve. Everything seemed cut from soft black velvet or gold or orange velvet. Smoke panted up out of a thousand chimneys like the plumes of funeral parades.

—"The Halloween Tree" by Ray Bradbury.

I spot the hills
With yellow balls in autumn.
I light the prairie cornfields
Orange and tawny gold clusters
And I am called pumpkins.
On the last of October
When dusk is fallen
Children join hands
And circle round me
Singing ghost songs
And love to the harvest moon;
I am a jack-o'-lantern
With terrible teeth
And the children know
I am fooling.

—"Theme in Yellow" by Carl Sandberg.

Black, and gold, and red and brown,
Olive, pink, and blue
What a riot of a gown—
What a medley hue!
What a way to go about—
Crimson cloak and vest!
October is a dancer
Dancing down the west.

—"October" by Annette Wynne.

INTRODUCTION

Hello, and welcome to Sweet Hollow.

This small and eccentric town is my home. At the edge of city limits, my wife, daughter, and I reside in a small cabin on Lake Ouspenskaya. It is autumn. Nearly Halloween.

The leaves dwindle from the trees, blanketing the ground in shavings of auburn. The sun is brilliant orange and melting into the russet earth, bringing on the twilight.

Within the following pages, I'll introduce you to many odd and gregarious characters about town, beginning with a strange man named Billy Rosenthal.

Then there's twelve-year-old Heather Beauregard, owner of the mysterious Haunted House Mystery Bank.

Not to mention Mr. Timothy Wallace, a local writer with a penchant for horror novels (his novelette, *In the Town of Sweet Hollow*, is available for your reading pleasure at the end of this book).

And let's not forget Kenny Vandermeer and his good friends, explorers of the legendary "Manor" on a Halloween midnight.

These are only a few of the characters I'll be introducing you to.

Listen: don't let the fact that Sweet Hollow is a small town make you think it isn't *enormous* in its scope of events and people. For here you will discover haunted toys, a ramshackle Manor, immortal creatures clothed in human flesh, a creepy old dance hall, human-sized mosquitos, and a man who transforms into a fish. (Yes, you've read that correctly.)

Now, I won't hold you back any longer. Let's take a walk down Main Street, you and me. Don't worry, I'll be there with you every step of the way.

Because good Lord, who *knows* what we might find?

Best,
Tylor James.

BILLY'S FIRST HAIRCUT

Billy Rosenthal caught his reflection in the barbershop mirror and smiled. Today was his eighteenth birthday. The laws of the land counted him an adult at last, capable of casting a vote, buying cigarettes, and going to war.

He would not 'officially' become a man, however, until his first haircut. This was the only sacred passage he was to endure—a silly, yet ancient rite designated by his religion. More precisely, his parent's religion.

Much like any child raised in a religious household, Billy hadn't been given a choice *what* to believe. 'Christian' children were only Christian in as far as their parents were, it seemed, and the same went for Jewish, Muslim, and Hindu children. Heck, if left to their own devices, Billy figured, kids probably wouldn't go along with any religion at all.

It'd always been his parents who'd taught him the ways of the Elder Gods. The rituals, the incantations, the sacrifices.

Yet even so much as mentioning their beliefs outside the house was forbidden, despite it being an impossible subject to avoid. With Billy's hair always unkempt and hanging down to his knees, the town's people wanted to know: *why, for God's sake?* What was he to say to them, if he couldn't speak of his religion? Billy's last resort had always been to switch the subject.

Home schooled for most of his life, Billy told his parents he wanted to attend public school. He desperately longed to make friends. His folks, although not pleased with his decision, believed in fostering independence, and thus agreed.

A terrible mistake. Billy hadn't made any friends at all attending Sweet Hollow High. Bullies were drawn to him like bugs to a porch light. They picked on him relentlessly—stealing his lunch, slamming his locker door on his fingers, and calling him names.

The names had been the worst. Every moniker referenced Billy's seemingly endless bedraggled hair. Sasquatch Billy, they called him. Or, take your pick: Sideshow Billy, Billy the Hairy Fairy, even Cousin Itt, from *The Addam's Family*.

Billy begged his parents to home school him again. Mother was agreeable. Father told him to stick to his guns. "A man's word is final, son," he'd said, lounging in his armchair with stoic repose. "Whenever you make a decision, it ought to be firm. Remember that."

Billy remembered all right—day after day, year after year, until Graduation Day.

Now, it was summer and he was free. He'd attend college in the fall, which meant even *more* freedom. With a haircut, he'd even have a chance to make friends. Heck, maybe he'd even land himself a *date*.

Billy's eyes flicked up to the mirror. Barber Carl, whom Billy had seen shuffle to and from the Barbershop since childhood, was a frowning old man with mile-long lines on his face. Carl worked the blades steadily, snipping away the mountainous cascade of brown hair which hung to the floor. Behind the overworked barber, Mom and Dad hugged each other beside the front door—all big, expectant smiles.

"We're proud of you, kid." Father beamed, briefly lifting his fedora.

Billy grinned.

Mother's hand lay over her heart. "Oh! All that beautiful hair …"

It was all she could say before breaking down into tears. Father held her, whispering consolations. Then he locked the door, pulling the shade down over the window.

Father had called a week in advance to schedule this special appointment at Carl's Barbershop. It was essential to the *Rite of Passage* that the only attendees be Mother, Father, Performer of Ceremony, and, of course, Billy himself.

Carl paused mid-snip, silver scissors suspended.

"Excuse me," he said over his shoulder. "Did you just lock my door?"

Father smiled handsomely. "Hope you don't mind. Intruders would only interrupt this special appointment we paid good money for."

"By intruders," Carl frowned, "do you mean, my *customers?*"

"You won't find any better customers than us, Carl."

The old man's forehead scrunched, as ancient and gnarled as tree bark. He scoffed, shook his head, then resumed cutting Billy's hair. Gritting teeth, he worked his fingers into the thick, filthy, greasy curtain, parting the bramble and snipping, snipping, snipping.

Weird family, Carl thought. *Nearly fifty years cutting hair, and I ain't never seen parents let their boy's hair get this long! He even outdoes the hippies that used to come in, back when they got their draft card. Long time ago, that was. Damn—the kid sure stinks, too. Hair like this cries out for a lotta shampoo. Bet he ain't ever used a drop of it. Wait a minute … what's this?*

Carl's scraggly eyebrows knitted into sharp, down-pointed arrows. Reaching into the thick fray of hair, he plucked out a monarch butterfly. His lips puckered as he held it eye level, examining faded, dusty wings from many summers past.

"Chrissakes, boy," he muttered. "Your hair is so long and dirty, it's got *bugs* in it!"

"Please," Mother said. "Let me have it, will you? As a keepsake?"

"Lovely idea." Father nodded.

Carl shook his head with incredulity, handing it over.

"How precious!" She smiled, delicately placing the butterfly inside her coin pouch before snapping it shut and burying it inside her purse.

"What religion you folks say you practiced?" Carl's brows raised into tall peaks.

"Just finish the haircut, Carl." Father winked.

The old man grunted his dismay, returning to his scissors.

Clip snip. Clip clip. Snip snip snip.

Locks, curls, and tresses floated down, forming a shaggy heap on the linoleum. Billy watched his identity slowly transform into a sharp young man. All those crude, merciless nicknames: Billy the Sasquatch, Cousin Itt, the Hairy Fairy—now mere blights of the past, and the past could just as well be forgotten.

The future lay ahead, bright and shining as the silvery gleam of Carl's scissors dancing in the light. Billy's heart pitter-pattered. He couldn't wait for this to be over. Couldn't wait to walk out into the summer sunlight as a new-made man, and ask the first good-looking girl he saw out on a date.

"Look, how *handsome*." Mother cried.

"Just like his old man." Father nodded appreciably.

Carl growled, muttering obscenities and wrinkling his nose. Further into the dense brush he foraged, buried up to his elbows at first, then gradually only to his wrists. The floor collected pounds of tousled curls, and the old man waded ankle-deep.

Suddenly he leapt back with a shout.

"What in blue blazing hell is *this?!*" Carl held the small, fur-matted skeleton up to the light.

"Link!" Billy exclaimed, his eyes illumined by recognition.

"Huh?" The old man wrinkled his nose, holding the rotten carcass at arm's length.

6

"My pet rat from when I was six," Billy explained. "Man, oh man. I always wondered where he went …"

"Well!" Father chuckled. "I'll be darned."

Carl tossed the damned skeleton over his shoulder. The bones clattered and rolled across the linoleum. Billy frowned, not appreciating the careless manner in which the old man tossed his once-beloved pet. Billy hoped when he grew old he'd be nice, not a curmudgeon like Carl.

"Holy balls, what now?" Carl muttered, unsnagging a '67 Convertible *Hot Wheels*.

"Jeez," Billy said, awestruck. "That was my favorite toy when I was four or five!"

"Ohh!" Mother exclaimed. "Let me have it!"

Carl chucked it impatiently across the room. Into the purse it went.

"Well, I'll be …" Father shook his head.

Carl spat, cursed, and grated his teeth through the job. The boy had so much hair, it was ridiculous. *Still, at least I'm gettin' nearer to done. Above the shoulders, at last. Another few minutes at most ….*

His fingers chanced upon something soft and rubbery. Billy winced as Carl yanked it out, along with a clump of hair that'd still been attached to his head.

"It's a friggin' *binky*," Carl said, numbly.

"Ohhhhh!" Mother began to sob. "That was Billy's first binky …"

"Bring it here please, Carl," said Father.

Carl snarled his dentures and chucked the binky.

Billy's father caught it high in the air, picked off the hair, and handed it to his mother. She kissed the dirty, smelly binky before dropping it into the deep, endless well of her purse.

Finally, Billy's hair was short enough for Carl to finish the job with his electric shaver—an antique Schick, produced way back in the 1930s. Billy's fingers dug into the leather armrests. He'd never touched an electric shaver in his life. The thing buzzed in his ears like an angry bumble bee.

Carl shaved Billy's hair incredibly short on the sides, with just an inch remaining on the top. Billy was amazed to see his scalp peeking through—as beautifully pale as freshly fallen snow. A few more strokes of the shaver would complete the ceremonial *Rite of Passage*. Billy braced himself. Mother and Father grinned and hugged each other tight, as if huddling for warmth in a cold wind.

Carl's brows knitted in a new onset of confusion. A vertical scar about seven inches long ran from the back of the boy's head to just past the topmost point of his cranium. *What an odd mark. This kid have brain surgery at some point? It'd explain why he'd be sensitive about cuttin' his hair short, I 'spose. Mighty pronounced scar ....*

Carl brought the shaver down for one last sweep, but not before his jaw dropped and his eyes grew large. The scar split open, revealing two rows of monstrous, jagged teeth. Carl froze, the shaver buzzing in his numb hand. He stared down into the slick red cavern of the boy's skull.

There wasn't even a brain behind those sharp, crimson-stained teeth. No, sirree.

However, there *was* a tongue.

The fleshy red tip jittered like a rattlesnake's tail, then shot up fast as a bullet, wrapping its warm wetness around Carl's neck. The antique shaver smacked the linoleum and broke, its buzzing immediately abated.

Carl shrieked. The tongue constricted tighter, cutting off his cries for help.

Billy's mother and father remained by the entrance, making sure no one outside got curious and tried the door. Billy watched this wild spectacle from the mirror, grinning with excitement.

Carl clutched the mucous-slicked tongue, attempting desperately to tear it away. His heart hammered, and his lungs felt on fire. The heels of his oxford shoes squealed, sliding across the linoleum as the tongue brought him dreadfully close to the open maw in the back of Billy's skull.

Placing his veiny, liver-spotted hands on either side of the gaping mouth, Carl began to push himself away. The tongue lashed tighter, and pulled hard. Carl howled, tears spilling down his gaunt face, as he was dragged closer, closer, closer ....

Sharp, bloodstained daggers glimmered—the last thing the old man saw before they sunk into the bones of his face, rapidly chomping like a pair of wind-up joke teeth.

Only, these teeth were no joke at all.

Carl's face shredded into unrecognizable, bloody soup. Strips of dark red flesh dangled from his forehead and cheeks. Eyeballs popped, running like egg yolk down the ragged contours of his face. The tongue pulled him inside Billy's head up to the neck, shoulders, ribcage ....

Frail old bones crackled and snapped, making it easy to pull the flaccid body through the mouth's narrow circumference. All the while, not a drop of blood splashed on the floor, the chair, or Billy.

Then the mouth snapped shut. Lips adhered. Only the oddity of a scar, or perhaps a rather strange birthmark, remained.

Silence. Billy turned his head this way and that, admiring his haircut in the mirror.

"All these years," he whispered, "and I hardly knew what I looked like!"

"Handsome, that's what you look like." Mother wrapped her arms around him, planting a kiss on his cheek. Father laid his strong, gentle hand on Billy's shoulder.

"You've done well, son," he shook his head, chuckling thoughtfully. "I remember *my* first Rite of Passage. Boy, had I been nervous as ever. You handled it bravely, son. Some don't handle the Passage well at all, you know. Some don't care for the blood. But now that you've completed the ceremony, you're a full-fledged man before the eyes of the Elder Gods. Ol' Barber Carl's sacrifice has satisfied Them, and shall satiate and sustain you well into old age."

"Will I look like Carl when I grow old, Father?" Billy asked, anxiously. "I didn't like the look of him, all wrinkled and ugly like a prune."

Father laughed. "No, son. The claws of time will inevitably leave their mark on you, but you'll never gain too many wrinkles, lines, or liver spots. Carl's blood, bone, and sinew will sustain you well into your one hundred fifties—take your mother and I, for instance. Then, once you get to be our age, you'll have children of your own, and you'll be there when they get *their* first haircut. Understand?"

Billy nodded. "Mind if I spend the rest of my birthday outside, Father? I wanna go down to Leo's Malt Shop. You get a free shake if it's your birthday."

"By all means." Father gestured toward the door.

Tearing off the plastic salon cape, Billy sprinted toward the door.

"William J. Rosenthal!" Mother scolded.

Billy's hand hovered above the knob. "Huh?"

"You forgot to give Mother a kiss."

Billy sighed, then strode over and gave her a peck on the lips.

"That's my boy. Now, go enjoy the day!"

She didn't have to tell Billy twice. Unlocking the door, he threw it open and ventured out into a cool summer breeze. He felt on top of the world, his smile as bright as the sun. Walking down Bradbury Avenue, the cracked street felt unusually strong and sturdy beneath his shoes.

He passed beneath the cool shadows of store canopies, their fringes fluttering in a breeze that tickled Billy's arms and whispered over his naked ears. He'd never felt more unburdened, happy, and free with all that hair gone.

The closed lips, tucked and obscured, tickled pleasantly beneath the sunlight pouring down like golden honey. With Barber Carl's blood flowing in his veins, he felt strapping and confident—thrilled to step into that vast expanse of future laying before him. One vaster and greater than that of any mortal.

"Get ready world!" Billy grinned, the bell above Leo's entrance door jingling as he stepped in. "Here comes the new and improved, Billy Rosenthal."

MOSQUITO SUMMER

*P*fffffft. *Pfffffft.*
Pffffffffffffffft.

"You gotta use so much of that stuff?" Kacy coughed.

Ted froze with the can of *Bug Off!* aimed at his forearm. A cloud of repellent hovered around them in the humid July air.

"M'yep," he replied, dousing himself. Their cabin porch filled with a haze of poisonous particles before he set aside the can.

Kacy waved at the air, launching into a coughing fit.

"Oh, stop that!" Ted grumbled, reaching into the plastic cooler beside his chair. He pulled out a can of Pabst. Cracked it open. "You're makin' it a big deal."

"You use too much of it," she said, getting up from her chair. At the bottom of the porch steps, she gazed out at Ouspenskaya lake. Their rustic motorboat bobbed gently at the end of the dock. Deep red clouds reflected upon the water. White plumes drifted on the wind—steam from Sweet Hollow's nuclear plant.

She watched the steam intermingle with the red clouds. Small cabins, much like their own, were scattered here and there on the opposite shore. Voices carried across the lake. Young, carefree, laughing voices. Kacy peered over her shoulder at Ted. He crushed the already emptied Pabst can, tossing it behind his chair. It clinked into an aluminum pile. He snagged another one. Kacy sighed.

Crack. He sipped the foam, took a long pull, then belched. Kacy turned back toward the lake.

Nnnnzzzz. A mosquito whined beside her ear and she swiped at it. The self-made breeze rippled her shoulder-length blonde hair. The insect went away for a second, then returned. *Nnnnzzzz.*

"Ted! Hand me that can, will you?"

"Ahhhhh," Ted said. "First ya accuse me of usin' too much. Now you want it, too."

"Just give it here." Kacy's mouth puckered with disgust.

Ted slowly set down his sweating can of beer on the side table. Picked up the *Bug Off!* Turned it this way and that, as if admiring it. He looked up. Showed her his gap-toothed grin.

Nnnnzzzz. "Come on!" she begged, swatting her arms at the air. "Please?"

"What'll ya do fer me if I give it to ya?"

"For Christ's sake, hand it over. I'm getting bit up, you asshole!"

A dry chuckle. Ted tossed the can.

Kacy caught it, aimed the can up into the air, and pressed the spray button.

Pfffft. Pfffft.

Pffffffffffffft.

A wind blew and took the haze of repellent up and away. Ted smiled as it disappeared into the clouds.

"Good sprayin'," he nodded. "Hope it kills the little bastards."

"They're *terrible* this year," Kacy said, now coating her arms and legs with a second coat. She collapsed into the chair beside Ted, feeling overheated, gross, and itchy. Her period was starting in too. The annoying cramps made her want to curl up into a ball and cry.

"Give me one of them beers," she said.

Ted did so. She cracked open the can, drank.

A tickle on her knee. Still sipping, she looked down the length of the can. A tiny mosquito, its long, needle-nose just about to—

SMACK! Beer spilled over the top of the can as her hand flew downward. A smear of blood was all that remained of the critter.

"Ugh." She grimaced, wiping the guts onto her denim shorts. "Let's go inside. The spray ain't helpin."

Ted guffawed. "No way. I wanna see the fireworks."

"Ain't even dark yet," she replied. "Might be another whole hour before they light 'em."

"We'll wait." His lips pursed over the can. Tipped his head back, Adam's apple bobbing.

"We'll get eaten alive if we do."

"Then so be it!" he shouted, beer-spittle flying from his mouth. "This is America's birthday, Kacy. We *always* sit and watch the young uns' cross the way light the fireworks. You wanna give up on our tradition? Fine by me. You go inside. Get!"

He crushed the umpteenth empty can, tossed it behind the chair.

Kacy stood, frowning. "You weren't always this way."

"What way, woman?"

"A mean old man," she replied. "I didn't marry a mean old man, you know. What's happened to us, Ted? Where did we go wrong?"

Ted gazed up at her. His cold blue eyes softened. His mouth opened, about to reply when—

POP-POP-POP-POP-POP-POP!!

Ted's attention snapped to the beach across the lake. A group of twenty-somethings were gathered, launching the first fireworks. Reds, whites, and blues flared up into the darkening sky, then fizzled.

"Whoo-hooooo!" Ted leapt to his feet, staggered a moment, then raised his beer. "The show has begun!"

The screen door creaked as Kacy flung it open. It smacked on the frame behind her. Then she kicked the inner door closed with the back of her foot. That way she wouldn't have to listen to Ted's inane cheering.

She kicked her shoes off, stuffing her socks into them. The cool, green tiles felt heavenly upon her bare feet. She walked through the main room into the back bedroom. Stripping out of her denims and t-shirt, she slipped into pajamas and got into bed. Tears streamed from her cheeks, wetting her pillow. A framed picture of her and Ted in mid-kiss at their wedding mocked her from the dresser. She turned away. The fresh bites on her arms and shins itched. She resisted the urge to scratch. Faintly in the distance, fireworks popped and snapped.

Darkening twilight shone through the window above the bed. Mosquitos tapped the window, hovered back, then tapped again. She fell asleep watching them.

Kacy patted Ted's side of the bed with fumbling hands. Still empty. She ambled out of bed. Put on her slippers. Stepped onto the porch.

Ted sat where she'd left him. The porch light attracted a cloud of mosquitos, moths, and tiny black bugs. Kacy gave the light a wide berth. Ted's mouth hung open. Red bumps dotted his arms and cheeks. She shook him. He moaned, smacked his lips.

"Ted, wake up! You're getting chewed up, you idiot."

A loud snore escaped him. Kacy rolled her eyes, then descended the porch steps on her way to the outhouse. Across the lake, the kids whooped and hollered over the blaring of country music. The sour smell of sulphur hung in the air. A mosquito landed on her neck. She swatted it dead. Her neck stung and itched.

She ran the rest of the way to the outhouse. Sat on the toilet and did her business.

Nzzz. Nzzz.

"Fucking A." She gritted her teeth. Tiny legs bounced against her forehead, which she smacked, then wiped the tiny entrails on the wall. Just as she began to wipe, something stung her left buttock. She shrieked, standing bolt upright. Looked down into the toilet's dark hollow. Several mosquitoes lingered inside, a few now hovering above the white seat. She could see them dance in the moonbeam shining through the skylight. They arose, bobbing in the air like corks on waves.

Kacy clapped the air with both hands like one of those wind-up monkeys with the tambourines. *CLAP-CLAP-CLAP*

"Die, you fuckers!" Pajama pants down to her knees, toilet paper still hanging from her butt, she clapped the bugs, making a sticky red mess of her hands. One of them landed on the bridge of her nose. Its thin, black proboscis poised to draw blood. She smacked it. Her nose stung, itched. Another on her ear. *Smack!* She winced, her ears ringing from the impact. One landed on her ankle. *Smack!*

They ascended out of the toilet by the dozens, swarming, buzzing, biting. She hadn't a chance. Quickly wiping her behind, she threw the paper down the hole, then ran outside. Across the lawn. Onto the porch. To hell with Ted. She slammed the cabin door shut, cutting off the noise of crickets, frogs, and the party across the lake.

The cabin was cool. Quiet. She slipped back into bed, her legs and face aggravated with bites. She started to itch every inch of herself with her long, sharp fingernails until the skin grew raw and bloody. Kacy tossed and turned, ruffling the worn sheets in misery. Then, a deafening roar.

Kacy froze in place. The walls and ceiling shook. Picture frames fell from the walls and shattered. She heard dishes from the kitchen shelves fall and crash. Heart palpitating, she grabbed a pillow and placed it over her head.

Everything became still. Looking about the darkened room, the place was a mess. Dresser drawers hung halfway out. Her bed had drifted five feet from the wall. A shattered piggybank and several pictures littered the floor. A crack ran along the ceiling.

Kacy's heart rate settled a bit. *What the hell just happened? An earthquake?*

Hardly possible. Wisconsin simply didn't have earthquakes. She thought about the kids partying across the beach. In the midst of their bacchanal, had they launched a firework at her cabin? If so, it must've been pretty big. She remembered Ted on the front porch.

"Ted?" she shouted. "Are you okay?"

What if he's been killed by the firework? His body mutilated, burned, smoking ...

Such thoughts arose in her mind like the answer to a mathematical equation—cold and emotionally vacant. Nonetheless, she knew the decent thing was to check on him. Make sure he was okay. She tiptoed around the broken shards on the floor, down the hallway, and into the main room.

NZZZZZZZRR! She jerked to her right. Outside the window, a glimpse of someone passing by. Her shoulders relaxed. *Must be Ted, assessing the damage. He's alive after all.* She sighed with relief, then grew tense again. *Ted's gonna be pissed at the damage done to the cabin. Probably pissed at all his bug bites too.*

Ted beat her when he was angry sometimes. Not often. But often enough.

NZZZZZZZRR! On her left, this time. Pine trees were the only scenery through the kitchen window. Except now ... a sickly yellow fog. It snaked around trees, caressing trunks and boughs with jaundiced tendrils. *Perhaps not a fog. Perhaps smoke.... . Oh, God. Is the cabin on fire?* She burst through the front door, stepping out onto the porch. Ted's chair was tipped over, as was hers. Empty beer cans littered the porch. Snapped branches, pine boughs, and other debris cluttered the lawn. Thick, yellow smoke hovered in a cloud over everything. The lake was obscured. Yet there appeared to be no fire.

Kacy hacked into her fist. The air tasted foul. Acrid. Worse than the bug spray. Her throat and eyes burned. She peered into the smoke.

"Ted?" She choked out his name. Her throat was irritated, dry as tree bark. The soles of her feet thudded to the end of the porch. Her toes skirted the edge. Balancing herself against the overhang beam, she peered over the side of the cabin, where she'd initially glimpsed Ted – *or was it him?* – passing by the window.

The smoke's too thick to see. No, wait …

A large black blot in the smoky distance. The blot swooped low, then zig-zagged upward, erratically moving through the air. Coming closer.

Not Ted. Definitely not Ted.

She dashed into the cabin. Shut and locked the door.

NZZZZZZZZZZZZZZRRRRRRR

The steady, obnoxious buzz was just outside the door. Kacy backed away. It sounded like an idling motor, yet oddly insectoid. Like a bumblebee trapped inside a microphone. The buzzing sound moved around the side of the cabin, then stopped at the window.

Its obsidian, compound eyes stared in at her. Hairy antennae scraped the glass. The thorax was bloated to soccer ball size. The abdomen was long, transparent, slick with fluids. Two prodigious wings with multiple cross-veins fluttered in place.

An inundation of shivers racked Kacy's spine. Her eyes widened, brimming with fear. It was difficult to breathe. She didn't know if it was due to the smoke she'd inhaled or the horror outside the window. The mosquito's impossibly large head cocked left, then right, as if taking mental notes on human terror.

NZZZZZRRRRRRRRR—a second unnerving buzzing, this time from the kitchen. Just like the other, it hovered outside the window, studying her as if she were an animal at the zoo.

Perhaps I am, she thought. Peach fuzz on the nape of her neck prickled. From above, an enormous burst of buzzing joined the insectoid cacophony. The noise was incredibly loud. She leapt back and screamed at the distinct sound of legs skittering across the roof.

Hot red pain surged in her foot and radiated up her ankle. She looked down. Glass from a broken dish stuck out of her heel. Gritting teeth, she removed the shard with one swift pull. Blood spurted. She hopped to the doorway and donned her sneakers, not bothering with socks. She looked up when the buzzing died away.

Silence. The creatures were gone.

She trembled all over, looking out the windows. She knew whatever conjured the sickly smoke, whatever caused the mosquitos to blow up a million times their size ... had nothing to do with fireworks. The kids across the lake were probably dead. Attacked by the ice dagger proboscises of a thousand, blood-thirsty—

Shaking her head, she pushed the gory images from her mind. If she wanted to survive, she would have to focus. *Keep sharp, girl,* her father would have said.

She whispered her father's advice. "Keep sharp, girl. Look both ways before crossing the street. Make good decisions. Keep sharp."

Kacy swallowed the lump in her throat and tried to think what to do. What to do.

Her eyes widened. *Ted's twelve-gauge. Should be in the back corner of our closet. Boxes of ammunition heaped in a pile beside it. Told him a hundred times to move it to a safer location. He never did ... thank God.*

She checked the closet. It was there. She pulled the string for the closet light. *Click.* Nothing. Power was out. The only light source came from the moonlight through the windows, dully dispersed through the yellow smoke. She wondered if the entire town of Sweet Hollow was out of power, as well. Then she gasped, half out of shock, half out of that exhilaration of fitting the last piece into a jigsaw puzzle.

The nuclear plant. It had detonated somehow. The yellow smoke was radioactive! And she had breathed it in. Her lungs suddenly ached, seeming to shrivel in her chest. She thought of Ted. There was no doubt now that he was dead. If the mosquitos hadn't gotten to him, the radiation surely had. She imagined him facedown on the beach,

BENEATH THE JACK-O-LANTERN SKY

choked with smoke, eyes wet and bulging, the radiation damaging his cells, rotting his brain and she would be next, by God, and she deserved it for leaving him out there on porch, didn't she? She was next, next, next—

"NO!" She closed her eyes, took a breath.

She repeated it, calmly this time. "No."

Keep sharp, girl. If you want to live through this. If you want to survive. Keep sharp.

Kacy loaded the magazine with four sabot slugs, just as Ted had shown her on the shooting range. She cocked the receiver, then stuffed a box of shells into the back of her pajama pants, drawing the waistband tight.

THUD THUD THUD THUD.

Someone pounded on the front door. Kacy froze, cradling the shotgun to her chest. Was it possible one of those *things* could knock on the door? Reflecting on the size and thickness of the insect's legs and antennae, she figured it was.

THUD THUD.

"For God's sake, Kacy … *Please!*"

Ted!

Gooseflesh rippled down Kacy's arms. She ran out the bedroom, sending fragments of fallen objects sliding across the tiles. Her hand reached the doorknob. It was cold to the touch. She shuddered and … didn't open the door. Ted continued to pound with his fists.

"Kacy! Let … me … the fuck … in! For God's sake!"

She sobbed, not understanding her hesitation. Doubling over, she gagged, nearly vomiting. As she forced the contents of her stomach to remain inside, she realized she hated Ted. Hated him with all her heart, all her guts. A part of her wanted him to die out there. Wanted him to suffer and choke on the radioactive smoke and even … Yes. She wanted to laugh. Just as *he* had so cruelly laughed when she'd coughed and hacked on the bug spray earlier that evening.

THUD THUD THUD THUD.

"KAAAACCCYYY!!!"

After a last futile blow to the door and jiggling of the knob, he was silent. Kacy's blood throbbed in her temples. Guilt overwhelmed her. Her stomach lurched.

I can't do this. No matter how mean and cruel he's been over the years. I can't just let him die out there. It's inhuman.

She unlocked and opened the door, peeking out into the yellow, smoky night.

WHACK! The door flung inward, brutally smashing into her right shoulder. She fell sprawling on her back, the shotgun clattering to the floor. A silhouette in the doorway. Ted.

… No. Not quite. The dark outline was of a man of identical height and width, except the head was grotesquely misshapen and bulbous. The figure stepped inside the room. Kacy saw it clearly.

She snatched the shotgun from the floor, aimed upward. Atop the shoulders, in place of Ted's unshaven, round head and cold blue eyes ….

Black compound eyes shimmered at her. The antennas, each three feet in length, scratched the ceiling. The spear of its proboscis pointed at her. It quivered, prepared to stab into her flesh and suck her blood.

The shoulders twitched spasmodically as it approached. Something burst out of the plaid fabric covering its back, now peeking from behind Ted's pale, limp arms—two wings, slick with blood.

Kacy's blanched face stared up at it. A trail of blood spotted the floor as the thing twitchingly approached. It stood over her now, lowering its quivering sword-nose toward her face. *NNNNNNNZZZZZZZZZZZ*

Kacy aimed at its head and pulled the trigger.

BLAM!! A flash escaped the barrel as her shoulder jerked with the recoil. The head exploded in a violent gush of blood and brains. Gore splattered the carpet, walls, and Kacy's face. She scrambled backwards before Ted's headless corpse could collapse on top of her.

Her chest heaved with sobs. Tears ran off her chin, red with blood. She wiped the snot dripping from her nose with the back of her hand. Shakily, she picked herself up from the gore-splattered floor.

NZZZZR. She aimed the shotgun at the doorway. The mosquito's wings fluttered. It pointed its long, black nose at her, and flew inside. She let out a breath, then fired. The thing exploded like a balloon of guts. Blood flew into her mouth. It tasted disgustingly of bitter copper and chemicals. She spit it on the floor.

To her despair, the collective buzzing returned, surrounding the cabin on all sides.

Keep sharp, girl. Her father's aged, trembling voice reminded her. She took a deep breath.

Pulling the dented ammo box from the back of her pants, she loaded two fresh bullets to keep the chamber full. She couldn't stay in the cabin. Even if she shut and locked the door again, it was only a matter of time before those buzzing monstrosities forced their way in.

As if in confirmation, the window in the back bedroom shattered. The buzzing was louder, invading the space inside the cabin. Kacy ran into the kitchen, fetched the keys to Ted's pick-up off the wall, and raced outside. She looked left, right. One of the creatures hovered at the far end of the porch, its form barely discernible through yellow haze. She fired the twelve-gauge at it. Its shadow dispersed, the guts appearing black in the dark as it splatted the walls and porch floor. Slimy innards dripped from the ceiling, hitting the floorboards with a sickening *plop.*

Inhaling the horrid smoke, she did her best to hold it so as not to breathe in more. Stumbling down the steps, then the hill, she collapsed on all fours onto the wet beach. She let out the breath she'd been holding, rapidly taking in air. The smoke rose with the heat. The air nearest to the ground was clean.

The buzzing was only slightly more distant. *Perhaps they think I'm still in the cabin. God, I hope so.*

The beach tapered off somewhere on her right, where a dirt road should be, as well as Ted's pick-up. She couldn't see the silhouette of the vehicle, nor the road through the smoke. But there were more vile bloodsuckers; zig-zagging and hovering to and fro like fleshy drones. They'd spotted her leaving the cabin after all. The truck wasn't an option.

Kacy groaned, getting onto her feet. Bent at the waist to escape most of the smoke, she ran off the beach and down the length of the dock. Hundreds of dead perch and northern pike floated fins-up on the water, underbellies white as snow. The small fishing boat buoyed against the foam breakers against the dock. She hopped in, setting the shotgun on the floor. Untied the ropes attached to the dock beams. Pushed off. She primed the engine of the Mercury outboard motor and yanked the pull cord. A fluttering rumble, then nothing.

NZZZZZRRR. Looking over her shoulder, she whimpered at the shadows descending onto the beach.

Keep sharp, girl. She concentrated on the Mercury. The cord whispered dryly when she pulled it. The buzzing behind her grew, creeping onto the dock.

She yanked. A rumble. Nothing.

She pulled again. Again. Again.

At last, the rumble turned into a gritty roar. She revved it, then squeezed on the gas, putting as much space between her and the dock as possible. A foul wind blew back her hair. Shafts of moonlight broke through holes in the smoke cloud. For a moment, it was beautiful. But then Kacy thought of those horrible photographs of Japanese men, women, and children who'd barely survived the bombing of Hiroshima. Their contorted bodies, misshapen heads, and discolored flesh brought nausea to the pit of her stomach.

She hadn't noticed the color of the water until now. It was dusky yellow, like the smoke hovering above. The gritty whine of the anachronistic engine drowned out the creatures behind her. She dared not look back. She throttled the gas trigger, hoping to reach the other side before ... she didn't want to think of it.

The burning in her eyeballs made it difficult to keep them open. She ignored the dry, constricting sensation inside her throat. She hunched awkwardly in the boat to escape the smoke. Peering eye level at the approaching beach, she spotted the dock. Several plastic boxes with burnt-out fuses sticking out the tops remained.

Afraid the mosquitos would catch up, Kacy let off the gas too late. The boat brushed past the dock. The propellers rammed into the bank, grinding violently to a halt and killing the engine. She grabbed the shotgun from the floor, then leapt over the boat's side. She sloshed through the urine-hued shallows, tromping up beach onto the lawn. Although she refused to look back (thinking of that Bible story where Lot's wife looks over her shoulder and turns to a pillar of salt), she heard them approaching.

NZZZZZZZRRR - NZZZZZZZZZRRRR - NNZZZZZZZZZRRR. They swooped and dived in the air, closer, closer. Kacy's heart pounded. Her eyes stung as if prodded with needles. Her head throbbed with a migraine. She raced uphill through the sickly yellow atmosphere. The front door of the cabin flew open. Several people appeared on the front porch.

The kids? They're alive? As she drew close, she realized this was not the case. Dressed head to toe in yellow hazmat suits, they nearly blended in with the smoke. For one frightening moment, she saw mosquito heads.

But they were only gas masks.

Kacy waved her arms in the air and screamed for help, then realized what a maniac she must look like. She dropped the shotgun onto the ground, and kept her hands in the air.

Muffled voices shouted for her to get down.

She dropped onto her stomach. Grass blades tickled her cheeks. The people in the hazmat suits darted down the porch steps and raised what appeared to be rifles with extremely long barrels up into the air. Vibrant jets of red-yellow flame burst continuously from the barrels.

Kacy's back was uncomfortably hot from the heat. A terrible screeching sounded above. She rolled onto her back, looked up. Dozens of the mosquitos zig-zagged in distress. Their bodies popped under the hot flames like knots in a log. Their wings shriveled. Each dropped to the ground with a dull *thud,* now little more than smoldering heaps.

The yard was soon littered with black, crispy corpses. A gloved hand grabbed Kacy's arm, yanking her to her feet. She faced a black gas mask. Behind the two ovals of thick glass, hard eyes glared, seeming to look her over from head to toe to make sure …

What? To make sure I'm not turning into one of them? One of the mosquitos?

"Ma'am, as you're well aware, you are in grave danger." His baritone voice was muffled, yet comprehendible. "You will come with us. We will do our best to keep you safe."

"Who is us?" she asked, afraid of where they'd be taking her.

"The Army Chemical Corps, ma'am," he replied. "In exchange for our protection, we ask that you peaceably cooperate. Though you may not have experienced any symptoms yet, make no mistake —you *are* infected. Atomic radiation is altering your cell DNA as we speak. Therefore you are to do as we say and when we say it. Understood?"

The man's voice was harsh and cold. His grip on her arm hurt. But she nodded complacently, knowing she hadn't much of a chance on her own. Somewhere on the smoggy lake, the noise of more mosquitos drew near.

Several soldiers seized her, dragging her to an army truck parked near the dirt road beside the cabin. They swung open the backdoor and extended a metal plank, guiding her up and into the back. Twenty or so people sitting on steel benches looked up at her. Their eyes were red, nearly swollen shut. Their lips purple. Their faces lemon yellow. Most of them were men.

One woman lay on the floor in the fetal position, twitching spasmodically. White foam cascaded over her lips and chin. Her eyes were shiny black saucers. Mosquito eyes. A low buzzing emanated from her bulging throat.

They pushed Kacy further in. She tripped, catching herself on a bench before she could hit the floor. She scanned the people staring up at her. Their convulsive, jaundiced, red-eyed countenances frightened her. Some of them were the young partiers. The metal plank slid back into place with a *clank*.

"Wait a minute!" Kacy spun around. They gazed up at her through the oval windows of their masks. Some appeared angry. Others melancholic.

Her stomach twisted in on itself. Despair washed over her. She heard somebody whimpering, then realized it was her.

CLANG! One of the soldiers swung the door shut in her face. Several bolt-locks clanked and rattled into place. It was pitch-black inside the truck. The space echoed with ragged, labored breaths. The sound of people trying to breathe with half-closed windpipes.

The engine started, and the motion of the truck moving uphill knocked her onto her butt. She sat kitty-corner to the door, crying.

Someone lay a hand on her arm. Kacy wasn't sure if it was a gesture of comfort or one of predatory intent. All the same, her eyes stung severely, even out of the smoke. Her body ached, the bones beneath her flesh brittle and thin. Sweat beaded from her pores, reactivating the itchiness of all those mosquito bites on her arms, legs, and face. Her migraine heightened into agonizing pain, as if her head might split open. She shivered in the corner, drenched in sweat, the twists and turns of the truck taking her God-knew-where.

She felt like a steer on its way to the slaughterhouse.

The hand on her arm advanced to her chest. Another hand touched her, then yet another. In the darkness, the clammy hands raced up and down her body. Touching her in places she didn't want to be touched. Next, she felt wet coldness.

Tongues of dying, radioactive men.

Kacy cried, shouted, demanded they stop.

They did not stop. The hands ripped and tore her clothes. Clutching, grasping hands of desperation. Anger. Sadness. Fornication. Hands of death that suffocated her more than the yellow smoke.

Kacy threw fists into the dark, her knuckles smacking cold flesh. It seemed to only encourage them. As they turned her onto her belly, she could hear that woman on the floor near the back … buzzing.

Her noise grew steadily, until even the truck's deep rumbling engine was drowned out.

Alone in the dark, the hungry and the desperate taking her all at once, she closed her stinging eyes and listened to the steady insect thrum.

NNNNNNNNNNNNNZZZZZZZZZZZZZZZZZZZZZ

To her utter horror, she realized the noise wasn't just coming from the woman.

It was coming from her own throat.

ONE MORE NIGHT
WITH SNOW WHITE

Sunlight streamed through the window, making dust motes glimmer like pixie dust. You would've thought the morning a serene and tepid affair. The kind of morning where you wake up, yawn, stretch, gulp down a pot of coffee, and greet the good day. Except it wasn't that sort of day. Not in the slightest.

Listen. I've been incredibly lonely since the day my wife of fifty-three years packed her soul into a travel bag and rushed away to the Pearly Gates—she'd taken a bus to get there, a big bus which she should've seen coming, but didn't, and although I wasn't there on Bloch Street where it happened, people say Saint Peter greeted her instantly—no suffering, no hospital overnights, and no goodbyes.

So, when I awoke to find a woman in my bed, you can imagine how surprised I was. I blinked six times and pinched myself, convinced I was dreaming.

I wasn't.

Her eyes were closed. Her face had a remarkable pallor, even in the dawn's amber light, and her features were placid, peaceful, and perfect. Long eyelashes, cute button nose, full lips, and a head of silk brown hair splayed on the pillow and cascaded down her shoulders. A white nightgown extended to her ankles.

I began to wonder if I'd done something crazy during the night. Maybe I'd gone down to Sweet Hollow Pub and got good and drunk and, apparently, extraordinarily lucky—for she was beautiful, laying there, a veritable Snow White.

She even held a bouquet in her hands, resting atop her bosom.

My curiosity piqued, I reached out and stroked the flowers, the yellow white flowers that weren't flowers at all, but petals of plastic.

The stems were green, brittle straws.

Clutching my head, I struggled to recall the previous night. What had this woman and I said to each other? What did we do, besides get so thoroughly drunk as to render me amnesic? My neurons fried with Sisyphean cognitive exertion. At last, I gave up the ghost.

I couldn't remember a damned thing about last night. I had no idea how we'd met, what we'd shared, nor how I managed to coax such a gorgeous, young lady into bed. Did we make love? She was clothed and I still had skivvies on, so it appeared not. Did we kiss, at least?

The only thing I remembered was drinking a hot cup of non-caffeinated hibiscus tea, drowsing through an episode of *Kolchak*, then crawling into bed.

My eyes bulged.

Of course! I hadn't gone to the pub. Hadn't gotten drunk. Hadn't met this woman. I'd simply went to bed, sad and alone, and slept. I used to pray before bed, but I hadn't done that since Donna died.

Had God, out of His infinite mercy, delivered this woman unto me as a companion in my time of loneliness?

I looked over at her and knew it wasn't true. I don't know how I knew, I just did. Besides, it was a rather sexist concept, wasn't it? Some Pimp-God delivering women into old men's beds during the night?

Nah. I don't think so.

So, what was the reason? Was this person homeless and simply in need of a bed? I imagined her wandering the shadowy streets, trying my door sometime after midnight, sneaking inside, lying down next to me and falling asleep. It was a crazy thing to do, but perhaps she was crazy. Perhaps I'm lucky she didn't grab a knife on her way through the kitchen and slit my throat.

Perhaps, perhaps, perhaps.

It was all I could think, watching her sleep.

Asleep. Was she?

My heart began to thump in my chest. *Oh, Christ!*

She was dead. I understood this with sudden, dreadful certainty. This woman had broken into my house during the night and lain down in my bed to die. Now, I'm lying next to her frigid, lifeless body. How will I explain this to the police? They'll think me a murderer, or someone deranged and perverted—a necrophile!

I reached over, placing two fingers under her wrist for a pulse.

I heaved a sigh.

Alive. Very much alive. Her flesh was cold, but not dreadful corpse-cold. Now, studying the flowers, I could see them rise and fall with the gentle swell of her bosom.

Her being alive didn't make her any less of a mystery. It was imperative that I wake her up and question her as to what the hell she thought she was doing in my bed.

"Excuse me?" I said.

Dust motes floated in the dawn light, one landing upon her luscious eyelashes.

"Excuse me," I repeated, loudly.

Her chest rose and fell, steady as sea-tide. I sat up and shook her with both hands, and kept shaking wildly.

"Wake up, miss! You must wake up!"

She did not wake up.

I made breakfast. A plate of scrambled eggs and two strips of bacon. Not for me. For her. I brought it to her while she lay in bed. Something I used to do for Donna, on occasion.

"Breakfast?" I asked, with a smile. "Breakfast, my dear?"

Silence. A bright eleven o'clock sunbeam slanted across her face; her snow-white face and red lips and closed eyes and comatose stillness.

Bringing the plate to her nose, allowing the steam of fresh eggs and bacon to enter her nostrils, I waited patiently.

She did not stir.

I sat at the edge of my bed, eating her breakfast. Rude of me, perhaps, but I was starved.

"Comatose," I muttered, chewing on the word as much as the eggs. "Is that the matter, darling? You can't talk, walk, eat, because … you're in a coma?"

Her silence seemed answer enough.

Afternoon settled into late evening, then the curtain of twilight sky drew back, revealing a cosmic arena of a million glimmering stars and a rising crescent moon. I carried her into the backyard and laid her beside me upon a reclining beach chair. The night was warm, but I noticed goosebumps rise on her arms and promptly covered her with a blanket.

We lay back, facing the universe together; one of us beholding countless burning suns, the other viewing the back of her eyelids.

"Isn't it beautiful, Snow White?" I asked.

I'm not exactly sure when I began calling her that. But she needed a name, and Snow White seemed fitting enough. I reached beneath the blanket and, for the first time in many years, felt the soft touch of another human being. Our hands rested one atop the other.

I wondered, vaguely, if Donna would be ashamed of me—holding hands with another woman.

But Donna is gone, I told myself. She would have wanted me to be happy. Right?

I took my eyes off of infinity, and gazed upon yet another infinity—Snow White's immaculate ivory face, the subject of a timeless fairy tale re-told countless times over in a million books and movies and plays and songs and voices. There I was, lying next to a living legend. An enduring myth that would not fade for as long as there were people on Earth and stars in the sky.

I leaned toward her, knowing I shouldn't, knowing that it was wrong, but I advanced closer, closer and she smelled of luscious lilacs, and my lips, at last, touched hers gently, gently as velvet petals falling, falling upon the moon-swept breeze ...

Eternity echoed in my ears.

Then I drew back, waiting for her eyelashes to flutter and her eyes to recognize the face of her one true love, the only person who could disperse the spell of her slumber.

And I waited still.

It was crazy allowing life to go on like this, day after day, and I knew it.

One more night with Snow White, I decided, then I'll call the police first thing in the morning. Tell them what's been going on. Somebody's gotta be missing this woman, after all. Yet here I am, a selfish old man keeping her all to myself.

I gazed across the dinner table. She sat in a chair, head slumped back, exposing her pearl white throat. On first sight, one would've thought she was dead. I knew better, though. It's of my nature to be a little paranoid, and over the past week, I had obsessively checked her pulse—once even laying my ear against her bosom in search of a heartbeat.

Thump-thump.

Thump-thump.

Strong and steady, like a river current that sweeps you up and takes you away. I listened for hours, and thought of Donna.

"It's nice having you in the house," I explained to her. "Nobody wants to live alone, Snow White, and nobody wants to die alone either. Still, I can't take care of you here. Can't feed you properly, and you need your sustenance. Can't bathe you either, lest someone should find out and that won't look very good on my reputation, what little there is. You understand, dear, don't you?"

Tears dripped from my chin, which startled me. I didn't know I'd been crying, until that moment.

"Forgive me," I said, getting up from my chair.

Then I scooped Snow White up into my arms and carried her to bed, where she would stay for one more night, and one more night only.

Sometime in the night, I got out of bed to pee. Trundling down the hallway, I halted. A shadow was cast in the night-light I kept plugged in the kitchen. I've lived in this house for half a century, and I know every shadow in this place. This shadow was utterly foreign.

It couldn't have been over three feet tall. A stout little body with a head that came to a point.

"Who goes there?" I hollered, heart hammering.

The shadow didn't move. Just remained stretched across the kitchen linoleum, as if in waiting.

I decided who or whatever it was wouldn't have to wait. My bare feet slapped the hardwood floor of the hallway, then onto the linoleum. Flicking a wall switch, the kitchen flooded with light.

An open package of saltines laid upon the counter. In the otherwise empty sink sat a bowl crusted with what appeared to be

34

tomato soup. My forehead scrunched. I didn't recall having any crackers or soup.

I moved toward the open package of saltines, then stubbed my toe and howled. Hopping around on one foot, gritting my teeth, I looked down to see what had obstructed my path.

There it was.

The shadow come alive.

"Chrissakes," I muttered, stooping low for observation. "How did you find your way inside my house?"

The smiling, ceramic face of one of my garden gnomes beamed up at me. Chunks of moist, black soil clung to its boots. Then, something appeared in my periphery. I straightened and looked all about the room.

Another gnome stood kitty-corner between the kitchen and dining room. Yet another sat atop my refrigerator, looking far and away, as if on a mountain top. One mischievously peeked from behind my waste bin, like a child playing hide-and-seek. Now that my eyes had adjusted to the light, I could see they were everywhere. I counted them.

Seven.

Seven gnomes in my kitchen. A package of crackers open, which I never touched. A crusty bowl in the sink, which I never used. How does this happen? Who could've done this? Neighborhood kids pulling a prank? Or were these gnomes somehow … alive? Animated in the night, until their owner shambles out of bed and they freeze to avoid discovery?

… Nonsense. Someone had obviously been in my house, damn it, and I was going to get to the bottom of it.

My sleep-crusted eyes focused, studying every oddity in the room. My pulse steadied, and the adrenaline flooding my veins took a backseat. I wasn't frightened anymore, so much as curious.

I walked over to the front door, checking to see if it was locked. I could've sworn I'd locked it. Ever since Snow White showed up, I've been much more attentive to locking up at night.

The door was unlocked.

Gazing down at the floor, a trail of dirty footprints.

Small, dainty feet. Not nearly as tiny as a gnome's would be—at least that crazy theory could be ruled out—but small, like a woman's. I traced the trail from my front door through the dining room, into the kitchen, and then down the hallway and, finally, into my … .

Snow White.

But it couldn't have been her! She was comatose. Gone on a long journey with the Sandman. Lost in an abyss of slumber, a sleep so deep not even a firetruck could've awakened her. But it made sense, in an odd way, didn't it? The saltines and soup out, because I never fed her and she must've been starving. And the seven gnomes were, in essence, the seven dwarves.

I darted into the bedroom, throwing on the lights.

Snow White lay in bed, her face pale and tranquil, and her gown straight and clean, except … .

The soles of her feet were grubbed with topsoil.

Stomping over to her side of the bed, I grabbed her shoulders and shook her.

"Snow White!" I shouted. "I know you're awake, so answer me!"

I bent over and shouted into her ear as loud as I could:

"WAKE UP!"

She winced, and my eyes widened. Snow White's face had actually *winced* in response to my voice. I could hardly believe it, yet at the same time I'd expected it. A sense of betrayal and confusion quivered in my blood as I leaned toward her.

"You moved," I spoke gently. "Your face twitched when I shouted just now. Give up the game, whoever you are, and tell me what you are doing here. Are you trying to drive me crazy? Are you trying to be cruel, tearing up what's left of this old man's heart?"

At last, Snow White's eyelashes batted open.

Her deep brown eyes shimmered with tears.

"Please, mister." Her voice quivered. "Don't make me go back. I hate it there."

I took her hand and squeezed. "For God's sake, lady, don't make you go back where? Where did you come from?"

"The Palace of White," she replied, swallowing a lump in her throat. "Everything there is white, you know. The walls, the floors, the ceiling, the uniforms, even people's minds … and the nurses, why, they won't let anybody in unless they're crazy! I can't have my true love's kiss if the only ones they let inside are crazy. Please, you're a nice old man. Let me stay, I beg you!"

I stared into her dilated eyes, which brimmed with fear and hope. Everything made sense now; a truth that threatened to crush me. Snow White was an escapee from the Sweet Hollow Psychiatric Hospital, no more than a few miles west. Out of all the places she could've hidden, out of all the houses she could've stumbled into, she'd stumbled into mine.

"The dwarves and I, we can help with all your chores too," she added, plaintively.

"My poor dear," I whispered. "You can't stay here."

"Why not?" She began to sob.

"Because, darling," I replied, my heart breaking at the sight of her distress, "When I kissed you beneath the stars, you didn't wake up."

I made the phone call in the kitchen, where the seven gnomes watched with cheeky, lunatic smiles. Snow White remained in the bedroom, sobbing her eyes out, and I'd be lying if I said I wasn't doing the same.

They came and took her away. I was holding her hands when they arrived, attempting to comfort her as much as myself. They ripped her from me, the orderlies, and I watched them drag the shrieking, writhing Snow White out of my house.

"I should've awoken!" she screamed. "You're my one true love! My one and only—"

The door slammed shut, muffling her cries with an abrupt conclusion to my final night with the beautiful, lost, and broken Snow White.

ONE WEEK LATER

The house was silent again—rooms of barren sunlight and floating dust. At night, the stars came out, but there was no one beside me to behold them with. Once more, I was adrift in a cosmos full of stars yet empty of meaning and devoid of love.

And yet life does take its turns, doesn't it? My bi-weekly visit to the laundry mat brought quite a surprise, point in fact. While transferring clothes from washer to dryer, there came a tug on my sleeve. I turned around, assuming it must be someone more in need of the dryer than myself.

She had kind blue eyes and a bright smile.

"Hello," I smiled back, thinking vaguely she must've been about Donna's age when she'd passed.

"Pardon me," she said, "I just wanted to let you know that I admire you for what you did."

"Oh," I said, searching my mind for recent heroic deeds and coming up short. "What'd I do, miss?"

"You took care of that lady who escaped from the hospital." She shrugged, as if embarrassed to bring up the subject. "I read about it in the paper. It's a sad story, of course, but you did the right thing, calling the police."

"You think so?"

"Absolutely."

"That's very kind of you." I beamed. "And I'm sorry, I didn't catch your name?"

"Marsha," she replied, with a smile so brilliant it deserved an award.

"Duncan."

We shook hands then and chatted for the next hour while we did our laundry. Marsha was a widow. Her husband, John, had died several years back from a stroke. Mustering up my courage, I asked her out to dinner.

Butterflies fluttered in my stomach the moment she accepted.

We enjoyed a spaghetti dinner at my place, our faces lit softly by golden candlelight. Then we walked into the backyard, and lay together in the beach chair, gazing up at the stars.

At some point, I'd fallen asleep.

Fallen asleep, only to be awakened at the gentle brush of Marsha's lips on my own.

My eyes opened, gazing up into her kind and tender face, backlit by a billion burning suns.

And as we leaned in for another warm, gentle kiss, I thought to myself, "Once upon a time ..."

IF FISH COULD SCREAM

A saran-wrapped turkey sandwich smothered with mustard. A zip-lock of unsalted cashews, pecans, and prunes. An apple, rinsed and delicately polished with a kitchen towel. These were the gifts of a loving wife who assured 'her man was taken care of'.

Susan's words, not his.

Lawrence Chaney would just as soon pack his own damn lunch. His wife, however, insisted she provide his sustenance. "Besides," she'd smirked, handing him his lunch cooler, "If it were up to you, you'd pack nothing but beef jerky."

She wasn't wrong. Beef jerky was an essential on any fishing trip. Still, the sandwich was delicious and he was grateful to Susan for preparing it.

Lawrence reached into the small red cooler, located on the floor of *Georgina*—his beloved boat. Cracking open a Pabst, he washed down the sandwich in one sudsy swig. Drinking alcohol went unadvised by doctor and wife alike, due to his heart condition. So, this would be his own little secret.

He'd been out in the boat all morning catching diddly-squat, and that was fine. He was just happy to be outside in this penultimate week of summer, bathed beneath the light of a dying star which would inevitably give way to a short autumn, followed by a long cruel winter. Should he pull up anchor for the final time, having caught nothing more than lake salad, Lawrence would be content. This last warm hug of the season was all that mattered.

He smiled now, even though the bridge of his nose burned from the harsh sun. Taking his eyes off the bobber, he gazed down inside the cooler. His pills lay couched between the full cans of beer.

Captopril was the prescription, though he referred to them as caterpillars. Every morning upon waking, he'd pop a few caterpillars into his mouth. Around ten o'clock that very morning, on his way out the door, Susan had called, "Don't forget your caterpillars! Once every four hours, remember?"

Lawrence knew not to mix alcohol with his caterpillars. Doctor Fisher reminded him plenty. And truth be told, Susan didn't like him drinking, period.

"It'll raise your blood pressure." She'd warned him, her eyes keen.

Lawrence understood his wife's concern. Still, he was a man— thus susceptible to negligence, stupidity and selfishness. Something kids these days deemed a *sexist opinion*, Lawrence knew, though it was a fault he fully recognized in himself.

Women, deemed crazy by their husbands, were angels and protectors.

Men, on the other hand, weren't just crazy—they were brutes and beasts and bastards. See referential evidence: every war waged on planet earth since the dawn of Humankind. All of them fought for the causes of men; men, stupid bloody knuckle-dragging, phallic-bragging, shit-throwing *men*.

But there were saving graces in this world.

Graces like Lawrence's wife of thirty-seven years.

"Susan." He spoke her name to the sun beating down on him, to the azure sky puffed with ivory mountains, and to the lake upon which they'd fished, swam, and water-skied over many years.

But he had a choice to make.

Finish his one and only beer, wait an hour, then take his

prescription. Or the far more enticing option: skip the damn pills and drink more beer.

CRACK. His fingers made the decision for him, pulling down the tab on his second Pabst. His lips suctioned to the opening—eyes shut, Adam's apple bobbing, gulping what might as well have been cold mountain stream.

Setting the beer beside him, he retrieved sunscreen from the cooler and smothered his arms, neck, and legs with the stuff. He smudged white paste on his cheeks and forehead like war paint.

Warrior fisherman, steering the battleship, prepared to haul in the enemy on a thirty-pound test and a Devil lure!

Lawrence chuckled, drained his beer, then retrieved a fresh one. Surveying the wide-open lake, he could just make out the boat launch. His red Chevy was the only vehicle parked in the nearby lot. In all other directions, hardly a soul stirred—except for a young couple canoodling on a distant pontoon. The girl was stark naked, save for sunglasses. Lawrence turned away out of respect for his wife.

Waves glimmered, undulating beneath the sun like green molten glass. Tiny stars sparkled in his eyes and made him believe, at the ripe old age of seventy-two, in the magic of a late summer evening.

A breeze ruffled his thin, gray hair and he knew it for what it was—the dying breaths of summer. Crisp, ragged wings brushed his cheek, promising to color and erode every leaf upon every tree the world over, followed by six months of snow shoveling and bitter iceberg winds and groaning pines and salt-rich roads which would rip away yet another year—not only from himself, but from his pick-up, rusting out the fenders and floorboards until the only choice left was either tow it to the auto graveyard or Flintstone the damned thing.

But for now, the sun was warm on his flesh and the lake shone like multi-faceted jewels. Draining his second (or was it third?) beer, he crushed the can, dropping it to the weathered, paint-chipped floor before his eyes widened.

The end of his fishing rod dipped, the line taught.

Lawrence snatched up the pole and gave a yank over his shoulder. The hook found purchase, and the purchase fought hard. He grunted, pulling and heaving, reeling whenever slack presented itself. Whatever was on the other end of his line was *big.*

Christ. Four hours and nothing but seaweed, yet the moment I drift off, the biggest fish in the lake bites!

Lawrence reeled the strained line in small increments. Gritting his teeth, he simultaneously cursed and praised whatever was down there. He prayed for a large-mouthed bass, and hoped it wasn't a turtle or some foul sturgeon.

If not for the anchor, the fish would've dragged him and Georgina half across the god- damned lake.

"Big fella, ain't ya?" He pulled, the pole bending dangerously close to snapping point. A little slack prevailed. He reeled, tugged, then reeled some more. His heart pounded in his ears. Sweat dripped down his face, intermingling with sunscreen to sting his eyes.

By God, I'm actually going to catch this thing!

The euphoric buzz of Pabst faded with the sobering adrenaline coursing through his veins. Now, stooped over the edge of the boat, he could see it.

It crowned at the surface, its enormous body weaving like seaweed in a gentle current.

Lawrence's seventy-two-year-old body ached and throbbed, on the brink of collapsing. Yet he wasn't about to quit, not with his prized catch close at hand. Snatching up his net, he lowered it into the silty water and captured the beast.

His pole clattered to the floor as he gripped the net's steel handle with both hands, heaving the overloaded net up to the rim of the boat.

Lawrence had never seen such a beautiful fish. It was a Northern Pike—long, slender, and glistening with olive-green scales. But he could not lift it into the boat. Thing must've weighed damn near fifty pounds. Not five years previous, Lawrence would've handled this just fine. But as he advanced in age, the breath seemed to come to him less and less.

He braced his arms around the net's metal hoop and heaved upward. The net was almost over the boat. Sweat poured off him, as if his flesh were melting. His heart rattled in his chest like a dying engine.

Lawrence groaned, bared teeth, the world running blurry.

With every ounce of strength in his arms, shoulders, and chest, he hefted upwards.

SLAP! The fish hit the deck, cloaked in the net's folds.

THUNK! Lawrence collapsed beside the biggest catch of his life. Perhaps even the biggest catch in the history of Ouspenskaya Lake.

The fish flip-flopped in the sun, gill flaps opening and closing, aching for water.

The man curled into a ball, hands clasped over his failing heart, aching for Susan.

Lawrence's heart felt as if it were on fire, writhing inside his ribcage and screaming. He prayed to God for it to settle. He couldn't breathe, couldn't take in air. He turned onto his side. An open beer can rolled past, spilling suds over the floor's peeling turquoise.

Lawrence lay face-to-face with the Northern now. Black, empty, staring eyes. The eyes of death.

A universe without stars.
That's where I'm going.
Oh, my heart, my heart.
Susan, Susan, Susan ...

His eyes closed.

Terrible sun smothered him where he lay on the boat's deck. Blinding white shrouded his vision—as if he were being born, emerging into the world's light for the first time all over again. Scrapes, thuds, vibrations, people's voices.

Lawrence tried to move, but his arms and legs were completely numb. He couldn't breathe. It took all the energy left inside him just to writhe and flop around. The floor was miserably hot and harsh, scraping against his belly.

Within the blanket of white:

"Poor old fella!" A woman's voice, choked with tears. "Come on, Paul. Help me haul him aboard."

Lawrence felt their footsteps as a series of alarming vibrations, scuttling through his body. He tried to tell these people that he couldn't breathe, but his mouth could only open, close, open, close.

"Ready, Marla?" asked Paul. "When I say three, we heave him onto the pontoon."

"I'll grab his legs."

A scuffle of feet, followed by a rocking bounce of the boat as Paul and Marla made about the work. Lawrence prepared to feel their hands on him, hoping like hell they'd already called an ambulance. Susan would be worried to death as soon as she heard the news of his heart attack.

At least I'm alive, he marveled.

Paula and Marla grunted, followed by another swaying of the boat.

"Now," Paul said. "Let's get him back to shore."

Wait! Lawrence wanted to shout. *I'm still here in the boat, aren't I? Don't leave me. I can't move, can't talk, can't breathe, help!*

The sun blinded him, flurried his world to static, roasted his flesh, and stole all the air from his gaping mouth.

"Wait." Marla said. "What about *that* thing?"

"The pike?" Paul asked

"It's suffering! Let's throw it back."

Hey! Who cares about the damn fish? Lawrence writhed in outrage. *Get me the hell back to shore. I'm hurting. The air, the sun, everything hurts.*

Suddenly, Lawrence felt large hands wrap around his body, sliding this way and that, as if he were naked and lathered in oil. Then, just as quickly, the hands were gone. Air rushed briefly at his sides before refreshing cool water enveloped him. He felt himself diving down into the lake. *Murderers! They've thrown me in to drown! Can't breathe—*

But he could breathe just fine. Ten feet beneath the surface, he took in oxygen without difficulty. Peering about his surroundings, the white shroud diminished into shapes, forms, shadows, three-dimensionality. The lake was incredibly deep and spacious.

Gliding through the water with the turns and twists of his body, he swam effortlessly. There were things, almost like tiny hands, attached to his sides. Adjusting toward the surface, he looked upward and saw the sun's white shimmer upon the waters, the bottom of the couple's pontoon, and beside it, Georgina, his rusty old boat.

He swam to the surface, eyes above the water. It was intensely bright, and he could make out only a few colors. His vision was altogether different, as if replaced by the lesser evolved visual faculty of some alien creature. Lawrence gazed above the small rise of the pontoon, at Paul and Marla's bare feet.

As a motor whirred and they began to drift away, Lawrence caught sight of familiar eyes.

Light, chestnut brown eyes, sunk into a pale, wrinkly face laid flat upon the deck.

His face.

He wanted to cry, shout, scream in horror, but his mouth merely opened and closed. The pontoon glided toward shore. His vision extended only so far, before that white shroud draped over everything. He dipped down into the lake, where he could see and breathe and collect his thoughts.

Feeling oddly at home in these cool waters, he dived near to the bottom, glimpsing tiny creatures scuttling through the muck. Soon, his vision sharpened and focused.

Crayfish, crawling away from him, disappeared into the crevices of algae-slicked rocks. There was an entire world down here, all dim, calm, and wavering green. Seaweed waggled like tapering green fingers reaching for the surface. Fish darted here and there, most of them sunfish.

Georgina's bottom loomed ten feet above. He swam up to it, and though his reflection was distorted in the bright aluminum, Lawrence observed what he'd become:

A long, slender olive-green body marbled with yellow spots and an underbelly pallid as the moon. A long, flat snout. Little black voids for eyes. He opened his mouth into an oval, revealing two rows of tiny sharp teeth. Lawrence stared at the reflection for a long time, feeling as if he were staring out of a mask, or an incredibly realistic special effects suit.

I must be dreaming. Must. Not only isn't this possible, it isn't fair ... maybe I've died up in that boat, but if that's true, then I should be in Heaven with the God I've diligently prayed to for seventy odd years. He swam about his reflection, disturbed by the surreal nightmare he found himself submersed in. *Am I dead, or asleep?*

No longer able to gaze at the horror he'd become, he dove down, down, down, until his fins grazed cold black muck. Water flooded into his mouth, passing through his gills. He wanted to close his eyes. Wanted to cease breathing and for the world around him to turn black, passing into eternal night.

Lawrence would rather have an afterlife of endless sleep over this bizarre manifestation: As the mind of a man, haunting the brain of a fish. A ghost living inside a machine.

A machine composed of tiny bones, lean meat, mucous-slicked scales, sharp teeth, and beady eyes. Lawrence hadn't ever been handsome, something he often cracked jokes about in his humble, self-deprecating ways. Now, he could say with utmost accuracy, he possessed a face not even a mother could love.

It'd been days, maybe weeks since that fateful afternoon Lawrence had died, only to be reborn, reincarnated, resurrected. He had no way of telling how much time had passed, except that many suns had touched upon the surface, and the lake's temperature had dropped substantially.

Lawrence had always hated the approach of winter. Now, he rather enjoyed the frigid waters—perpetually caressing his body, sliding over his fins, assisting in an effortless glide through the green abyss of flickering seaweed, undulating current, and the veritable wilderness of lake creatures.

Many creatures resided in Ouspenskaya Lake. More than he'd expected. There were crayfish, of course, but also loons that kicked legs upon the surface, fluttered their wings and cried lonesome moonlit odes. There were turtles, bass, sunfish, minuscule zooplankton and phytoplankton, and at least a dozen species of plant life.

Within the north end shallows there lived big, fat, nasty bullfrogs. Lawrence had been ferociously hungry one night, hovering motionless beside the outer beam of a dock. Seeing a frog pump his back legs at the surface, he'd shot upward with his mouth cast wide like a net, scooping the creature inside.

Lawrence's tiny teeth jabbed and shredded the juicy amphibian to pieces. Tendrils of blood drifted upward. After swallowing the meaty lump, he continued swimming about the lake, searching for further morsels to feast upon.

There were minnows, snails, insects, leeches, and obscure nests of fish eggs resembling strange alien larvae. Lawrence gobbled them up, savoring each bite. On one occasion, he'd spotted a serpent slithering along the surface. Darting up sharp as an arrow, his jaws chomped down just above the arrow-shaped head. The snake writhed and twisted a terribly long time.

It hadn't sat well inside Lawrence's stomach. The sight of the ragged, half-chewed serpent floating lifeless in a billow of red made him feel sick and ashamed.

Never again would he eat snake.

From then on, he stuck mostly to minnows, bullfrogs, and crayfish. They were healthy, nutritious, and carried with them a feeling they were *intended* for him to eat.

Sometimes, he'd swim up to the surface and look around. The forms and outlines of beaches, trees, and private cabins became distinct whenever clouds obscured the sun. Leaves danced from the limbs of overhanging birch trees, falling to make ripples upon the lake. Back when he was human, Lawrence occasionally wondered what the world looked like to fish. What it felt like, or if they felt pain.

Now, he knew. His world was one of shadows, but there were colors and forms. Sensory nodes upon his head detected nearby prey. He sensed coldness and warmth. He delighted in raw flesh.

Recalling the terror of the bright sun in the suffocating air upon *Georgina's* floor, he understood that fish felt pain too. Oh, yes. They could feel pain.

It's only that they couldn't shriek in distress, like a slaughterhouse pig or cow, say. All a fish could do on a hot sandy beach, or at the end of a fillet knife, was stare up with blank button eyes and flop about the place, hoping and aching to touch water and breathe again.

At night, Lawrence nestled within a forest of tall reeds. Dark serenity cloaked him while ivory moonlight shone from above. Sleep never found him, although he rested contentedly, as if dosed with tranquilizers.

Beneath wavering moonlight, blanketed by cold darkness, Lawrence reflected on his wife of thirty-seven years. How he longed to hear the melody of her voice flow into his ears (*what ears?*). Wished to stroke her face with his affectionate fingers (*fins*). Tell her how much he adored and missed her (*without a voice*).

But Susan was as gone as the world he'd left behind ... *up there*.

An entire civilization, up there. A tumultuous species called Man, struggling, scraping and striving after money, status, and happiness. Sometimes such things were secured. More often they were not.

Society and its teeming billions. Smoldering cities coughing black smoke into the stratosphere. Thunderous stampedes crowding streets with frenzied feet, either walking, running, or crawling for those high, lofty distractions—sturdy illusions of an ape-like species hell-bent on their own destruction. The death instinct compounded and declared custom. Eternally frictionless pursuits which slipped one's hands like fish in a stream.

Elementary survival, once a reigning priority, had become the shame of man's ancient past—a stamp of lowly origins. Humans couldn't simply mate, sleep, and feed. Such things were too base on the hierarchy. Too rudimentary for their character and drive. Evolution had propelled them into expanded consciousness. As a result, they smoked cigarettes, made love, wrote symphonies, waged war, philosophized, burned coal, gurgled alcohol, shit tacks and rocketed to the moon.

The moon—Earth's aborted fetus, its alabaster ghost now peeking behind dark lily pads, illuminating across millions of miles of space from out of dead lunar craters.

Lawrence felt as if he were inside such a crater. Hunkering, hiding, hoping desperately this under-the-sea nightmare would end and he would wake up warm in bed with Susan cozied beside him. She'd smell of lavender and peaches, her skin pruned and old, yet feather-soft, her lips hungry for Lawrence's kisses.

It was all he could think in this endless stream of nights and days, rotting away like petals from a discarded lotus flower.

Down here, there were no flowers.

Down here, only the silty dark and the cold and the living dead—hungry creatures, floating through a mindless existence, feasting and mating and drowning ad infinitum. The plights of fish and the plights of man, though worlds apart, seemed equally arbitrary.

I wish I had taken my pills.

I wish, I wish, I wish.

Oh, Susan ...

Lawrence burst into tears, except they did not pour from his eyes. The tears were squeezed, tugged, and wrung from his soul and there was nowhere for them to escape. That was the maddening thing. There was no place for his tears to run, nor for himself to run, for he could only float and hover and swim.

Lawrence swam in a lake of tears.

The lake felt unseasonably warm. Lawrence took great joy in darting around bushels of water thyme, scaring the hell out of schools of perch. Their bodies shimmered—little panicky arrows of phosphorescent glass darting away in an explosion of bubbles.

Lawrence hadn't spent his life as a 'big fish', but now that he was one, intimidation tactics came naturally. He'd gone from existing as one man in a big, industrious world, to an enormous fish in a relatively small pond. Having died and been reborn, he'd become King of Ouspenskaya Lake.

Granted it wasn't the most prestigious of royalties, but at least it was something. If Lawrence couldn't have Susan or his old life back, at least he could be ruler of an underwater realm.

Dusky silt danced all around him, occasionally illuminated by a sunbeam streaming through the surface—a liquid veil between this world and its opposite. Lawrence's existence consisted of three primary elements: silence, solitude, and silt.

He dwelled about the lake bottom, catching crayfish as they scurried through muck and snuggled between rocks. At the bottommost point of the lake, which the sun barely grazed even on the clearest of days, was the wreckage of a small airplane.

Propellers were buried deep into the muck. Algae cloaked cracked wings. Verdigris tinged the faded yellow sides. Two skeletons sat strapped in the cockpit, their clothes mere tattered rags undulating in the currents. Minnows swam into the hollow of their eyes, exiting their open mouths, weaving between their ribs. A playground of bones, dyed green with perpetual plankton.

Lawrence studied their forms in the dim light, wondering who the pilot and co-pilot had been: Aviator and student? Father and daughter? Intimate lovers? How did fate manage to yank them down into this silent watery grave? They must've sat down here for decades, half-buried in muck and obscured by the brackish water. Perch, sunfish, bass and pikes, maybe even a few as big as Lawrence, had picked their bones clean long ago.

A perverse way of returning the favor, Lawrence surmised.

For this once, fish had devoured the humans, leaving only bones.

Watching the tiny creatures dance within and without the skeletons, Lawrence thought of himself and Susan. He wished they were together down here, like these two. The pilots had died of a tragic accident, true, but at least they'd been together when it happened.

No one wants to die alone.

Neither does one want to live alone.

Swimming up into the dusky light, Lawrence caught a bright,

silvery flash in his periphery. His body twisted toward the source. *There!* A long silver body flashing through the waters. There were no salmon in Ouspenskaya Lake, but that's exactly what this creature resembled. Lawrence hadn't eaten in days. Depressed, bored, and deranged, no common bullfrog nor minnow nor crayfish could've excited him. Now that bigger prey was in sight, his predatory instincts loomed supreme.

He chased the quivering quicksilver as it swished across the lake.

Speedy little guy, Lawrence thought. His aqua-dynamic body thrusted forward, his vision never straying from the creature. Opening his mouth wide, he promptly overtook the fish, and bit down.

Bit down, and tasted cold hard steel.

Lure! Lawrence's bottom lip stung as the treble hook pierced through. He was tugged, yanked, reeled toward shore.

Doom and panic threatened to consume him, yet he fought back with all his strength. He prayed the hook would tear through his lip. It'd be painful as hell, but it would set him free.

Attempting to swim in the opposite direction, the line only pulled him toward shore. Lawrence heaved backward, drew down into the lake, the line persistently tugging him back up. He darted left, right, then down again, erratically flailing and writhing and twisting.

All futile. The line summoned him to the surface. A net enveloped him, scooping him up into suffocating air and blinding light.

Lawrence's gills ached for water to pass through them. His operculum, the piece of hard flesh covering his gills, throbbed relentlessly. Beneath him, the hardness of a dock, though he couldn't see it. He couldn't see anything, except the silhouette of a human floating above him— the fisherman.

Hands darted down upon him, seizing with a grip sharp as a vulture's talons. Fingers crawled into his mouth, working the hook free. Next came the gentle thud of footsteps on the dock.

Being taken toward shore. The fisherman isn't going to throw me back. Why would he? I'm the biggest fish in the lake—was.

I was *the biggest fish in the lake.*

Lawrence's heart, located behind his gills, pounded with terror. All around him, the air burst with sounds: twittering-tweet of birds, rush of wind, high-whine of cicadas, footsteps.

Coolness passed over him as the blinding light dialed down into dimness and shadows descended. A rattle of dead leaves, crunching like bones beneath the fisherman's feet.

The back of a pick-up truck opened with a distinct *pop.* Lawrence was laid out upon a cutting board. *The coolin' board,* Lawrence thought vaguely. *Like the old bluesmen sung about. Or the killing floors ...*

Outlines concretized into distinct forms and colors. The world stared down from above. Vast silhouettes of giants—trees, swaying in the eddying winds. A grey curtain had drawn across the sky, blocking out the sun. Looming just above ... the fisherman.

Gentle blue eyes. Slim, angular face. Aquiline nose. Pretty, thin lips. A familiar white blouse open at the second button, despite the crisp autumn air.

Energy surged through Lawrence's body as he flipped and flopped upon the board, attempting desperately to communicate. Susan's azure eyes teemed with tears and her lips formed a delicate smile.

Lawrence stared up at her, wishing he could say something—anything!—to let her know he was here, he was alive, that she'd caught him—hook, line, and sinker.

Susan. Lawrence's mouth opened, closed. *Susan ... please. Susan!*

"What a magnificent creature you are." Susan gazed down at him. "My husband of thirty-six years had a large pike in his boat the day he died. Maybe *you* were the one he had exerted all his energy trying to catch."

Susan's smile waned into a taut, sad line. She didn't get much sleep these days, Lawrence could tell by her eyes. He wondered how she spent her time since he'd been gone.

Tears splashed her cheeks. Lawrence's heart throbbed with grief, just as much as his gills ached for water. He wanted to reach out and wipe away her tears, whispering to her, "Everything will be fine. I'm here now—it's me, Lawrence. I'm here, my sweet."

Shiiing. A silver flame glinted between Susan and Lawrence; a long, thin blade glimmering in the autumn light. Lawrence twisted his body, beginning to flop and writhe.

Susan's jaw clenched. Her soft, sad eyes set into hard marbles. A sharp sting pierced beneath Lawrence's tail fin as the blade inserted into his anus.

Please don't do this. Throw me back. Throw me back, please!

Susan frowned a moment, looked deep into Lawrence's eye, then withdrew the knife.

She knows. Tremendous relief radiated through him, and he ceased writhing. *Thank God, she knows.*

"Almost forgot," Susan said, pressing the back of the fillet knife against him. "Lawrence always told me to start with the scales."

The knife scraped hideously against his flesh. Scales fluttered, spindling in all directions as she methodically worked the knife down the length of his body. She flipped him over, repeating the process. Susan thrilled at the dissection, taking all her aggression, sorrow, and grief out on what she mistook as a mere fish, one potentially responsible for making her a widow.

Lawrence lay there now, raw and stripped and naked. He wished not for Susan's love, nor for the cool rush of water over his gills, but to die— that very instant. He wished it more than anything in heaven or on earth.

Stinging, wrenching pain stabbed every nerve in his accursed body. The knife slid deep into his underbelly, spilling blood. Susan grunted, pulling the knife lengthwise. The blade tip rippled across his ribs, cleaving meat from bone.

Lawrence basked in horrendous agony, discovering he could no longer move. He could only lay there, feeling red hot pain wash over him like a sea of boiling lava. Susan filleted him, peeling his flesh into meaty strips and dropping them into a bucket beside the cutting board. Next to the bucket, a black marble urn sported a silver plaque:

Lawrence Chaney.

Born July 3rd, 1948.

Died August 29th, 2020.

The urn lay emptied on its side, faint grey powder dusting its rim. Susan had come here not only to fish, but to dispense with his bodily remains. She was unknowingly killing him … *in his own honor.*

Her hands reached inside him, yanking out his gonad, spleen, stomach, liver, bladder—all of it splattering over the tailgate and onto the ground. "My husband taught me how to do this, once." Susan said. "Probably not doing it perfectly, but he'd be proud. When I get home, Mr. Pike, you're going straight into the frying pan."

She grabbed an old meat cleaver from behind the bucket and raised it high. Lawrence watched in terror, helpless. She swiftly swiped it down just behind Lawrence's gills. A shockingly loud *CRUNCH!* echoed through the air, the trees, the wind, the universe.

Lawrence watched numbly as Susan hefted the headless body of a Northern Pike into the air. The spine, ribs, and bits of dangling innards were all that remained. Susan nodded admirably before tossing it into the nearby ditch. Then she looked down at his decapitated head, and a strange glimmer shone in her eyes.

A moment passed between them.

"Huh," Susan said and plucked up Lawrence's head and tossed that into the weeds too.

He watched from behind dry, crisp weeds—a mere discarded fish head piled with bones and guts, couched in autumn foliage. After packing up the pole, tackle box, and cooler, Susan climbed into Lawrence's old pick-up and drove away in a cloud of dust.

Everything was silent.

Until …

BUZZZZZZZZZZ

Dozens of them, at first, then hundreds all circling and landing. Like minnows swimming inside the skeletons of Ouspenskaya Lake, the flies danced and hovered, tickling Lawrence's lips, crawling inside his mouth, their tiny legs pricking and prodding his black glossy eyes.

Eyes that would never close.

Bare, raw, automatic nerves worked Lawrence's mouth.

Opening, closing.

Opening, closing.

A scream raged within him, drowning his soul in agony and outrage. There would be no God coming to save him.

No blessings bestowed, for he wore a halo of flies.

Bird twittered.

Wind blew.

Leaves stirred.

Flies buzzed.

Lawrence screamed.

Not a soul in the world heard a thing.

NIGHT OF THE CHILD

For every small town there are a few universal traits; the pretty girl next door, the downtown drunkard, the old man with the snarling Doberman (*mailmen beware!*), the English teacher who pens mystery novels, and then ... have you guessed it yet?

Yes, of course — *the haunted house.*

Like a malignant growth surrounded by small-town perfection, the hideous tomb-like dark of an ancient Victorian looms its shadows over lush green grass and towers its blackened chimney into crisp blue sky; a grotesque obelisk; a rotting spine that shivers in moonlight.

Even in mid-summer, a breathtaking October chill consumes every child who bicycles past the Manor. If particularly daring, they'll glance up at this anachronistic monstrosity and wonder ....

Did they see something twitch the dusty curtains, just then? Did they hear skeletal fingers scratch the window? Or was it merely wind turning the rusty weather vane?

The heart pounds in such moments.

The heart pounds, the skin crawls, and all the mystery of the world doubles. For a child, that which constitutes the natural and unnatural, the real and unreal, are contentious prospects—ones that will not be settled until they reach adulthood. A child's world is one of magic and paradox and impossibly spooky things.

For adults, the Manor was merely an eye sore. Something to be cursed and eye-rolled for lowering the real estate value. Adversely, the children found the decadent old house on the corner of Bloch and Leiber Street inestimably frightening. Its very existence seemed to rage and rebel—an expectoration in the face of natural order. There was no name for this tumorous estate, save for *The Manor*, a simple enough moniker which, nonetheless, sent chills down the spines of any kid who saw it, or even so much as listened to its legions of legends.

To the Manor's left, Kenny Vandermeer's house stood with its two-car garage, well-manicured lawn and white picket fence. Kenny spent most of his time alone, reading books. To the Manor's opposite side, Anna's house appeared identical to Kenny's, save for a turquoise front door as opposed to lacquered azure.

A conformity of houses, strategically aligned into columns and streets, squared upon immaculately trimmed estate, formed the Natural Order of Suburbia. The Victorian Manor, with its weathered clapboards and grimy windows and black, shingle-checkered roof and sagging porch and paint-chipped door, remained a monster, a misfit, and a metaphor.

To all the children in the Midwest town of Sweet Hollow, this gigantic, squalid structure represented, quite simply, *the Unknown.*

Kenny, lying in bed reading a science book, gazed out his window at the ramshackle manor and felt as if he could gaze upon the face of the Unknown itself.

What's hiding in there? Kenny's brow pinched studiously. What looms and lingers behind those crud-covered windows? What about the noises? Those weird high-pitch notes, like the short-lived blare of an alarm, or the bleep and bloop of a robot. How about those mechanical clanks and shuddering whirs that resound at all hours of the night? Maybe a mad scientist lives there. One who's creating a machine to take over the world. Maybe it's Dr. Frankenstein, conducting experiments in the interest of re-animating dead tissue. Or perhaps—

"Kenny?" Mother stood in the doorway, a black witch's hat atop her head. She held out her cell phone. "It's Anna, she wants to discuss trick-or-treat plans."

Kenny groaned. This was the fifth time she'd called in under an hour. Confirming, re-confirming, then cancelling, then re-re-confirming. *Now, what?*

"You be nice to this girl," Mrs. Vandermeer warned with a smile. "She's a sweetheart."

Kenny sighed with resignation before accepting the outstretched mobile. Mom winked, then padded down the hall to assist Kenny's little sister in putting on her Cinderella costume.

"What's up, Anna?"

"So, I know you're probably sick of having me in your ear, but listen. I just talked to Erick Justison, down at the library. He was helping set up tonight's Halloween story-hour display, and we got to talking, you know, and he was all like—"

"Anna, c'mon. Cut to the chase, please?"

"Okay, okay!" Anna huffed. "Long story short: Erick's going to explore the Manor with us. He'll bring along his Dad's heavy-duty flashlight. Plus some provisions, in case we need them."

Kenny could hardly believe his ears. Erick Justison? The sports jock? Why would someone who'd built their life around playing quarterback for the Sweet Hollow Robins want to hang out with the two most unpopular kids in school—on Halloween night, no less? Erick being there seemed as weird and unlikely as the house they sought to investigate.

"How come you were talking to Erick, anyway?" Kenny asked.

"Oooh, somebody sounds ... jealous?"

"Me? Nuh-huh! I don't care who you talk to."

"Well, why *wouldn't* I talk to Erick? He's our neighbor, you know."

"Anna, in a town this size, everyone's our neighbor."

"Shush. You know what I mean."

Kenny knew what she meant. The crumbling old Manor squatted on the corner of Bloch and Lieber Street—Kenny's house to its left, Anna's to the right, with Erick's house located diagonally behind the Manor. Whenever Kenny ambled into the backyard (usually to mow grass), he'd sometimes glance beyond the four-foot fence line and see Erick playing catch with his big brother. *Guess it isn't much of a mystery why Erick wants to join us after all,* Kenny reflected. *He, too must lay awake nights, listening to the strange noises erupting from that supposedly vacant house.*

Kenny wasn't fond of jocks. He found them narrow-minded and unimaginative, plus they didn't read books. Yet Erick's curiosity in the Manor surprised him; Kenny wondered if he wasn't judging the kid unfairly ....

"Yoo-hoo," Anna chimed. "Still there, space cadet?"

"Sorry," Kenny shook his head as if clearing his brain of cobwebs. "Let's meet on the corner at 7:30, okay? We'll get our candy first, then go about tonight's business."

"Isn't it supposed to be business *before* pleasure?"

"Yeah, but this is Halloween. People used to call it 'Mischief Night', you know. Anything goes."

"Does that include breaking and entering?" Anna teased.

"Oh, come on," Kenny chuckled. "It's not like we're criminals."

"Aren't we?"

He considered her question uneasily, only just now realizing they *would* be breaking the law. "Touché, I guess. See you at 7:30?"

"See you then! I'll call Erick and let him know our plans."

Kenny returned the phone to his Mom. She sat at the kitchen table, applying rouge to Suzanne's cheeks.

"I'm Cindy-rella." Suzanne grinned, exposing pink gums and a couple of teeth.

"Very nice, Suzie-Q." Kenny kissed his sister atop her head.

"So?" Mom asked, adjusting her witch's hat. "What's the plan?"

"We're meeting at 7:30 for trick-or-treating."

"That's awfully sweet. I'm glad you and Anna have become such good friends. If you're as smart as I think you are, Kenny, you'll keep her around. Ask her out on a date, maybe?"

Kenny outwardly scoffed, yet not without a flutter in his heart. Secretly, deep down inside the part of him he hid from the world, he longed to take Anna out to a movie. Not as friends, like they did most Saturday nights, but as a couple. They'd sit close together, so close he could smell her hair, and then he'd put his arm around her shoulders and she'd smile at him, even snuggle up beside him a bit closer.

"What will you go as?" Mom smiled, snapping Kenny out of his daydream.

"Hmm? Oh ... I haven't decided."

"Well, why don't you get out of your head and into a costume? The trunk is up in the attic, remember."

After Mom and Suzanne left for early trick-or-treating, Kenny went into the garage and stretched on his tippy toes, pulling the string to the hatch. He unfolded the accordion steps, then climbed into the dusty attic. Boxes and plastic tubs cluttered the floor space. He slid these out of his way, hunching so as not to bump his head on the cobwebbed rafters. A ventilation grate was fastened to the attic's southward wall. Dying sunlight splayed through its open slits, throwing amber stripes upon the battered antique trunk.

Flipping up the unlocked latch, Kenny opened the lid and shuffled through the trunk. A sea of rubber masks gazed up at him— all strange, monstrous eyes, screaming mouths, and long, warty noses. An odor of dust and silicone flooded his nostrils, forcing a sneeze out of him. His hands dug through the soft velvet of a black cape from many Halloweens prior, scrabbled across plastic make-up kits, rattled extra pairs of vampire teeth, fluffed a collection of white, curly wigs, then—

The disguise he desired was in his hands.

A lime green alien with black eyes, tiny nose, and a puckered mouth gazed upward with wise suspicion. After a half-minute's search, Kenny located the black tunic with a tall green collar that accompanied it.

Closing the trunk, he slid the tunic on over his clothes, and donned the mask. His breathing resounded against its concave walls. Gazing through the eye-slits, the ventilation grate now caught his attention. He pressed his new face against the spaces, peering out.

The elevated position of the attic allowed Kenny a closer view of the Manor's second floor. There was a window directly across, spotty with dust. His heart palpitated because of what he saw in there.

A face.

A gaunt, pale face with beady black button eyes staring out from sunken pits.

Kenny blinked. The window was empty.

Empty, save for still, unwavering curtains—its grey, shabby fabric soaked in one hundred years of sun, holding in the dust and rot as efficiently as a mummy's wrappings.

A nauseating churn inside Kenny's stomach made him step back from the vent. Probably my imagination, he thought, attempting to comfort himself. He knew the truth, nonetheless. Someone was living inside the Manor. Someone with a slim angular face and the complexion of a vampire.

The Manor was supposed to be condemned; a *No Trespassing* sign stapled to its front door. Kenny now wanted to cancel his plans with Anna. What if they ventured into the house and encountered this person? Would he be dangerous? Violent? If they entered the old Manor tonight, would they *die?*

Kenny swallowed the lump of fear in his throat, then peered through the grate again.

The window remained empty. The curtain hung just as limp,

tattered and lifeless as a cadaver's shroud. Kenny ripped off the alien mask. Checked his watch.

Twenty minutes until his meet-up with Anna and Erick. He would tell them about the face. Let them know they couldn't go on with their plans; it was too dangerous.

Surely, they'd understand.

Right?

Kenny snagged an orange latex bag from the kitchen cupboard above the sink. The black etching of a toothy Jack-O-Lantern mirrored both sides. He unfurled it, shaking a year's worth of dust from its crinkled crevices.

Seven-thirty p.m. arrived as fastidiously as a black cat hunting down a barn mouse. Storing the alien mask beneath the crook of his arm, Kenny raced into the waning blue twilight.

On the sidewalk, he met a pretty, young witch wearing all-black attire and a pentagram necklace. Brett Favre, former quarterback for the Green Bay Packers, stood across from her. Clutched in his hands, a pillowcase that fluttered in the chilly breeze.

Mom winked at Kenny as she walked past, holding his little sister's hand while she skipped and hopped.

"Look, Kenny!" Suzanne held up a small orange bucket. "Cindy-rella gets all the candy!"

"Only two pieces tonight, Suzanne," Mom reminded her. "It's bedtime in half an hour. You kids have fun, now! Just don't get into any trouble."

"We won't, Mom." Kenny half-smiled, unsure if he was telling the truth.

"Have a good night, Ms. Vandermeer!" Anna waved.

Then it was just the three of them on the corner. The derelict Manor stretched long its tombstone shadow … almost to the sidewalk, as if it desired to seize hold of their ankles. The sun settled into the horizon, an orange pumpkin descending into darkness. Streetlights flickered on, illuminating the sidewalks with bright ellipses. It was time. Kenny put on his mask. Older children and teenagers began to flood the street, chiming doorbells and posing that eternal, mischievous query: *trick or treat?*

Is it a question, or a threat? Kenny wondered. Or is it a mantra, even?

The shrill cries of 'Trick or treat!' echoed throughout the town, spoken with such verve and reverence as normally reserved for chanting or sacred prayer. In a way, Kenny reflected, Halloween night is a prayer unto itself—an appeal to the immaterial forces that lay behind reality's gossamer veil, separating this world from the next.

Kenny thought of the curtains then, and the glimpsed face behind it, then shuddered. He took a breath, about to inform the witch and the quarterback about what he'd seen, when—

A rusty Ford pickup rumbled up the street, pulling up to the sidewalk.

"Hey, kiddos." Erick's teenage brother leaned out the window with a Cheshire grin. "Forget that begging for candy crap. Y'all wanna come to a *real* party?"

"Oh, hell yes!" Erick shook his fists enthusiastically, climbing into the cab.

Anna and Kenny stood there, a witch and an alien exchanging uncertain glances.

"Come on, you two," Erick said, waving them into the cab. "This'll be a lot more fun. Promise."

Kenny gazed out of his eye-slits over at Anna. Is this really a good idea? They seemed to ask each other. Anna shrugged and Kenny followed her into the cab, slamming the door shut. The four of them were packed as tightly as canned sardines.

"Name's Cody," said the long-haired teen behind the wheel. "Now, buckle up!"

Anna and Kenny looked down, discovering there were no seat belts. Erick laughed, shaking his head at his brother's antics. Then Anna and Kenny were laughing too, out of nervousness.

The truck rumbled down the road, headlights cutting into the fresh-fallen dark. Where they were going, or what they'd do when they got there, Kenny hadn't a clue. He felt apprehensive but excited. Anna sat so close beside him their knees touched. Her smile was carefree and, for Kenny, had a tonic effect.

Cody drove straight through town with its goblins, princesses, werewolves, vampires, and white-sheeted ghosts parading the sidewalks. Finally, they descended deep into rolling pastures where a pale crescent moon arose into the star-spun heavens and made sacred shadows of everyday objects. Brittle fence posts, mailboxes, and swaying pines transformed into magnificent specters from another world. A chill wind blew through the open cab, ruffling their costumes. Anna crumpled her pointy hat between her knees, so it wouldn't blow out the window. The night chirruped with cicadas. The wind howled over the horizon like a werewolf. Large-winged bats flittered across the moonlit sky, and everything, in that moment, seemed a perfect pinnacle of gothic ghoulishness.

The essence of Halloween lay within these surrounding fields, its ancient corpse awakening with marble eyes rolling, rolling beneath the moon, and rising, rising like an insidious tide to swallow them up — and they would indeed be swallowed, thrilled by a sense of excitement and danger, as eager as any kid who slaps down his ticket for a roller coaster ride.

A surge of freedom coursed through Kenny's veins. Riding in a stranger's pick-up to some unknown destination – *without seat belts!* – was thrilling. The future lay ahead, a long black ribbon winding through the countryside. Kenny found himself smiling when Anna stretched out, putting *her* arm around *his* shoulders.

Kenny, Anna, and Erick climbed out of the cab, returning to the corner of Bloch and Lieber. They stood within the flame-yellow circle of a street lamp.

"Later, little buddies." Cody drunkenly leered out the window before driving off. The pick-up's chugging staccato faded into the distance, giving reign to quiet streets.

Quiet, save for a wind moaning like a sorrowful phantom through the Manor's crooked rain gutter. Leaves rattled across the porch, the crisp dead foliage turning and flipping, as if a ghostly broom swept them along. The three children broke the unsettling ambiance with laughter and roughhousing, their spirits crescendoed by the night's bonfire, heavy metal music, and beer.

Kenny had never imbibed until tonight. He hated the taste, finding it bitter and gross—what he imagined urine would taste like. Still, he'd managed to gulp down a can of Budweiser, and he was pretty buzzed. Erick, a far more experienced drinker, had downed four cans, while Anna partook in only a sip before handing it over to Kenny.

Kenny's eyes now widened at his wristwatch. It was eleven-thirty, two hours past his Mom's established curfew.

"Crap."

"'Sup?" Erick smiled behind the grate of his football helmet.

"He's late," Anna answered for him. "He was supposed to be home by 9:30. I was too, but I don't care. I'm having too much fun."

Kenny felt a sudden tug at his heart. He knew what would happen if Anna didn't go home. Her father was a brutish, vulgar sort of man who imparted lessons through hurtful words and insults. Kenny had a mind to tell her to go home, then realized it wouldn't matter. Whether Anna ran straight home or showed up at dawn, her father would reprimand her with curses.

Despite this dismal realization, Kenny was having more fun than he'd had in a long time. Retiring to his bedroom seemed a dreadful waste. Halloween night was still young.

Not even midnight, the fabled witching hour when that threadbare veil thinned to but a single strand; an ethereal division which any searching mind could cut, rendering the world of the living and dead indistinguishable. Or, so claimed the esoteric philosophies Kenny had read about online. All superstition, of course, but there was a romance to it, a poetic sensibility that made one's blood rush.

Perking his ear to the wind, Kenny felt he could hear the howl and whine of a million spirits, all gliding their way through eternity. Glancing at his house, a single light glowed in the kitchen. Then he stared up at the Manor—its dark form hulked in the moonlight, casting shadows that oddly appeared more real than their source.

Despite the pallid face he'd seen, or imagined, earlier that evening, Kenny wasn't afraid anymore. He was exuberant. After all, it was Halloween night, he was accompanied by friends, and there was a haunted house—in the flesh and blood, in the nails and pulp wood—practically begging to be explored.

"*Trick or treat?*" The Manor seemed to whisper, beckon, entrance, drawing them with irresistible gravity, like an enormous black star pulling in comets to blaze with color before disintegrating in its atmosphere.

The house stood silent. Not a rattle or clank resounded behind its walls, as on so many nights prior. Somewhat restless, Erick pulled his father's flashlight from his pocket. "Well, are we going to do this or what?"

Anna and Kenny locked eyes. Understanding passed between them. The matter was settled.

"Be right back, guys," Kenny said. "Hold tight."

Kenny ambled inside his house, receiving his Mom's scolding. He apologized with all due appearance of humility, then shuffled into his bedroom. His Mom yawned, stretched, filled a glass of water, then went to bed. Kenny quietly slid up his window, hopped out, shut it, then re-joined his friends on the corner.

"Smooth, Kenny," Anna laughed. "Real smooth!"

"Thank you, m'lady!" Kenny bowed proudly.

"Hey!" Anna frowned. "Where did …"

Erick was nowhere to be seen. They looked up and down the street. Stray orange-black streamers rolled across the asphalt, assisted by a gentle breeze. Open candy wrappers gleamed like precious quicksilver beneath street lamps. As if the darkness had swallowed Erick Justison whole.

Creeeaaak.

Their heads turned. Erick had mounted the squealing porch steps and now stood before the Manor's large ebony door. Gazing over his shoulder with glimmering eyes, he gestured for accompaniment.

Kenny stuffed his still-empty candy bag and alien mask beneath Mom's hedgerows, along with Anna's witch hat. Side-by-side they walked up the weedy, cracked pavement of the footpath, then mounted the noisy porch.

The three of them stood before the door. Kenny squinted into the dark, noticing something ornate carved into the top frame. It resembled a half-open eye, or possibly a flying saucer. Before he could point it out, Anna pressed her hands against the door.

"One …" she began, then the rest of them joined in on the chant, placing their hands against the rugged timber, "… two … *three!*"

With a pterodactyl-like screech, the door swung open on rusty hinges. Darkness lay beyond the threshold. Kenny had expected –

perhaps even hoped – the door would be locked. He longed to explore the Manor and yet longed not to. His stomach turned uneasily, but when Anna grabbed his hand, all thoughts of desertion dissipated.

Anna's hand was warm, even a little sweaty. He'd daydreamed of this moment. Now, the dream had become reality.

"All right, love birds," Erick snickered behind his helmet. "Let's see what this old house has to offer."

They stepped into the house of dust and shadows. Erick flicked on the flashlight, shining a beam over a torn up couch with a water stained floral brocade. The beam floated over the room's contents. A fireplace, large and dark, like the mouth of a monster. Beside it, a small table with nothing on it but dust. The rest of the room was empty, except for a tall column in the corner—a grandfather clock, its golden arms perpetually frozen at one minute to midnight.

Erick's beam rested upon the filthy glass overlaying the clock face—

CLANG!!! ...

CLANG!!! ...

CLANG!!! ...

Erick cried out, dropping the flashlight. It rolled in a circle, the beam sweeping across the floor like a miniature light-house. Kenny and Anna huddled together, clamping hands over their ears, attempting to block out that dreadful tolling.

The grandfather fell silent after the fifth chime, its bell no more than a lingering resonance. Kenny's heart pounded in his ears, louder than the bell. Anna hugged him tightly.

Laughing, Erick bent down and reclaimed the flashlight.

"Don't you guys see?" he asked. "That stupid clock is probably the cause of that noise we keep hearing at night. It's just a dusty antique!"

He tilted back his head and laughed. Anna loosened her grip on Kenny's waist, and now they were all laughing at themselves—expelling the fearful tension which had paralyzed them for no good reason.

71

"Bunch of freakin' scaredy cats, aren't we?" Anna smiled, shaking her head.

The front door slammed shut behind them, once more launching their hearts into overdrive. They spun around with widened eyes. Erick ran to the door, grabbed the rusty brass knob, and found it locked.

"*Oh, no!*" Erick tucked the flashlight under his armpit, then braced his foot against the frame and yanked with all his might.

The door wouldn't open. He walked over to the window beside the clock, where a shaft of moonlight fell upon the floor. Erick heaved and pushed, hammering the heel of his hand against the lip of the frame.

At last he turned around, panting with a nervous smile. "Don't worry, guys. Some wise-ass is having fun with us, that's all. Heck, it's probably Cody."

"Right," Kenny nodded, finding this explanation far more assuring than the one he had in mind — that the Manor really was haunted, and whatever spirits remained there would not allow them to leave. "It's trick-or-treat night, after all," Kenny smiled weakly. "Guess we just got the 'trick' end of the bargain."

The house of dust and shadow creaked and groaned beneath their shoes. Venturing into blackened rooms with Erick's Dad's flashlight, they hoped to locate a window they could open, providing an escape.

It was as if the Manor had swallowed them. Now, heading deeper into the belly of the beast was their only option.

Armed with the flashlight, Erick led the trio from the front. With plodding footsteps, they toured a great many rooms. Every darkened corner brought not only cobwebs, dead flies, and scrabbling spiders, but a lurking fear that traced their spines with an icy finger.

The Manor was larger than they'd expected. Not only was there a parlor room, a spacious kitchen, bathroom, multiple storage closets, and a billiard room—there was a library. Sagging shelves covered the walls from floor to ceiling. Old books with yellow, water-damaged pages and cracked spines. A round table held the room's center, piled precariously with weathered tomes. The children cloistered around the table, and Erick shone his light upon the titles.

Intricacies of Human Anatomy
The Sociological Encyclopedia
Geography of Planet Earth

"Science books!" Anna beamed, flipping through the pages of a textbook detailing the rich contents of Earth's biome. "Way cool."

Ever since Ms. Huppert had assigned Anna and Kenny as teammates on a science project, they realized they shared a mutual passion for discovering things about the natural world. This led to many after-school hours at the public library, sharing books with each other—everything from astronomy books by Neil deGrasse Tyson to evolutionary biology texts by Richard Dawkins.

"Why would someone leave all these books here?" Erick asked, shuffling through the stacks.

"Maybe they *weren't* left here," Anna suggested.

"Whaddya mean?"

"Well, suppose whoever these books belong to never really left. Suppose they come here sometimes, to read in solitude."

"Pffft." Erick shook his head and laughed. "Nah, these are *old* books."

"Old," Kenny interjected, "but not that old. Look — this physiology textbook is only from a few years back! Plus, notice something?" He dragged his index finger across the book, then showed it under Erick's beam.

Erick cocked his head. "Huh. No dust."

73

"I don't like this," Anna frowned. "Whoever these books belong to might return at any moment. Or they're already here ... watching."

The children straightened. Erick swept the beam across the room, investigating the dark corners for surprises.

Elaborate spider webs with twitching insect prey.

A few red-eyed rats, scraping along the trim and nibbling at the soft wood.

But there appeared no one lingering in the dark, watching, waiting for the perfect moment to strike ....

"Time to go," Kenny announced.

"If we can just find a window that will open," Anna said. "Or a back door?"

"Not many windows in this place," Erick said, "but I did see one in the kitchen. I noticed because it looked straight out into my backyard."

They followed Erick into the dilapidated kitchen. The cupboard doors hung open. Inside were dusty plates, ceramic mugs, and couple of mice skittering across the grimy wallpapered shelves. Collected inside the sink, a pool of black water lay stagnant and smelly. Above it, the window overlooking Erick's backyard.

Despite gazing through dusty panes, the back lawn sparkled with dew in the aquatic moonlight. Erick's house was dark, just as asleep as its inhabitants. No one waiting up for him, it seemed. Although Kenny slightly envied that Erick wouldn't receive a scolding, it did make him feel sad.

"What time were you supposed to be home?" Kenny asked.

Erick shrugged. "Anytime, I guess. They don't care." He paused, then added, "My step-folks don't, that is." He swiped aside the curtains, lifting at the window.

He grunted, pushed, hammered, blew out his cheeks.

"Shhh!" Anna hissed, "You're making too much noise. Someone will hear!"

Erick turned from the window, shoulders drooped, sighing with resignation. Then his forehead scrunched. "Kenny, what time you got on that watch?"

"Midnight," Kenny said, eyeing his watch. "On the dot."

"But wasn't it midnight when we first came in?" Anna frowned quizzically.

"Yep," Kenny nodded. "The grandfather clock informed us of that rather loudly ... we overlooked that."

"Overlooked *what?*" Eric was becoming more confused by the minute.

"The grandfather clock," Anna answered. "Someone's been keeping it on the correct time."

Erick shook his head. "Jesus, we've gotta get out of here. Whoever's been hanging around this place, I don't want to meet. Besides, what if he's still—"

Their blood ran cold. Above their heads, the distinct knock and creak of footsteps. Fine grains of dust sifted down from the ceiling. Anna coughed. The footsteps entered another room, then ceased.

Erick shuddered, his eyes wide and roving.

"That's it," he nodded, determined. "We're getting out of here."

"How? What are you going to do?" Anna asked warily.

Erick charged out of the kitchen, leaving Anna and Kenny in the dark gloom. They looked at each other.

"You look as scared as I feel," Anna whispered.

Kenny nodded. "You're not wrong."

Erick returned, flashlight in one hand, and a large tome in the other.

"What's that?" Kenny nodded at the book.

"*The Complete Guide to Victorian Architecture,*" Erick replied.

"No, duh," Anna interjected, hands on her hips. "He means, what are you *doing* with it?"

"Oh." Erick handed Kenny his flashlight. "I'm going to smash in this window with it."

"That's a *terrible* idea." Anna scrunched her face. "That guy upstairs, he'll hear and come find us. *Then* what'll we do?"

Erick shrugged. "I don't know, Anna! But we've gotta get out of here, otherwise whoever he is will find us anyway. And who knows what kind of person he is? My guess, if he's squatting in this old creepy dump, reading textbooks in the dark, probably not a sane one."

Eric darted to the window, raised the book over his head, then slammed it against the glass, then again and again.

A mild *booonnng* resounded upon each impact.

The glass didn't even rattle in its frame.

Exhausted, he dropped the book onto the cracked linoleum floor. *Thump.* "I give up! That glass looks old and brittle, but damn if it isn't strong." Erick disappeared through the doorway into the adjoining parlor. Kenny and Anna followed, not wanting to be left in the dark for a single moment.

Erick now gazed sullenly out the window beside the grandfather clock.

A clock that should've given up its senseless ticking long ago, yet was still keeping time, still abiding the attentive hands of some mysterious personage.

"Look," Kenny said, running his hands over a portion of the crumbling wall. The plaster had cracked, and beneath were the rotting boards of the house, and beneath those …

A silvery glimmer, like the sparkle of a diamond.

They joined Kenny beside the hole in the wall.

"Here," Kenny handed Erick back his flashlight. "Keep it trained on my hands."

Erick nodded, aiming the light while Kenny dug away brittle plaster, termite-infested wood, and exposed, beneath the wall, yet another wall ….

Kenny reached in, sliding his palm over its smooth, polished surface. "Some sort of titanium maybe," he mused, tearing down

76

more of the wall, revealing a metal shield that appeared to encompass the entire southward wall of the house.

"Uhm, guys?" Kenny's eyes stared widely. "This house is not what it seems."

"W-what do you mean, Kenny?" Anna quivered.

"I mean, these old crumbling walls are just for show. The *real* walls are behind them. Every detail of this place is decoration. The cracked linoleum. The chipped paint. Even the crooked rain gutter, and the spiders, and the rats in the kitchen. All of it ... in the service of an illusion."

Erick shook his head rapidly. "No way, dude. That's crazy talk."

"Yes," Kenny agreed. "But you don't need to take my word for it. Here, *touch*."

Leaning into the ragged rent in the wall, Erick and Anna placed their hands upon cold metal. They knocked. Pushed.

Solid. No common aluminum, nor was it some defunct air vent, barricaded and forgotten. This was incredibly durable, non-corrosive metal. Titanium, like Kenny surmised, or steel. Or perhaps even ... a different material altogether.

Erick stepped away from the wall. "It all makes sense now."

"Explain it to me, then." Anna threw up her hands in frustration. "I don't understand."

"The windows," Erick replied. "They look old, brittle, but I couldn't even smash one in. They're made of bulletproof glass or something. Made to *look* old, but like Kenny said ... just an illusion."

The house began to shake. Dust (or was it merely made to *look* like dust?) cascaded down from the ceiling. The floor quaked beneath their feet. All three of them cried out, grasping onto each other.

Kenny's stomach plummeted while saliva collected in his mouth, thinking he might throw up. Dishes in the kitchen cupboard fell off the shelves and shattered. The table in the parlor room dumped onto its side. Yet the windows did not rattle. The metallic walls, some unimaginably solid exoskeleton, vibrated with a soft, steady thrum.

Anna and Erick lost their footing, collapsing to the floor. They clambered across the hardwood, over to the ripped-up couch, and held on for dear life. Kenny caught the window sill, holding tight. The room tilted. Then came a sudden *lifting* sensation, as if he were being thrust a thousand miles up. The acrid taste in his throat caused him to turn aside and vomit. When he turned back to the window, he gasped.

Kenny could see his house far down below, as well as Erick's, and Anna's, and all the surrounding neighborhood. He really *was* thousands of miles up, and getting higher by the moment. In place of where the Manor had stood only seconds ago lay a square of plain brown dirt.

Houses, streets, patches of lawn—all of it immensely tiny, their outlines visible beneath the blue moon that now came into direct view of the window.

Kenny met the moon eye-to-eye.

Soft, blue clouds floated across the window. Finally, Kenny's feet lifted off the floor — inches at first, then several feet. A split second ago, he'd felt heavy as an iron anchor. Now, he was a child's balloon.

He clutched fast to the window sill, gazing out at the brilliant stars and the blue-green earth beneath. Erick and Anna floated about the room, attempting to grasp each other's hands, fingers sprawling, screaming with terror and confusion.

They didn't understand, but Kenny did. Gazing down at his home planet, everything became crystal clear.

They were being kidnapped. Not by ghosts or a coven of witches or some clichéd boogieman, but by unearthly visitors — beings of extraterrestrial origin.

The Manor was *not* a haunted house.

It was a UFO; a highly advanced craft designed to attract only particular members of the human species – children – on the night of Halloween, the night when children are most vulnerable.

A spaceship.

A trap.

Kenny's eyes welled with tears. He felt like a rare insect, captured in a jar and being taken far, far away from home.

The Manor flew through the silent, star-spewed fathoms of outer space. It might well have been fueled by phantasms, for its energy source was utterly unknown to humankind. Its brick chimney was not of brick, nor its windows glass, nor were its walls, clapboards and shingles composed of any earthly material. The house was a *chimera*, cleverly planted within an earth-suburb.

Adrift in zero-gravity, three children attempted to make sense of these things. The flashlight had died an hour ago, now floating useless in mid-air.

They'd been on a mission to explore the unknown. Such is the nature of what attracted them to the Manor. Now, they were face-to-face with the *ultimate* unknown — flying at light speed through the vastness of interstellar space.

Beyond the windows, they were witness to what no human had ever seen; cosmic depths yet unexplored, populated with colorful planets, brilliant suns, pocked moons, porous asteroids, and blazing cerulean comets.

Who, or what, was taking them through these celestial deserts? Would they ever return home? Would they see their parents ever again?

Questions boiled in their brains. Gurgled in their stomachs. Floating in darkness, all they had left was each other. Linked at the hands, they used their legs to bounce off the walls and swim across the space of the parlor. Kenny grasped onto the stair banister, began pulling them up to the second floor.

Gravity had abandoned them, as had most of their fear. They were going to get to the bottom of why they were here in this dark, strange ship, where they were being taken to, and who was taking them.

Hovering at the top of the stairs, a dark and narrow corridor stretched beyond them. Sweaty palms pushed against the walls, shooting them to the end of the corridor. They were light as feathers. Kenny glimpsed into an open room to his left. It was the room with the window, the one he'd seen the white face staring out of.

The fake white face.

He'd been shuffling around in the attic when he'd spotted it, wearing his alien mask. Similarly, the alien had been wearing a *human* mask.

Maybe, Kenny thought, the alien thought I looked equally weird and creepy.

At the end of the corridor, another hallway with more rooms, each one shabby and empty. Reaching another stairway, they floated up the steps, then paused before a door.

Not an ancient, paint-flaked door like the others.

A door of smooth, polished metal. Above the entrance, a series of strange characters belonging to a language none of them had ever seen.

"Look!" Erick shouted. "Those hieroglyphs or whatever they are! They're *changing*." The black squiggles writhed like worms, transforming into English characters. "'Welcome Aboard', it says."

They studied one another now, floating before the door which would lead them to a place from which they may never return.

Kenny grabbed Anna's free hand and gazed into her eyes. "I don't know what's going to happen to us," he spoke softly, "but I hope we'll survive tonight, that we'll be able to hang out and share books again. And I hope ..."

Anna's eyes shimmered, visibly touched, as well as a little frightened. Kenny was talking like they were going to die. She hadn't considered that possibility, until this very moment.

Kenny pushed onward and finished, "I hope you'll go on a date with me sometime. To a movie, if you'd like?"

"I'd love to." Anna's grim expression lightened with a smile.

"Erick?" Kenny turned toward him, slowly, so as not to float away. "I'm sorry you got yourself involved in this mess. I hope you'll be able to play football for the Sweet Hollow Robins next year."

"Bah." Erick rolled his eyes. "I don't care about that. I just wanna see my brother again."

Kenny nodded, hoping to see his mom, and his adorable baby sister, Suzanne.

"Ready?" Kenny asked, rather needlessly. The three of them had experienced such a range of emotions tonight – from absolute fear and trembling to hilarious laughter to dreadful tears – they were now ready for anything.

They locked eyes on the door, knowing it would open on its own accord.

And it did.

The pneumatic door slid into the wall, exposing a vast, cavernous attic — the ship's command center. Kenny, Anna, and Erick floated inside. Behind them, the door silently slid shut.

An enormous panoramic window formed the attic's walls and ceiling. The transparent dome provided a glorious view of the cosmos, surrounding them with endless burning suns, each sun the size of a million Earths. They were reminded that Earth itself was merely the size of a grain of sand, a speck, an atom.

A dozen towering creatures with slim white faces turned from the translucent control panels and stared. They appeared almost human, wearing charcoal suits with collars buttoned about their throats. Their pitch-black eyes shimmered.

"Take off your masks, please." Kenny floated between his

friends, rife with fear, yet managed to speak confidently. "You aren't fooling us."

The aliens exchanged glances, then their smooth, white faces writhed, bubbled, contorted. Their bodies boiled like scalding seas of ivory flesh, dripping into pliable beads which floated all around the room in a mist before evaporating into thin air.

Now, their true visages hovered all around the dome—hazy orbs of brilliant white, pulsing with energy and glimmering like freshly strewn tinsel. Spheres of light, composed of an intelligence both beautiful and terrifying in its unfathomable amplitude.

The spheres drifted and circled in a dance of welcome. Their thoughts transmitted into Anna, Kenny, and Erick's minds with an effortless telepathy. The children nodded with understanding. The messages were crystal clear.

Their hearts pounded. Not with fear this time, but hope. They smiled, as the Spheres' knowledge drifted like white clouds over a pure blue sky. Every fear they'd held now dissipated completely — for they *knew*.

Knew they were not being brought to the Sphere-being's home planet to be cooked into rare meals of human delicacy – *fresh meat from planet Earth!* – nor were they destined to become slaves to some technocratic society, nor would they be designated as curious specimens, imprisoned behind glass for the entertainment of extra-terrestrials.

No, only humans would commit such cruelties.

For this was the truth which Kenny, Anna, and Erick delighted in: they were being flown across billions of light-years of space and time to a planet whose name, if rendered in English, would approximate, *PZULU*— all in the service of liberating and enlightening the Sphere-being's civilization.

But how? The children frowned at one another. We're just kids! We haven't any wisdom. No great knowledge to liberate anybody, especially beings with immense intelligence and technological advancement.

The Spheres pulsed like brilliant quasars, scintillating thoughts to flit through space and blossom inside the children's brains. Answers arrived in the form of a gentle, androgynous voice, the words rendered in English:

We, the Sphere-beings of PZULU, have reached the summit of progress — the highest achievements in space travel, energy resource, and communications technology. Yet we do not know how to have what earth-children call 'fun'. We do not know how to enjoy, to marvel, to daydream, to dance, to play for the sake of play.

In short, children, we do not understand the charm, mystery and wonder you feel on October 31st of every earth-year. We do not understand the cultural oddity of dressing up in gowns and rubber masks and parading the streets, roving from door-to-door, begging strangers for sweet delights which melt in one's mouth. Nor, still, do we fathom the intrigue a child feels before a ramshackle old manor — a thing of materially no value, all termites and brittle wood and checkered shingles.

What of that special, magic emotion of the child that is more pure than our telepathic thought? Stronger that our greatest warp drives? More special than anything in the known universe, save for that curious emotion Homo sapiens call 'love'?

You children shall serve as the enlightened teachers of our vast, multi-planetary civilization. Your expertise will be in and of yourselves — how to marvel, how to play, how to appreciate existence. It is this perspective, this knowledge, we Sphere-beings shall find invaluable. Our species has perfected everything else. Now, our final frontier is not of space or time or technology, but of philosophy; how to deem this life as worth living.

Kenny, Anna, and Erick floated adrift, gob smacked and honored. The Spheres were quick to assure a return trip to Earth— when the time was right, when every bit of invaluable knowledge was gleamed. And when the illusory 'haunted Manor' finally landed in its vacant lot between their houses, no time would've passed on Earth whatsoever.

For the Spheres were masters of the fourth dimension, manufacturers of perfect paradoxes. The three children would walk out of the Manor unscathed on a chilly, Halloween night, the full moon pocked and sea-blue, and the green grass of home lush and sparkling. They would laugh, and hug, then bid goodnight.

Life on Earth would continue just as before, with its struggles and hurtles, its pains and cruelties. And yet, floating in the dark of this life, the children knew they had each other.

Their hands, the very same which held close in the Manor, would unite time and again over the years—to hold, to comfort, to lift one another back onto their feet.

Never again would such a night be so magical, so mirrored with memories, delicious in dreams, fantastic in phantasms.

For it was *Halloween night*, and their youth was so young, they seemed eternal. The moon, the grass, the crinkled candy wrappers, the Manor's grotesque facade, the odor of dead foliage in a whining, wet wind echoing with the distant screech of bats – all of it! all of it! – exulted in that timeless night of childhood.

A night of magic and mystery. A Night of the Child—like a wild comet blazing through a strange world that has forgotten how to marvel, burning up in the atmosphere, exploding in the fieriest, most astonishingly brilliant colors.

Dedicated to Ray Bradbury,
for there will never be another like him.

BELLS ARE RINGING AT
THE TRANSIT STATION

T̶he following letter, composed circa 1870s by amateur artist, John R. Clarkston, was recovered among the crumbled ruins of an historic building on London's Fleet Street. Stored for several decades in the basement vaults of the Archive for Historical English Documents (AHED), the letter's contents have now been released into the public domain. The physical letter itself, a yellowed, crinkled, tattered seven pages of parchment, can be observed under glass display in London's Buckingham Gallery. The sketching purported to have accompanied this letter was, unfortunately, never recovered.

My dearest Julia,

Your considerate father may underestimate my character, as well as my ability to provide for you. Yet as of this moment, I believe he will no longer have cause for doubt. Your future husband is bursting with good news, at last! For I've procured dependable employment within the dirty, grimy, beating heart of the City of London—on Fleet Street, no less. The job pays quite handsomely, undoubtedly due to its macabre nature.

It is not a *morgue*, per se, my dear, so do not fret. No, indeed. *Not a morgue*—so my employer gruffly reminds me whenever the word slips my tongue. Mister Hogarth (a great-grandson of the famous artist, so he claims) calls this place the "transit station". I find that to be a rather charming euphemism, and it is this peculiar locale from whence I write to you now.

Hogarth is a bilious, broad-shouldered, brooding, dark-eyed man who, having poor lungs and foul breath, huffs and puffs a most unimaginable stench! His personality and manners lack charm as well— yet I must remind myself to be grateful to Hogarth. He has, after all, rescued me from that lowly state in the alley (specifics on this matter a bit later, but rest assured, I am fine). Hogarth, weary and hunchbacked from a day's work, left for home a half-hour ago, and so I am left to my own devices at the 'transit station'.

The desk upon which I write is elegant: an antique, its copper-red mahogany well-polished and the surface large enough to spread one's arms. It is the nicest piece of furniture in the building ... certainly more handsome than the caskets. I can work on my sketches here, perhaps even smuggle in some paints and canvas, if I am fastidious. I am all alone here (save for all those moldering bodies in the nearby rooms), and my responsibilities are simple.

The Transit Station is a holding place for the presumed dead— *presumed* because doctors have, on rare occasions, made mistakes in their mortal pronouncements. Surely, you too have heard those horror stories of some poor man or lady buried alive? A grave, sometimes, is dug up for relocation, and upon opening the coffin—hideous claw marks on the underside of the wood, and the fingers of the corpse all chewed up, as if the person had been alive and starving, desperately resigned to self-cannibalism. Horrible! Dreadfully macabre! I shall spare you further ghastly details, my darling, for which I am sure you'll be glad. Rather, I will describe only the station itself:

A brick-and-mortar building. Quite old. Spacious. There are thirteen rooms (apparently, the architect was not privy to the silly superstitions of Londoners, or if he was, did not care a whit). Within each room is a row of upright coffins, in each coffin a body, and upon the right hand of each body is a string that tapers out of the coffin and is thereby attached to a small bell secured to the adjacent wall. Should one of the dead not be dead, the man or lady has only to move and the bell shall ring and I shall be notified—upon which I am to help the poor soul out of the coffin, provide care, then promptly contact Hogarth, who will, in turn, call upon his friend, the good Dr. Seewald, a trusted family doctor.

"Has such an event ever occurred here?" I'd asked Hogarth, as he led me from chamber to chamber, explaining my duties.

"What?" Hogarth's voice was rough and ragged as tree bark.

"I mean," I spoke quietly, for one's words echo and reverberate off of these brick walls, "has anyone awoken in their coffin and rung the bell?"

"Never, young fellow John!" Hogarth laughed. "Not in all my years in this place. Those stories you hear regarding the alive bein' buried ... it's happened, from time to time, but it's *exceedingly* rare. Still as yet, people read or hear of such ghastly tales and become frightened, and thus willing to pay for such a nonsensical service as this ... their decayin' hands attached to strings attached to bells. How ludicrous! What folly! Though I mind it none, young fellow, for it provides me my means of livin'. Thank God, I say, for the folly of the livin' and the quiet of the dead."

"Indeed," I muttered, a chill coursing my veins at the thought of the dead *not* being quiet. Hogarth walked with an uneven gait, his footsteps heavy, echoing, leading me from crypt to crypt (for they were all the same, all dark and brooding and the walls wet and growing black spores), his hand clamped on an oil lamp burning bright and making shadows stretch from the coffins and crawl across the grimy floors, as if to slither round our ankles and take hold! (Only my artist's imagination, of course).

The building is in a poor way. The ceiling leaks. Rain drips into the coffins and splashes about the gaunt, sallow faces. Yes, I have seen the bodies—Hogarth, morbidly curious about all things cadaverous, has opened several of the coffins, eager to reveal the still-fresh remains.

"Why! I thought you looked familiar, young fellow John! This body quite resembles you, yes?" He stood back so that I might admire the poor soul, resting in the tilted back coffin. I shuddered, for the man indeed shared a striking resemblance with myself. If you saw him, Julia, you would've screamed! Dimpled chin, like mine own. A goatee finely trimmed. Black, wavy hair. Approximate equal weight and height. Even his clothes perfectly matched what I am wearing now: a wool grey herringbone coat, black trousers, white cravat, and brown shoes beginning to wear through. Good heavens! It felt as if I were gazing into a mirror, although upon some sickly day in which my complexion is ghostly white, white as ivory, as opal, as the sun blinding one's eyes ….

Hogarth cackled, abruptly snapping me out of some sort of trance— I'd drifted off with widened eyes, staring at a corpse so eerily similar. Turning to Hogarth now, he winked, closed the coffin, and moved on to the one directly next to it.

"Here," he grumbled. "Seeing as you are night guard from now on—if you can manage it, for many have not due to their weakness in fortitude—you must accustom yourself to the sights of the dead. It is not much, but it *is* something. Look! See you, this wretched old face?"

I nodded, for I could see just fine. The old woman's face was scrunched, dirt and grime between every fold and wrinkle, her eyelids halfway open, the opaque irises eerily peering out. Her veiny hands, pallid as moonlight, lay at her sides. Secured to her ring finger, a string tapered out of the coffin and up to an old bell plated and bolted into the wall. The string was taught. The slightest movement and the bell would ring.

"Strumpet," Hogarth grinned. "She was carried in only yesterday, but for the longest time she peddled her wares, so to speak, right on this very street."

"On Fleet?" I drew in a breath, slightly taken by Hogarth's casual vulgarity.

Hogarth's grin spread wider revealing black, rotting teeth. "Margaret was her name. Used to stop in here when I was doin' night duty. Peddled her wares, if you mark my meanin', and I paid her handsomely. She'd get down on her brittle old knees and, havin' no teeth—"

"That is quite enough, I think, Mister Hogarth." I held up my hand, hoping he'd cease his obscene discourse. Hogarth's belly quaked with laughter. "Tender-footed fellow, I see." Closing Margaret's coffin, he led me into the next damp, smelly, cavernous chamber, and the next and the next. The sour, meaty odor of decaying flesh merged with the chill air. I breathed only through my mouth.

"How many bodies reside in this dreadful morgue, Hogarth?" I asked, upon our return to the cozy front office. Hogarth sat behind the desk, myself in the chair opposite. "Transit station, not morgue," he corrected me, then opened a drawer, took out a roll of paper, like a map, and slid it across the desk. I unrolled the parchment and studied it. For it was, indeed, a map. Rendered in thick black ink, it facsimiled every room in this building, as well as every coffin, each one assigned a number. Two hundred coffins exactly. Adjacent to the map, the numerical list was accompanied by tacked on sheets of paper featuring the names of the deceased, as well as the name and address of relatives who so dutifully committed their loved one's bodies to the 'transit station.'

"How long are the dead to stay?" I asked.

"Never more than three days, young fellow. Should their bell not ring, and it never does, I load the coffins into my hearse wagon—which you shall assist me with tomorrow morning. 'Tis part of your job, you know, and you bein' strong and full of vicious young blood and all. Then I ride up to whatever churchyard of the family's choice, where the corpses are arranged for a burial."

"I see."

"What?" Hogarth leaned forward, quite suddenly, frowning. "*What* do you see?"

I gazed up from the map, astonished by the sudden glare in Hogarth's beady eyes. "Why, I ... I merely meant that I clearly see the duties of my employment, Sir."

Hogarth settled back into his chair. "Fine. Good then."

"If I may ask, Sir, what did you think I—"

Hogarth stood tall from the desk, and suddenly I felt like a little boy in the chair, gawking up at an angry father. "Remember, you are to make one round of each room, each coffin, once *per hour*. You are to write a brief report concerning all tasks you've accomplished on your shift. And you are to alert me should anything go awry. You've my address?"

"I've written it down, Sir. Indeed, I will contact you should anything go ... awry."

"Fine." Hogarth nodded, satisfied. "I shall see you at five o'clock tomorrow morning, bright and early. And should I catch you snoozing on the job, young fellow John, you'd better expect immediate termination!"

I arose from the chair with a slight bow. "I shall not disappoint you, Mister Hogarth."

One foot nearly out the door, Hogarth turned with a most curious look. A peculiarly sensitive and haunted expression creased his forehead. The left corner of his mouth twitched. "Some souls, young fellow," he said, thickly, "are fitted for jobs like this. Some are not. Tonight, you shall discover your soul's constitution. God willing, I'll find you well tomorrow morning."

The door closed the moment I began to inquire as to his meaning. Hogarth, as I have described him, my dear Julia, is a rather crude old man, yet little did I expect to hear such elegant phrasing as "your soul's constitution" uttered from his blubbery, spittle-speckled lips.

Having writ these pages, I have passed the time astonishingly quick! It is six-ten in the evening. The sun is setting, gleaming in shafts through the front windows that look out onto the street. It is cold, so I have lit the logs in the fireplace. I see no other cordwood to burn, however, which means tonight I will be positively freezing. Ah, but such cold is minimal in comparison to being outside, is it not? My heavens—*the time!* And I have yet to make a round of the building. Off I must go then.

I hope you are well, still attending those fabulous little book parties with your friends, and that you are enjoying my library whilst I am away. I cannot wait, truly, to return and feel your warm presence enrapt in my arms again. I love and miss you dearly.

To think, in another month or two, your fiancé shall return as a well-to-do artist!

Give your father my best. Tell him I've procured excellent employment, and that I am ascending to the highest of artistic circles in London, just as I had stated I would do, and that his future son-in-law is on the path to success. God will surely forgive a slight fib, my dearest Julia, should such a fib soon become honest truth.

Lovingly yours,
John

Even now, a terrible chill traces my spine like the tip of a frigid blade. Strangest thing, Julia! Forgive me for what may be a lengthy post-script, but it is not yet midnight in these gloomy quarters, and I've many hours before Hogarth relieves me. I suspect, as well, that only by epistolary means may I alleviate this lurking unease in my heart.

I'd been making my fifth round of the night, taking mark of each coffin, one by one. How detailed and textured these old boxes, when one stops to study them! I may want to paint them, if only to capture the fractures in the wood, the multitudinous splinters, the yellowed warping caused by water damage, and that ominous black shadow between cover and frame when the coffin is slightly ajar … yet this is not the dreadful thing I have to tell you:

I heard a bell.

I swear it. A particular one of these two hundred bells gave off but the faintest, the slightest, the dullest of dings—as if someone were to nudge a dinner bell with their elbow. Still—I heard it! My eyes widened about the room, my heart raced. The lamp in my hand, I toured the room and its every coffin, opening them up to see who—*who,* by God, could be one alive among so many dead?

Upon inspecting each body, I found them all stiff and pale and lifeless. I know now what I heard must have either been my artist's imagination at full work, or a draft of some kind, strong enough to sound one of the bells. When raising my hand up toward each bell, however, I found not the slightest rogue air.

Admittedly, I am tired. Yet now I must keep awake and perform my duties. God forbid I attempt a bit of rest, only to oversleep, and be awakened at dawn by an ill-tempered Hogarth!

Still, I hardly think I should even be able to sleep. Not in such an uncomfortable straight-back chair, and *certainly* not after that chilling moment in the crypt. It was in room thirteen I'd heard, or thought I'd heard, the bell—go figure! Perhaps a black cat will cross my path next. And have I walked under any ladders lately? I cannot recall. Oh, how silly! How foolishly imaginative your fiancé can be! Ahh, but just as well, my dearest. So long as you remember that you are to marry this fool.

Again! And again! And again!
DING! … DING! … DING!

Thrice rung the bell as I was sitting here at the desk! I took up the lamp, sped out of the office and down the hall, my footsteps echoing into the open chambers. Stopping mid-path, I cocked an ear to listen. The bell sounded no more.

Someone is *alive* in here, but how am I to know which someone? I must go to room thirteen (it is, I believe, from whence the bell is tolling). I must open every casket and check for a pulse. If I only had a mirror, a piece of reflecting glass, I could test for breath.

What a thrilling letter this will be for you to read, Julia! Although I doubt it will chill you as much as I am chilled now. My tortured heart gallops madly, rapidly, as if it were about to explode out of my chest! Thank your lucky stars these pages are not inked in my blood.

Ah, but some poor soul is in desperate need. Off I must go.

I was diligent in my search. Very, very diligent indeed. Not one of the bodies (how acutely I examined them!) revealed any trace of life. I pressed my fingers against their cold, clammy wrists, then beneath their frigid jaws. I took their heads in my hands, turning them side to side, and they made not a noise, nor a shutter of the eye, nor the slightest twitch of the mouth. They are dead, Julia ... dead, dead, dead.

It *must* have been a draft, then.

But if so, why did Hogarth not warn me? Surely this is something one would share with a novice? Of course, Hogarth *is* quite old. He might well have forgotten. For how cruelly does age prey upon the mind. I pray, Julia, neither of us will become so neglectful in our twilight years. Ah, but you have good blood, do you not?—Your father is to be seventy-two in the spring and his mind is sharp as a tack. So sharp, in fact, I sometimes wish to dull it. As for my own parents' mnemonic vitality, I cannot say. My parents and I are not on friendly terms, as you know. Only fools and bums are artists, they tell me, and that if I am to live my life as a fool or bum or artist (it is all the same to them) then they'd rather not know me.

Too bad. Having lived and strived and painted in London for three months now, I have made many artist friends, many worthwhile connections with museum curators and gallery hosts, and it will only be a matter of time, really, before—

... *What?* No! Again—the *bell!*

This cannot be my imagination, nor can it truly be a draft, for it is repetitive, and *loud!* Obscenely and grotesquely loud! O, how the bell rings dark and dreaded, winding through these old halls to pool like filthy vermin inside my ears! O, dreaded brass tongue upon dreaded brass shell! Horrid, blackened tolling! My heart, my wearing aching pounding heart ....

I shall follow its sound and discover, at last, the poor soul alive, and help him. Then, promptly, I shall call upon Hogarth (even at so late an hour, I must)!

Margaret. The strumpet, as Hogarth called her. She is alive! Oh, but her poor soul is weak, weary, and worse for wear. I have settled her into the chair beside the fireplace, the flames still burning warm and strong. Her milky eyes blink at the flames. I have offered her water, and bread from my satchel, yet her lips refuse my charities. The string tapers loose from the ring finger on her left hand. The poor old dear's chin rests upon her chest. Imagine, Julia, awakening inside a coffin in some cold, darkened, damp room! Thank God she rung the bell so adamantly, otherwise she would have been buried—a far worse fate, indeed.

"My dear old lady," I've told her, "Rest easy, and I shall bring help."

She barely manages a nod, for Margaret is so very tired, pale and cold (even by the fireside, disturbingly clammy!). Still, she is rather beautiful in her misery. I should wish to paint her portrait, if only time and circumstance were not so inopportune ....

Hogarth lives but down the street. He'll be asleep, I imagine, but I shall knock upon his door and roust him.

"You are a bastard fool!"

So declared Hogarth, after feeling for a pulse and finding none. Margaret, slumped in the chair, did not stir. Plucking a small mirror from the pocket of his waistcoat, Hogarth held it up to Margaret's nostrils. The mirror remained clear, did not fog in the slightest.

"She is dead." Hogarth stuffed the mirror back into his waistcoat. He stood tall, fixing me with an accusing glare. "Have you no respect, man? Snatching the poor lady out of her coffin and sitting 'er here to slump and rot?"

"I swear to you Hogarth, she *was* alive! She rang the bell thrice—"

"Shut your trap, fool! And grab hold her legs."

Daresay, if Margaret *was* alive, she wasn't any longer as we carried her into the crypt. Upon our return to the office, Hogarth placed his meaty hand on my shoulder and shoved me down into the chair behind the desk. "Now listen, lad," he growled, and it took every bit of determination not to wince, for Hogarth's breath was awful—a mix of alleyway bilge and rotten trout. "'Tis only the witching hour and you've disturbed my sleep ... over what? Nothin'! The lady is dead when you claimed she was alive. What rubbish! I knew full well I was takin' a chance on hiring a well-dressed bum like you, but what caught me unaware was how utterly bonkers *mad* you are!" He paced back and forth, huffing and puffing, face beat-red, then he stood straight and scowled. "Stamp it! It is late. I must return to bed. For one requires sleep all the more when one is older. I trust you will keep guard here and not do anything *foolish*. Should you roust me from the comforts of my home again, I shall fire you and pay you not a shilling. Not one! Am I understood?"

"Understood, Sir." I nodded, eyes downcast, utterly ashamed. Hogarth muttered curses under his breath, then promptly stomped out of the room, slamming the door on his way out.

The flames in the fireplace flickered, danced. Then the clock struck one and I got up for another round.

Oh, how stupid I am! Upon acquiring a job in this accursed city, I am but inches away from being thrown back into the gutter where Hogarth found me. Yes, my dear, it is true: I have not been doing well for myself, although my letters have led you (and your father) to believe otherwise. I will now open my heart to you. I shall spare you the slightest fib, revealing only the truth: I am living in the street. I subsist on hard, stale bread. I haven't enough money to purchase paints or canvas. Not one gallery in the city of London has any desire to see my paintings—for I haven't any paintings, nor even a place to store them. I've sold them all cheap for food. Yet I did not buy food from the pitiful revenue I earned from my paintings—I bought drink. Now all I have is this job at the Transit Station, this one chance to lift myself up out of squalor. I must not be a clown anymore, Julia. I must be strong, diligent, and do the work Hogarth has hired me to do. Margaret is dead. She has been dead all along. My imagination has betrayed me.

Please, do not relay these details to your father, unless you desire that he forbid our marriage entirely. I love you, dearest Julia. I beg you—Forgive my fibs.

It is but only pride that has put lies into my heart.

The clock above the hearth has struck two. Three hours before Hogarth relieves me of my duties. Then where am I to go, you ask? Back to the alley, of course. I shall sleep in the dirt, my head resting upon my satchel. Ah, but all is not so bad, after all: I have discovered a blank journal in the bottom drawer of the desk. Quite suitable for sketching.

After a few false starts, I've drawn what will surely be the subject for my next painting once I can afford paints and canvas again. My expensive brushes I still possess, however. I keep them safe in the inner pocket of my herringbone. How I treasure them so (and to think I had even considered selling them!). For if I ever parted with these brushes, I would never forgive myself. Their bristles are of the finest Arabian horsehair, and their handles are ivory—oxen bone, I believe. Such a merging of beasts into an artist's brush makes one feel wild and invigorated.

The sketching, rendered in but iron gall ink, depicts the fellow in room thirteen who sports a disturbing resemblance to me. I have opened his coffin for a closer inspection: How sad his closed, grey-shadowed eyes! How sunken his cheeks! How dapper his clothes, although spoiled by splatter of mud, just like my own attire. He was young, about my age, in fact, for the wrinkles in his face are minimal, only a few lines clustered about the eyes, like mine. I wonder how the poor soul died?

The winds of life blow steadily, sometimes in vast gales. I have felt such vicissitudes, such storms as of late, here in London ... but I know, so long as I can sketch and hope and dream, all will be fine. I will return to you one day soon, my belle, and we will be married together in a life of bliss. I am sure of it.

I—

My mouth trembles and yearns to open wide in a scream, though I dare not.

Unspeakable!

I wish to shout, exclaim! Yet I must sit in this chair by the fireside, must keep quiet, must pen this letter to you. The air is chilly, the fire burns (impossibly, it burns, for I have not added any wood to the flames since I first arrived many hours ago, and when placing my hands near the dancing fire, am not warmed). The hour is late, late, oh so desperately late! I cannot bear to think that I am hearing the bell again ... only it is not a single bell this time, but all of them, *all* of them! Every bell in all thirteen rooms of the crypt is tolling, the strings tugged by the convulsions of the living dead. The air positively quivers in the clamorous reverberation of their obscene *Clang! Clang! Clang!*

What ghastly clatter! What unearthly din!

And that I should believe it is all my "artist's imagination". What a laugh! What a fright! I wish to throw myself into the flames of the fire and roast my brain until I hear the bells no more—alas, I cannot do even this, for they are cold flames, ghost flames, phantasmagoric flames. I wish to take this quill, then, and jab it into my veins and bleed into silence, sweet, heavenly silence.

Bells, bells, bells!

How they toll and for whom they toll, I know not. I wish only they would cease, and be dead, at long last, dead; the bells become wisps of smoke to dissipate into nothing, nothing, blessed *nothing!*

Must remind myself—it is all in my brain.

All an illusion.

A neuroanatomical concoction.

Perhaps it is something I ate? The bread in my satchel is a month old and molding—some alien, green spore that causes one to hallucinate upon digestion, perhaps. Yes, of course!—The manufacture of illusion by the mysterious organ that is the human brain. It is the most rational explanation I can think of to explain this, this, this accursed *cacophony!* On and on! I can hardly hear myself *think!*

If there is a God, Julia,
may He be damned to the Hellish
fires of his own creation!!!

I wish to run out of this building screaming into the chill October air. For the bells were torture enough! The tolling has all but ceased, and for the moment, I hear something worse, something far, far more ghastly ....

I am a very sick man, Julia. I require a doctor's care and attention. I hear things—Horrible, dreadful things which cannot be.

Still, such noises persist ... the dull rattle of bells dragging across the floor, and footsteps, hundreds of footsteps echoing out of the rooms and down the main passageway that leads to this very office from whence I write. Betwixt the din of dragging bells and the echoes of shuffling footsteps, arises the moaning and groaning of the dead come to seek a life ... mine own.

I shiver, scrawling this letter so messily I am unsure you will find it legible. No matter. To write, to sketch, anything to distract myself from the madness of my mind—this unmerciful, malevolent, and macabre madness at long last come home to roost!

Moaning. Groaning. Calling my name: *John ... John ... young fellow John* ....

Harsh, rotting voices grow and loom closer, approaching the door that I am certain shall swing open at any moment, and all of the rotting corpses shambling in to feast, feast, feast upon my flesh and choke the night with terrible blood-chilling screams; mine own!

Quiet.

Silent as the grave, really. (isn't *that* a laugh?

HA! HA!

HA!

HA! HA! HAAA!

Not a thing stirs, save the wild pounding of my heart. The groaning cadavers scraped their bodies against the door, and the scuffed brass knob did turn, and the door opened wide on screeching hinges. There, the ominous dark yawned silent before me, beckoning that I come hither ....

The clock's hands have slithered to three. Time, I am afraid, for another round. Must keep my head. Must remember, it is only the night, only my imagination playing cruel tricks. Must keep this job, must regain Hogarth's trust, must save money, must survive and make it home to you—oh, how I long for your warm touch, your tender kisses! God knows I would benefit from your affections this very moment.

Now, I place the quill upon the desk and leave for a time. I will return, I am sure I will, indeed, I must return, for there is nothing, really nothing to be afraid of, I'll return presently, soon, in a minute or two, but soon, I will, I must ... return.

I am not who I thought I was, dearest Julia.

I am not who I thought I was at all.

What year is it? The dawn came, yet no Hogarth came with it, and now it is night again, and how long have I lived here, roaming these darkened halls and crypts, lingering about the office with its false flames, staring out the windows at the turtle-paced peasants groveling in the mud?

Here I am, at dawn, and at night once again, moaning and groaning, and what is *this*? Attached to my finger, the finger that is to wear a ring in honor of our love and commitment? Why, it is a yellowed old piece of string! About four feet long, and at the end of the string, a bell that jitters and trembles as I drag it 'cross the floor.

I am not the John Reilly Clarkston I thought I was, my dearest—no, no, *no!*

Upon making my previous round, not fifteen minutes ago, not fifteen years ago, not fifteen eons ago, I entered the dreaded Room Thirteen, and was drawn, steadily, like moth to flame, to the casket— *you know the one.*

I was drawn, as if a string were attached to my heart, and being pulled, and my heart was ringing. Slowly, dreadfully, a chill quivering my body, I opened wide the creaking coffin. Inside it, lying perfectly still, and cold, and dead, the poor soul that so perfectly resembles mine own.

Sunken cheeks, a few wrinkles about the eyes, finely trimmed goatee, mud-splatted herringbone coat, a morose mirror image, a sickly spitting image, a fracture in the glass of life and time, and I reached not toward him, but toward myself, into the inner pocket of my coat, and discovered my pocket vacant. My treasured brushes, gone!

CLANG! CLANG! CLANG!

I leapt backward, body fumbling, nearly dropping my lamp, as the bell above the coffin jangled obscenely. I stared wide in horror, all breath snatched from me! My heart stopped in my chest, the very moment the bell ceased its tolling.

The eyes of the dead fellow were wide open, and you know, Julia, the color of his eyes, for you have gazed into those sky blues for hours at a time, laughing and flirting and sharing jokes—You remember.

I stared into those eyes; mine own, and they stared back into mine, like a haunted reflecting glass between us. Slowly, as if drawn by a taut little string, I reached my hand into the casket … into the pocket of the fellow's mud-splattered herringbone, and his eyes did not leave mine, and there, my fingers grazing the silk lining of his inner pocket, I felt them, and pulled them out—my fine ivory paintbrushes with the Arabian horse-hair bristles, some of them round, some flat, and I bunched the brushes in my hand like a bouquet of rotten roses, for that is quite what they were; a thing beautiful dead in my hand, and myself, my spirit, dead in the hand, and I looked slowly up from the brushes, up to the face of the poor fellow in the casket, and the face was mine own.

Utter darkness descended and I blinked, and I was holding not the brushes nor the lamp, but only the string with the bell that dangled from my ring finger as I walk these halls, these horrid hellish halls with all their lost spirits moaning and groaning and slinking across the dripping walls, the bells clattering in the dark in a most grotesque cacophony!

It is midnight of the soul here.

It is midnight everywhere, and dawn is never to come.

My lovely Julia, what have I become?

(London, it turns out, is no place for an artist!)

Please, do not relate these details to your father.

The midnight madness of my soul has come home to roost. Roost home, where I am presently, home, and I have always been—home.

Hogarth arrives at random intervals, bringing with him a shaft of gray London light, as he huffs and puffs, shuffling out the corpses— alas, their spirits remain eternally fixed here. For the Transit Station, as it is called, is a joke: its transitions are of dead matter only; yet it chains the souls, succumbs the soul like a sickly succubus, soaks all souls into its mold black bricks and never let's go.

This letter I write to you now has been written and re-written, and has always been written, forever afloat in the flotsam of time, adrift in the eternal mirror of death; a mirror that does not fog over with the breath of life. Do you remember, as I remember, the zenith of our lives, Julia? How I used to lay you down among wildflowers, both of us unclothed, your pliable breasts in my hands, your smile on my lips, O, how blissful we were in mad, fervent, passionate *love!*

Harken! Do you hear, even across the sea, *this,* my old coffin bell, dearest Julia? How it tolls an eternity—*only for thee, for thee, for thee!*

This story is dedicated to Edgar Allan Poe,
who has touched, and will continue to touch,
grasp, and clutch, and squeeze
each and every one
of our tell-tale hearts.

AN OBSOLETE ART

I hadn't received an honest-to-God handwritten letter since I was a kid. As a thirty-four-year-old woman living in golden wheat country with no partner, friends, or career to speak of, human communication remains dubious. I ain't much for phone calls ('cept with Mama), and I don't text, email, or any of that social media stuff.

As for a handwritten letter? Hell, I plain forgot such a thing existed.

It was nearly ninety degrees the day I rolled down my window, reached into the mailbox, and discovered Bobby Aveeno's letter. Bobby was a fellah I'd dated in high school. Hadn't heard from him in damn near two decades. I smiled big and must've looked like a maniac, all covered in blood and smellin' to high heaven of death.

But that's how anyone looks, fresh from the slaughterhouse. I kill chickens. It's a downright brutal industry and I don't like it much, but there ain't shit for jobs round here and I don't got money to move to any other town.

So I work the slaughterhouse, and I live in my quaint cottage, and on weekends I sit on the porch and drink coffee and read.

Books, mostly. Never letters.

I shoved Bobby's letter into the back of my blue jeans, parked in the driveway, then went inside to shower. All clean, I poured a glass of iced coffee and sat in a warm breeze on the bottom porch step. Then ripped open the envelope.

Bobby Aveeno's neatly penned words conjured up an alternate universe when we was both sixteen, in love, and tryin' out new moves in the back of his '71 Chevrolet. I sat there dazed. Sunlight gleamed off the ripped out notebook pages. Paper fringes came off in my hands, fluttered away on the wind like dandelion fluff.

It was a charming letter from a man whom, for all these years gone, might as well have been a fiction.

"Bobby Aveeno." His name slipped from my lips and there was only the wind rustling through the honeyed wheat to answer.

I read over his letter twice, three times. Bobby had gone back to livin' in our hometown of Sweet Hollow. He'd had a wife and kid, too, 'cept he and the wife got divorced and she turned the kid against him and now he don't got a family. But it wasn't all bad, he said, 'cause he bought a house just a block down from where my Mama's living. They see each other in passing, and it was from Mama he learned my current address.

Thought it'd be nice to communicate by old-fashioned epistolary, he'd written, *instead of over a plain old boring phone. Letter writing may well be an 'obsolete art', as they say, but it'll come back. Remember how vinyl records went away? Now all the kids are buying them again. It'll be the same with letters. Just you wait.*

I got so excited about practicing an 'obsolete art' that I scrounged about my office for sheets of paper. Then I snatched up a black ink pen and got to writing:

Dear Bobby,

Receiving your letter has been a wonderful surprise. Your words bring a great deal of warmth and joy to my heart, and here I'd thought you was lost forever to time! You know how it is, right? Friends and lovers pass in and out of one's life constantly. Like whirls of smoke, here then gone, or like paper fringes loose to the wind.

Here I paused in my scribbling. I sipped my iced coffee, then took another run at it.

Or like phantoms, popping in and out of existence, like them quantum particles I learned about in a documentary. That's you, Bobby Aveeno. A lovely little quark that just popped into my existence. I hope we'll be able to continue this 'epistolary' thing. I'm finding it novel and exciting. Exactly what I needed.

I went on to tell him about my life and found myself lacking in material. God, what was there to say? I told him about my cottage, that I worked hard, that I read novels.

I neglected mentioning the slaughterhouse. Comin' home day after day covered in blood and feathers didn't do much for one's dignity.

I wrote a lengthy letter, mostly philosophizing about stuff, and asking Bobby questions about what he did with his time, if he liked being back in Sweet Hollow. I closed the envelope by licking the bitter-dry seal, applied a stamp, then walked the thing to the mailbox.

What a satisfying feeling, sliding up that red flag! The silver box gleamed harshly in the afternoon sun, but that little red flag was respectable—like a proud pedestrian downright determined to hail a cab.

That night I lay in bed and gazed out the window. Stars shimmered in the black night. I thought about Bobby's slim frame and pimply face and wondered how he looked these days. Maybe he'd aged handsomely, with silver in his beard. That's the unfair thing about men—they age well. An aging female movie star knows she'll be offered less roles year after year, but an aging George Clooney or Denzel? They'll have work the rest of their life.

Maybe it was that way for Bobby.

In my next letter, I'd ask him to send me a picture of himself, pretty please.

As for myself, I hadn't had any kids and therefore kept in good shape. I didn't eat much either. Workin' at the slaughterhouse deterred appetite. I lived on Cheerios in the morning, bread and veggies at night, and black coffee in between. If Mama ever got wind of my diet, she'd curse up and down. But we only ever talked on the phone.

Due to livin' three states away, Mama and I only visited at Christmas. "Girl, you're skinny as a rail!" she'd say, but I was smart at switching the subject.

And heck, Christmas was only four months away! Maybe I'd drop by Bobby's house on my way to Mama's. We could have us a nice little one-nighter. It's been years since I've gotten laid, and a woman has needs.

I took care of those needs lyin' in bed, thinking of Bobby. We was getting hot in the backseat of his Chevy. Only he was older, handsome, an aging Clooney. In my mind I straddled him, while my two fingers did the work.

Satisfied, I closed my eyes. Darkness swept over me. My last thought before the oblivion of sleep was of the letter I'd sent. It was the most exciting thing that'd happened in a while. I hoped to hear back from Bobby soon.

I get to thinkin' deeply in the slaughterhouse. I wander in my imagination, while my hands pick up the wild screamin', wing-flappin' chickens and shove them upside down onto the conveyor shackles. Once they're hung, the conveyor moves them down the hall, where their heads will be dipped in electrified water to stun.

By midday, I'll be switched to a different station, but I like shackling best. It's the least messy and I can daydream of the future, or the past ...

I moved South when I turned eighteen. I don't know why, 'cept that I'd been the only black girl in a nearly all-white school. My parents, both black, had grown up in Chicago, and upon marriage decided to raise me far from the city.

Daddy had been a good man. He'd made Mama and me happy, until passing away of a heart attack when I was nine. A handsome headshot from his military days hangs on my living room wall.

Sometimes I wonder how the hell I got here. This rinky-dink town. This hot, stupid, gory job in the slaughterhouse. I can hardly believe I'm thirty-four years old either, but arithmetic don't lie.

Bobby and I had shared classes and graduated the same year. We'd discussed starting a future together, but in the end, realized we weren't right for each another. Bobby had plans to attend Michigan State. I didn't want anything to do with Michigan. I wanted to see the country, new faces and lands.

Bobby went his way. I went mine.

I rambled around and saw mountains and fields and rivers and oceans. Even went all the way to the Gulf of Mexico. I hopped trains, just like in the old movies, and went hobo-in' from town to town, workin' odd jobs just to save enough money to split and go somewhere else.

In my late twenties, I drifted into Wheaton, Tennessee and never left. I made friends here, but now they're all dead or in jail or gone off somewhere. Like I say, friends are phantoms in disguise.

My first year in Wheaton I'd worked at a gas station, savin' enough money to put a down payment on the cottage and the five acres it stands on. When I got the slaughterhouse job, I kept it because it was more money. And I *still* need it. My mortgage ain't paid off and every year the Government sees fit to increase my land taxes.

These days, I don't go nowhere but for work and home, and my only escape is daydreaming. Today, stringin' up chickens, I daydream about Bobby Aveeno and his charming letter.

Strange how people come in and out of your life! Little quarks, all of them. Every person you meet. Every town you enter or leave, or why people do the things they do. One little mystery after another.

"Michelle!"

I let out a shriek of surprise and spin around.

It's Coleslaw, comin' over to take up my station. He's a fat albino in a blue apron slick with blood. The yellow-white hair piled atop his head is what gives him his moniker.

"You're on cuttin'," he says, and shoves me out of the way. He stoops into the trough, picks up a chicken. The animal screams shrill as it's shoved hard onto the shackles. Sometimes the bones in their legs snap. Coleslaw doesn't care none. He just repeats the action, over and over.

The shackle conveyer glides between walls, into the next room. I leave for the cutting station. You have to move fast when switching stations—the conveyor doesn't stop for nothin', as our company needs to produce as many cook-ready chickens as feasible.

I pass the shackle corridor and the electrified trough that stuns the chickens (well, most of them—some chickens are good at craning their heads above the water), then take up my station just past the automatic throat-cutter machine. The ceiling lights are sickly yellow, casting everything in a cancerous hue.

Sometimes the throat-cutter doesn't cut all the throats, and the chickens are left flapping their broken wings and screamin'. That's where I come in. With a razor, I simply step forward and slice through their feathers and skin, down into their jugglers. The blood pours out, dripping all over my rubber gloves and apron.

I'll cut throats for the next three hours. No break.

All I've got are dreams.

Bobby Aveeno and I walkin' hand in hand down my driveway and I show him my cottage and he smiles, says, "You've done well for yourself, 'Shell! What a lovely home." I then tell him I got a lovely bedroom, too, and that's where we go next.

So much blood and feathers and screamin', you'd think it might be hard to drift away, but it ain't. The sickly pall of jaundiced light and the inhuman screaming and the hot, hard-to-breathe agony of the slaughterhouse only makes it easier.

Like John Lennon once said, *you might say I'm a dreamer, but I ain't the only one.*

It's the smooth sweep of Bobby's hand that I admire. The ink is slick-black, almost like it ain't quite dry. The delicate curl and curve of his pen makes me dream of what else Bobby's hands might be capable.

His second letter was twice as long! My nerves jangled as my eyes roved the pages, devouring every word. It was another hot day in Wheaton, and I contented myself with iced coffee. Come about the middle of his letter, I began to cry.

I'll tell you a secret, Michelle, one I've not shared with another living soul. Up until recently, I've been a sad, lonely man. With my wife and kid out of the picture, I didn't have anything left. I felt empty inside, like a zombie. About one week ago, I'd considered swallowing a bottle of sleeping pills. Then I thought about you. How much fun we had back when we were kids, smiling and laughing in that eternal summer. Remember how we'd smuggle in a bottle of wine at the drive-in? Or go skinny-dipping in Ouspenskaya Lake? I recall fondly those hot, sticky nights in the backseat of my Chevy. All these memories of your soulful brown eyes full of dreams and your smooth ebony skin and your tender smile saved me. So I took up writing you a letter, and sent it immediately, hoping you'd reply.

Lo and behold, you have. Now, I've got a reason to live. Maybe I've gone crazy, 'Shell, but for now, let it be. Craziness has never felt so good.

"Bobby," I whispered, dropping the letter onto my table. Wiping tears on my sleeve, I realized it was true—I'd saved Bobby Aveeno's life. And, in turn, he'd saved mine.

Saved me with dreams and fantasies of what *could be.*

Now, a ravenous spirit seemed to course through my body. I jumped up from the table, fetched a pen and paper from the other room, then sat down and got writing. A few tears dripped off my cheek onto the paper.

Bobby,

I've been waiting for somethin' to break for a long time. My cottage home is fine and all, but all I've got is work and wild dreams and wheat grass. I want something real, see? I want connection with another living being, something physical, something I can hold and call mine.

Your letters do that for me.

I hope mine do the same for you.

It's been twenty years since I've seen your face. Would you send me a picture? I'll bet you're handsome as a fox. I'll send you a picture of me, too, taken by my Mama at last Christmas.

And yes, I remember those intimate times in your Chevy, and at the Drive-In. All those cool, moonlit nights come cascading through me, time after time. Do you remember those promises we made to each other, while we was laid out on a blanket on the hill? The grass tickled our naked sides, the future was an infinite horizon. Then life came and did what life does—mess things up.

The universe is a home to chaos, as I see it, and human beings must learn to navigate through it. Impossible as it is to navigate chaos.

But the future is looking bright, Bobby Aveeno, because you're in it.

I know you feel the same about me.

Let's plan to meet in person, okay? At Christmas? I'll be in town.

Love,

Michelle

P.S. if you like my picture, I'll send you more … only they won't be the kind Mama would take!

Summer of blood and feathers.

Summer of love, daydreams, letters.

Our relationship, a blossoming flower amidst the chaos of the world.

I bloodied my apron yet opened my heart. The months passed like a sea breeze over a mainsail, and I was coasting through the waters of the world. Such mountain highs of fancy, such soaring eagle-winged heights—all those evenings out on the porch, or at my table, writing letters to Bobby with butterflies in my stomach!

I'd never had a long-distance relationship before, but I suppose that's what it was. It's a strange phenomenon, to feel so connected to an ideal in your mind. God knew, Bobby was a figment of my imagination—that part of the mind that deals with one's past. But the Bobby of my past is not the Bobby of my present. I wouldn't truly *know* who he was until I got to meet him again.

As summer turned to fall, Christmas seemed farther away than ever. I longed to take off for Sweet Hollow yet needed to save money for the trip. The slaughterhouse didn't offer P.T.O., and so I scrimped and saved every penny.

No extra expenses, 'cept for stamps. I saved gas by walking the two miles to work and back. Bobby's letters came in every week, and I'd reply the very day I received one.

It was in October, after the third or fourth time of my pestering him for a picture, that Bobby told me the truth.

Michelle,

You insist on a picture. How I'd love to send you one that I was proud of. But I'm afraid I can never be proud of my appearance, my face.

I hope you will not be too upset to learn I have told you a lie. I never did get divorced and had my kid taken away. The truth: a car accident killed them both a few years back. I'd been driving the car. A truck came zipping out of an intersection. Took us rolling across the road, into the ditch.

Several days later, I awoke in a hospital room hooked to a machine. My wife and child, whom I love dearly, are gone. I'd barely survived the crash, myself. My scarred face is testament to that fact. You say you expect me to be 'handsome as a fox', but I cannot in good faith agree with you.

I wish I could. God, Michelle, you have no idea! I am sorry.

Once again, I wept at Bobby Aveeno's letter.

I paced the floors, imagining what Bobby's face looked like.

Was he truly so hideous that I could not love him? Was I so vain *not* to love him?

I skipped coffee that evening and went straight for the bottle of bourbon beneath the kitchen sink. I poured a glass, downed it in a gulp, then poured another.

At midnight, a thunderstorm broke. Rain lashed the windows. Purple lightning flickered and flashed. Thunder boomed like an angry god stomping about the heavens.

When the power went out, I fetched my coconut-scented candles, the only kind I had layin' around. Felt like I was inside some old Western movie, all cold and huddled in a blanket at the table beside candlelight.

I thought about Bobby Aveeno's face.

Scars. Bunched tissue. A crooked mouth.

I drew a terrible image in my mind—yet found it tolerable, even loveable. How come? Because no matter how his face looked, it was Bobby! The same Bobby who'd saved my life from ennui and dreariness with his letters, his love, his wanting.

Yes, Bobby *wanted* me.

And I wanted *him*. Drunk, I took up the pen and gave him what for:

Damn you, Bobby Aveeno, I don't give a damn for your scars. Perhaps I'll even find your scars handsome in all their ruggedness. They bring you memories and pain, but what if they bring me pleasure? Am I so terrible to suggest it?

If not a picture, how about a phone call? How I'd love to hear your voice! I can't wait until Christmas. Give me a call some evening: 731-377-0101.

Words are just tools, Bobby, and they possess that paradox of bein' both powerful and inefficient. Words cannot express my blossoming love for you, even though we've not seen each other in such a long time. And words cannot explain how truly sorry I am for you and your loss.

I would be happy to talk with you about your dear wife and child, should you ever feel like sharing. If not, I understand.

I'm enclosing a photo of me that I've taken. I know how much you've enjoyed those last ones. This one isn't sexy, so much as just plain cute. I took it before goin' into work a while back. Isn't that sunrise behind me glorious?

I stuffed the polaroid I'd taken of myself (a 'selfie', the kids call it) into the envelope, licked it shut, then applied address and stamp.

When the storm subsided, I ran out into the drizzling rainy dark, protecting the letter beneath my blouse. The driveway was muddy, but I slogged through.

Shoving the letter into the mailbox, I smiled and flipped up that little red flag.

Like a pedestrian in the rain, doggedly resolute for a ride.

Aren't we all, sometimes?

Next morning after the storm, I'd just got around to pourin' a cup of steaming coffee when the telephone rang. Damned near jumped out of my skin! The antique rotary clanged in the living room. Each sharp jostle of the bell made my heart flutter.

Bobby?

But I'd only sent the letter with my phone number last night. It couldn't be him. Illogical though it was, a sliver of hope agitated my heart.

I picked up. "Hello?"

"Michelle, my bell! How are you?" Mama's voice, raspy from a life of smoking, sounded in my ear with its usual overemphasis on joy. That's the way it was with her. Everything had to sound joyful, even when things were the exact opposite.

"Fit as a fiddle." I sat in the recliner, wishing I'd brought my coffee into the room. The phone's pigtail cord didn't reach as far as the doorway. "How about you, Mama?"

"Oh, I can't complain."

I rolled my eyes. She never did complain. Most folks make a virtue of that, but I don't. Complainin' is cathartic to the soul.

A silence fell between us, and I sensed Mama grasping for a topic.

"Sure am excited to see you this Christmas!" she squealed, adroitly.

"Mama," I said, "Christmas is two months from now."

"Right! Only two months, 'Shell. And you know what? I'm gonna have some guests over this time."

"Really?" I was surprised. Every year it was just me and Mama hangin' around the Christmas tree, exchanging presents over glasses of wine. Lonesome.

"Who's all comin'?" I asked.

"Roberta, my next-door neighbor, and Tom and his wife Sara, from across the street and—"

"Bobby Aveeno?" I'd blurted, giddily. I'd thought of seeing Bobby separately, secretly, but the idea of the three of us spending Christmas together made me warm and tingly inside.

"*Who?*"

"Bobby," I repeated. "Bobby Aveeno? C'mon, Mama, you remember! I grew up with him, we dated. Lives right down the street from you?"

Christ! This woman could be so clueless.

Another long silence, then I leaned forward. "You still there?"

"Oh, *Michelle!*" She scolded me—a welcome departure from her constant pretense of joy.

"What's wrong, Mama?"

"Bobby Aveeno's been dead a *year* now."

My breath caught in my throat. Only the hum of the telephone wire between us.

Then I laughed. "Mama, that's crazy!"

I went on to tell her about the letters. How Bobby lived in the old Victorian down the street from her, the one we'd called 'The Haunted Manor' when we were kids.

"Listen." Mama weighed her words, speaking carefully. "Bobby died of a car crash, along with his wife and child. They're buried in the Sweet Hollow Cemetery. You can visit their headstones if you don't believe me. And there isn't anyone in that old house. That place has stood empty a long time."

"But Bobby said he'd talked to you, and that's how he got my address and began writing me letters—

"Michelle Lynn Connors!" Her voice heightened into a scream, and I yanked the phone an inch away from my ear. "*Enough.* I don't know *who* you've been exchanging letters with, but it's not with that poor Robert Aveeno! For Lord's sake, girl, can't you let the dead be dead?"

Mama's plea buzzed in my brain like a fat, sick fly. *Can't you let the dead be dead?*

When the next letter from Bobby arrived, I read it with Mama's shrill claims overshadowing his words. The power of his sentiment, the grace of his hand, all now subject to conspiracy. *Was* this Bobby Aveeno writing to me? Or some freak pretending to be him, for a perverse joke, a laugh?

I'd arrived home, fetched the letter from the box, and read it on the porch. My arms were splattered with blood. I was sweaty, sticky. My red fingers stained the edges of the paper.

How I dream of you, Michelle, and think on the bright times we've had and the even brighter times to come. I so look forward to being with you on Christmas! Best not to tell your Mama this, though. She might not approve (as you'll recall, she didn't approve twenty years ago either!)

I look forward to having you at my house. Do you know the neighbor kids still consider it haunted? Can't say I blame them. There's something creepy about Victorian houses. Something dark and mysterious about the windows, the peeling clapboards, the weathered porch stairs. I'm hoping, together, we can make this old house a merrier place.

May the months speed by, until you are here, and warm, and safe in my loving arms.

You mention a telephone call, but I'm afraid I can't do it. I don't have a phone in the house, cell or landline. And I don't think there's even pay phones anymore, do you? We'll content ourselves with letters then, until we meet—and oh! What a time that will be.

I love you, Michelle Connors.

XOXOXXX.

I cried, coming close to ripping up the letter.

If this wasn't Bobby Aveeno, then who was it? Who could know the intimate details of our past, about our nights in the Chevy, the lake, the drive-in? Some old friend of Bobby's? Someone who'd been his closest confidant, and who, upon some perverted desperation and loneliness, reached out to me with a forged hand?

Perhaps.

Or was Mama mistaken? Maybe she'd picked up on some neighborhood gossip about Bobby dying in a crash and took it to heart. That, I felt, was more likely.

Mama meant well, but she could be gullible. I folded up the letter and stowed it in its envelope. After hopping into the shower, I began to feel at ease. Hot water flowed out of the showerhead, ran down my tired, aching shoulders, arms, and legs. I felt silly for believing Mama, even if for just a short while. What did that old woman know about *anything?*

You can visit their headstones if you don't believe me.

And I bet if I visited Sweet Hollow Cemetery, I'd find some headstones that belonged to the Aveeno's—his wife and daughter. But Bobby's name wouldn't be chiseled on any of 'em.

Tell a person a lie, and if they want to believe it, they will. And so Mama saw Bobby's tombstone next to the others because she *wanted* to believe it. It made sense to her, somehow.

I shampooed, rinsed, toweled off. Then I sat down at the table in my robe, and wrote Bobby my most luxuriant, lovely, love-struck letter yet.

Two days before I was to leave for Sweet Hollow, I received Bobby's Christmas card. Handsome red trim bordered the sides. Two cartoon reindeer kissed at its center. I sighed, butterflies quivering in my stomach, and opened the card. A photograph slid out onto my lap.

I picked it up, studied it in the lamplight.

At first, I thought it was a picture of nothing. Just a black photograph, maybe a mistake in development, but then I saw the outline of Bobby's face. Only his chin was clearly visible, the same dimple chin I remember kissing so long ago.

He was pale, and what appeared to be a deep fracture ran slant-ways across his chin. I could barely make out his lower lip in the dim light.

It was a crappy picture, but it made me smile. Bobby was being vulnerable, and I loved him for that. His card read:

Merry Christmas, Michelle, and a Happy New Year!
I so look forward to being with you.
I love you more than life itself.

To think, I'd see him in the flesh in just a few days! Time had passed quickly. Summer had whirled by in a blur. Autumn had fluttered down and away. Now, it was the dead of winter. I magnetized Bobby's photo to my refrigerator, then fetched my three hundred dollars cash savings and stuffed it into my wallet. I packed a duffel bag with clothes, my prettiest dress, a toothbrush, perfume, a book, then crammed in a winter coat on top.

I wouldn't wait around no more.

I'd leave tonight.

After preparing a thermos of coffee, I climbed into my truck and took off. It was sixty degrees. I kept my window partly down, letting the cold night air rush through my curls.

I thought about Sweet Hollow and how surprised Mama would be to discover my arrival on Christmas Eve morning—a day earlier than expected!

I'd surprise Bobby too. I'd drive to his house, knock on the door. When he opened it, I'd jump into his loving arms and give him a long, deep kiss.

I'd drove thirteen hours straight, stopping only for gas, snacks, and to stretch my legs. At nine a.m. on Christmas Eve, I drove past Bobby Aveeno's house.

Just as I'd remembered it—an empty, haunted shell.

Crows cawed in the calm morning, fluttering black wings in the barren trees. Bobby's windows were dark. The driveway was empty and drifted over with snow. *Where's his car? Why isn't his drive shoveled?*

Likely he was still asleep, I thought, and hadn't gotten around to shoveling. As for his car, maybe he didn't have one. Lots of folks depended on public transit, after all.

Oh, my heart surged. How I wanted to knock on his door that

very instant! I gazed into my rearview mirror. Heavy bags under my eyes. My hair a disaster. It was better to wait.

I parked in Mama's driveway, beyond ready for a nice long nap.

I slung my duffel over my shoulder, walked up the salted steps, and knocked.

I waited, shivering in the Wisconsin winter winds.

Knocked again.

Mama's face peered out the long rectangular window beside the door. Her brown eyes widened as she let out a muffled scream of delight.

Opening the door, she leapt onto the front step in her nightgown and slippers.

"Oh, Michelle, my bell!" she squealed, wrapping me in a hug. "You're early! What a wonderful surprise!"

"It's nice to see you too, Mama," I said, and meant it. Taking up my bag, she rushed me inside out of the cold. Soon, I got comfy on her couch with a cup of hot cocoa.

She sat across from me, in her recliner. The Christmas tree beside us glowed red, green, blue, and purple. Antique ornaments, candy canes, and an angel on top. The tinsel shimmered so bright it hurt my eyes.

"I missed you so much, Michelle." Mama smiled, blinking tears.

"I missed you too, Mama. I'm also real tired from the drive. You still got my room made up?"

She nodded, sipping her cocoa. "Dusted and changed the sheets just last night. Come on, girl, I'll make sure you're comfy."

I set aside my empty mug of cocoa and stood, stretched, yawned. "That's okay. I know my way around, Mama."

She ignored this, guiding me up to my old bedroom. I lay down in the soft bed, cozied beneath covers that Mama pulled to my chin. As if I were seven years old again, home with the flu.

"You get some rest," she smiled. "Later, we'll put presents under the tree."

She closed the door.

I shut my eyes. Slept.

I told Mama I was goin' into town to buy us a big fat turkey.

Even though I don't eat meat no more, on account of that damned slaughterhouse. I've seen enough of what goes on to know better.

No, I wasn't goin' into town for turkey.

I was goin' to Bobby's house, to hold him, to touch him, to make love.

"Why're you dressed so *nice?*" Mama frowned.

"Be back in a while!" I replied, ignoring her query. I drove to the end of the block, parking outside the Manor.

I'm not much of a makeup gal, but I'd spent damn near a half hour prettying myself up. I wore a dress, a tight-fitting thing, dark blue with black polka dots.

I walked through deep snow in my high heels, as the driveway still wasn't shoveled. Snow wetted the tops of my feet, and I hissed at the cold. Bobby's windows were darker than ever.

My heart sunk. Was he even home?

At last, I glimpsed a soft yellow glow shining through one of the front windows. Candlelight, perhaps. How romantic! I imagined spending the evening with Bobby over a candlelit dinner, toasting glasses of champagne. But in my mind, three-quarters of his face was hidden in the dark, just like his photograph.

The porch stairs creaked beneath me, noisy in the otherwise silent dusk. Christmas lights gleamed on the roofs and porch banisters of neighboring houses. Plastic decorations of Santa Clauses and elves and snowmen and reindeer and candy canes glowed softly. Snowy lawns glistened with kaleidoscopic colors. The street was empty. All was silent, save for a muffled voice or laugh from a neighbor. Everyone cozied inside their homes, awaiting Christmas Day.

I knocked firmly on Bobby's door. Grey paint flaked off, powdering my knuckles with ash. I flinched as the door creaked open.

Like a gaping mouth, the door stood wide.

Nobody there.

I frowned, shivering in my dress. Had the door been partly open when I knocked, the force of my knuckles pushing it in?

My heart pounded.

I was nervous, frightened, hopeful.

"Bobby?" I called, stepping into the house. It was dark and cold as a grave. I shut the door behind me, cutting out the draft that made the fringes of my dress flutter.

Mama was right. Just an empty old house.

But what about the light in the window? My eyes adjusted to the dark, and sure enough, there it was. A soft golden light flickering from an open doorway on the opposite side of the room.

"Bobby?" I approached the doorway.

A voice returned. "In here, dearest Michelle!"

It wasn't Bobby's voice.

It couldn't be, for it was deep, and wheezing, and rusty. Like water dripping from an old pipe, a sound both quiet and loud, and if you listened for very long it would drive you mad.

In here, dearest Michelle!

My body was all shuddering ice, yet my face blushed hot.

Nervous, frightened, hopeful.

I'm getting out of here, I told myself.

I'm going into that room with the light, I told myself.

A dual force raged in my heart, and as my feet stepped closer and closer to the glowing doorway, my soul screamed: *Stop. Turn around. It isn't Bobby Aveeno in that room, but somebody else! Some creep who's been writing letters from this address claiming to be Bobby, but it ain't, it ain't, it ain't.*

I entered the room.

A table with napkins, bowls, glasses, and silverware laid out. Three tall candles burned bright. At the end of the table, sat a man.

Why didn't he jump up to hug me, kiss me, hold me in his arms like he promised? Beside the man's filthy hands lay an open notebook half-filled with ...

And then I knew—*yes!* This was, indeed, Bobby Aveeno. Even in the dim light, I could recognize that hand anywhere. The same handwriting on my letters, the same in my high school yearbook, the one that said, *Many great times to come, 'Shell!*

"Please." Bobby's voice was a drip, a leak, a rugged gurgle. He gestured toward the chair opposite him.

Slowly, I pulled back the chair. I squinted at him in the dark, unable to make out his features in the light. Reluctantly, I sat.

His voice is ruined from the crash, I realized. His vocal cords were damaged, maybe from his throat being sliced by glass or shrapnel. As my eyes adjusted, I began to *see* him.

Bobby resembled the Invisible Man, for his entire head was wrapped with white bandaging. All save for his eyes, which appeared as little dark holes in the white bandages. Black pitted caverns.

"Bobby," I whispered. "I've been waiting so long for this moment."

He nodded, as if to say, *yes, me too, my dear.*

But he dared not say anything, for then I'd hear his dreaded, corroded voice. I now felt guilty for requesting a phone call with him, but how was I to know about his voice? He'd never mentioned it.

I licked my dry, chapped lips, no longer certain I wanted to kiss him. He frightened me in that dim light. Just a silhouette in the dark, covered in bandages.

"Honey," I said. "Won't you take off the bandages? You don't need those. Not around me, you don't."

Bobby stood and walked to the kitchen counter. He opened a can of I-don't-know-what, then brought it over to the bowl before me. I felt like throwing up, due to the way the cold mush *slopped* into my bowl. I thought of chicken livers, hearts, intestines. My stomach curdled. Next, he fetched a bottle of wine from the cupboard. He poured his glass, then mine, and the moment he ceased pouring, I looked up at his bandaged face and into his pitch-black eyes, feeling as if I were gazing into an abyss.

I touched his pale, frozen hand that seemed covered in dirt, or soil, as it clung to his skeletal fingers in frozen chunks, almost as if the dirt were *part* of his fingers, his flesh, and I wondered if it weren't dirt after all, but some sickly ulcer that accumulated upon damaged skin.

I didn't know anything, except that I wanted him to remove his bandages and show himself.

"I love you," I said. "You don't need to hide."

And I stroked his hand. His frigid, cold-as-ice hand.

Bobby's shoulders hitched with a stifled sob, and I nearly crumpled into my chair. I can't bear to see a man weep. It tears me up inside.

I wondered, randomly, what Mama was doing right about now. Probably sitting in her recliner, sipping her evening's third cup of cocoa, awaiting my return with the turkey.

Suddenly all thoughts of Mama cut away—Bobby began unraveling himself.

He wept with a noise like a flood from a pipe, a maddening flow of emotions that thickened into a cascade and racked his body.

"Oh, Bobby," I whispered. "Honey ..."

He tore his hand from mine, ripping ferociously at the bandages.

A sprout of black hair atop his head. He was bald, save for a few wild strands.

His forehead, slick with sweat, or mucus, and not pale so much as brown—like frozen soil beneath the snow.

His eyes—I inhaled sharply, my breath stolen. He had *no eyes!*

His nose, too, was absent—only black, teardrop-shaped ovals remained.

His lips, mauve and mossy and moldering.

His chin, the sweetly dimpled chin that I kissed when we were young, in love, both of us *alive.*

The tail end of the bandage fell to the table. My chair screeched as I shoved it back. Wet sobs exploded out of me—Mama was right!

Bobby died of a car crash, along with his wife and child. They're buried in Sweet Hollow Cemetery.

I backed through the doorway into the living room. Bobby followed in jerky, sporadic movements, pivoting awkwardly on broken legs. He fell forward and gripped my hands tight, jerked me close to his face, so close my nose touched his cold, wet cheek and his breath wafted over, and it was the breath of deep soil, moth-eaten satin lining, earthworms and damp wood.

The fetor of death washed over me as I stared up into hollow sockets, slick with the jelly of putrefied eyeballs, and I screamed.

His skeletal hands locked around my wrists.

"*It is lonely being dead,*" Bobby Aveeno rasped.

I kicked hard at his right knee. Something audibly *snapped*—he crumpled to the floor, holding his horrible face and weeping, his voice croaking and grating, the sound of insects scurrying up his throat, tumbling over his lips, and even in the darkness I saw the shimmer of beetles squirming out of his mouth, his nostrils, his hollow socket eyes ....

I tripped over myself, landing hard on my tailbone. I gasped as a shot of pain radiated up my spine. Despite the wind being knocked out of me, I picked myself up, ran to the door, flung it wide.

Frigid December air blasted in my face, chilling me. I sprinted toward the porch steps yet found myself caught. I spun around, expecting Bobby's undead hands to be clutching the fringe of my dress.

One nail, loose from a floorboard, clung to the fabric. I yanked it back, the dress ripping. I bounded down the steps into the snow, then climbed into my truck, fumbled keys into the ignition.

I looked back once, only once. Bobby's emaciated form leaned out the doorway, his skeletal jaw opening, closing, and on the wind arose a bone-chilling banshee wail that I won't never forget. Stepping on the gas, my tires spit up clods of snow and ice.

I sped into town, all the while wanting to pull over and vomit.

At last, I pulled into the parking lot of H. Phillip's Grocery Mart. The sun had long liquified into the blackest of nights, and I sat in the darkened cab covered in sweat and gooseflesh, hardly able to suck in air.

I palmed my eyes, breathed deeply, tried not to think of Bobby's freakishly festering face. Tried not to think of having to explain to Mama why I'd been gone so long, why my dress was torn, my makeup ruined.

Life's chaos stirred my brain, my heart. I wished I hadn't knocked on the Manor's door. I wished I'd never replied to Bobby's letters.

Why can't you let the dead be dead? Mama had shouted over the phone.

I shouted it to myself now, my own anger and self-condemnation drowning out the luminous lights, the glittering garland, and beautiful baubles in the grocery display windows.

Here I was, a thirty-four-year-old woman back in her hometown, used up, letdown, screaming in the cab of a rusted truck. I hadn't even come all the way here to spend time with Mama—not this time. I'd come to rekindle a relationship that'd died twenty years ago. Died well before Bobby himself had died. I fell back into my seat, tired and weeping.

After a while, I grabbed Kleenex from the glove compartment. Wiped runny mascara off my cheeks. Then, numbly, I walked inside H. Phillip's Grocery, my high heels clicking down the polished aisles. I hefted the biggest turkey I could find and paid in cash and brought it home to Mama.

She took one look at me and frowned, asking what on earth the matter was.

I replied, "Just let the dead be dead, Mama, all right?"

On Christmas day, Mama's neighbors came over. I drank more wine than all of them put together, and we had ourselves a merry holiday. I pretended to be merry, anyway, and was so convincing in my joyful demeanor I even outdid Mama.

Guess I won't be writing letters no more. An obsolete art, Bobby had called it, and I'm content with that. I don't care to resurrect it.

Let the dead be dead.

THE HAUNTED HOUSE MYSTERY BANK

M r. Burgess trembled as he placed the Haunted House Mystery Bank in the display window of the curio shop. He'd purchased the elaborate tin-and-plastic bank when he was a kid in the fifties. Now, in the twilight years of life, he knew it was time to bequeath it to someone who would treasure it just as much as he had.

The House was no common novelty item. It was no toy, as any adult walking by the window might be inclined to believe. It was, in fact, a *real haunted house*—scaled down to the size of just seven inches high, seven wide, and nine deep.

A circular indentation was visible just before the weathered front door. Place any coin there and a mechanical whirr erupted from the house and all the windows lit up white and the door creaked open and out *it* came ....

The hand. A little yellow hand with sharp fingernails that clawed the coin and dragged it into the house. Once the door clicked shut, the lights blinked out and all was silent, dark, and gloomy.

That is how Burgess felt now, blinking glossy brown eyes behind spotty spectacles; dark, and gloomy. Stroking his snow-white goatee, he wondered if he'd find the right home for it in time. Not many days left now. His breath was short, and soon his twilight life would settle into a vast dark.

It'd been there for him all these years, the House; a loyal bulwark against life's encroaching waves that, time and again, threatened to submerge the ship of his soul.

Only five dollars and ninety-five cents! So read the advertisement on the back of his big brother Tom's tattered *Archie* comic book. Burgess' eight-year-old self had lit up just as bright as the House's windows when you placed a coin on the step. Straightaway, he knew he'd had to have it.

From that point onward, he'd worked hard delivering newspapers and mowing the neighbors' lawns for a small allowance. Two months of golden summer afternoons had been used up in the process, but as soon as he'd mailed in the $5.95 (plus .35 cents for postage and handling) he knew all his sweat, blood, and tears would prove worth it.

The House arrived on a summer's day inside a wooden crate packed with straw. The sun was bright and hot on the back of his neck. Burgess yanked the (surprisingly heavy) House out of its crate and knew the moment he held it in his hands that it wasn't just any old toy. Somehow, this thing was special. Special in a way he didn't understand but would soon enough. Inside the crate, lying atop the straw, was a slip of paper inked with a black scrawl that made him chuckle:

This house devours souls. Feed it coins every-single-night ... lest it devour yours too!

A silly superstition, perhaps, but Burgess dutifully fed it coins every night. Well, *almost* every night.

One evening after baseball practice, he'd kicked off his tennis shoes and went to bed exhausted. Next morning, Burgess discovered something so ghastly and hideous that he never forgot to place a coin on the doorstep again.

Despite that harrowing memory, he'd treasured the House all through college, three failed marriages, and a career as an independent businessman. Now, as he neared the winter of life, just as the October season grew bitter and chilly and the last of the leaves were falling, he knew he couldn't shuffle off the ol' mortal coil without ensuring the House fell into respectable hands.

Burgess sighed deeply, his soulful brown eyes now studying the wet October streets. He knew whoever deserved this house would come along soon. The house would be safe from harm, and so, in turn, would the world.

It wouldn't be a grown-up, though. Adults weren't responsible enough to take care of things like this. Only a child, bright in spirit, big in soul, and great in imagination could be trusted with the House. Mr. Burgess laughed quite suddenly, his entire face lighting up. The child he'd been waiting for had arrived! And much earlier than he'd anticipated.

As if out of a lovely dream, little Heather Beauregard sped by on her bicycle, slowed to a stop, then circled back to gaze through the display window. A smile spread across her face. Her blue eyes sparkled with fascination.

Burgess slunk back into the shadows, not wanting to distract her. Not wanting to intrude on that magic moment of first seeing the House in all its ghoulish, gothic glory. Slipping into the kitchen behind the shop, he put on a pot of tea. The girl would be cold. It was a gray, dismal day. A spine-chilling gust had been blowing through her crimson hair. A hot cup of cinnamon tea would warm her spirit. Burgess set out the cups, listening for the bell above the door. After a minute, he frowned and sped back into the shop's main room.

Heather's admiring face no longer peered through the window. But how, Burgess wondered, could that be? Opening the front door, he looked up and down main street. She was gone.

Quietly, he shut the door.

Quietly, he gazed down at the House with all the sadness of the world welling up in his eyes. He wondered if he'd been wrong about the girl. Maybe she didn't feel the magic like when *he'd* first seen the house—heck, when he'd first glimpsed the tattered advertisement, even.

Not quietly, the teapot shrieked from the kitchen. He didn't fetch it off the burner just yet, merely stood gazing at the House of magic, mystery, and money. The streets outside were strewn with soggy leaves, desolate, and empty, and now his heart was empty, but at least the house would never be empty. He'd make sure of that, wouldn't he?

The shriek resounded through the old shop. Burgess paid it no mind and reached inside his pocket. Pulling out a shiny new penny, he placed it delicately before the front door.

An offering to the Things within. A token for the *horror hand*—for that's what the advertisement had called it, all those many years ago.

The windows illuminated, flashing white like an electric shock. The mechanics of the house grinded noisily, and the door creaked open and out of the black rectangle of the doorway ....

Sharp, grimy, yellow cuticles.

It preyed upon the penny, dragged it into the dark just as it had once dragged in his big brother, Tom. Shrunk him down to the size of a quarter, then pulled him inside to fill its dark hollow belly and never let him out again. Sometimes, Burgess could still hear Tom smacking his palms against the windows, his little face screaming behind the clear plastic panes. Sometimes, although not as much as he'd used to. As if Tom had resigned himself to the basement, long given up hope.

The door slammed shut, then, and the House quieted.

Burgess sighed long and deep; his heart warmed a little, but not much.

Finally, he stepped into the kitchen and fetched the frantic teapot off the burner. Poured himself a steaming mug. Then he let out a gasp, dropping the teapot onto the linoleum floor. Scalding water spilled all over his leather shoes, but luckily did not seep through to burn his feet.

The jangle of the bell had frightened him, the one he kept above the shop door.

Could it be? *No!* he told himself. Don't get your hopes up, old man. The little girl showed vague interest, then rode on home. Just a customer come to inspect the place for its meaningless trinkets. So it goes, day in and day out.

Burgess stepped over his mess and entered the shop. Adjusting his collar, he prepared the greet the visitor with a friendly welcome. Yet there was no one at the door.

He looked all over the place, eyes roving the trinkets, knick-knacks, colorful glassware, and dusty kitsch paintings. At last, his head darted toward the corner of the display window, at the House, and there *she* was.

Heather kneeled, admiring its ramshackle roof of checkered shingles, its weathered porch stairs, its rotting clapboards ....

"Why, if it isn't little Heather Beauregard!" Burgess exclaimed. "What brings you inside a dusty old shop like this?"

But he knew very well what brought her into his shop. He knew because Heather's eyes lighted on him like fireflies in the dark. Magic, glowing, in awe of the little house of haunts that would take anything: pennies, nickels, dimes, quarters, even your soul.

Especially your soul.

Heather lowered the House into the wagon tied to the back of her bike. The moment she'd spotted the miniature gothic abode, she'd raced home to fetch her wagon to haul it. She'd also brought along her every dollar of savings, but Mr. Burgess was too kind to accept the money. He stood behind the display window now, waving goodbye—not to her, it seemed, but to the house. Are those tears in his eyes? Heather thought they were but smiled anyway, shouting, "Thanks again!" then made for home through a gusty wet wind. Crimson leaves swirled and fluttered all about her.

With a pleasurable shiver, she biked down Main Street, then turned onto Bradbury Avenue, passing the Credit Union, Karl's Barber Shop, and the Old Gem Theater. Riding through downtown Sweet Hollow during this time of year was a treat. She loved the look of ancient brick buildings on a chill fall day. Loved to wonder at the second-floor windows, the curtains parted, sometimes catching the flash of a television or a person walking by. Occasionally, she glanced behind her shoulder, making sure the marvelous House hadn't fallen out.

It shuddered in the wagon, responding to every bump and dip in the pavement. How fantastic, to have a creepy old house to store change in. Mr. Burgess had even given it to her free! She could hardly believe it when the old man looked her in the eyes and said, "This house belongs to you, young lady. It always has, I can tell. But you must always do one thing. You must feed the house a coin – doesn't matter what kind – every night of your life. If you do not… well…, let's just say, there will be dire consequences. Understood?"

Mr. Burgess had scared her a little, but she'd nodded as if she'd understood perfectly, and Burgess seemed pleased enough. Now, as she passed Sweet Hollow Cemetery and the Protestant Church upon the hill and circled onto Hodgson Street where she lived in the big yellow house, she'd never felt happier in her life. In just a few days it would be Halloween—her favorite holiday. The one day a year when Sweet Hollow became a veritable ghoul-town, full of witches, ghosts, skeletons, and fairy-tale things.

She breathed in the odors of rain-damp leaves, relishing every moment. Black and orange streamers coiled around streetlamps. Paper jack-o'-lanterns hung in nearly every window. Front lawns brimmed with Styrofoam tombstones and blow-up Jack Skellingtons and large sheeted ghosts that rippled in the wind, always on the cusp of blowing away, the white shroud rippling off into the gray skies like a lonesome kite freed from its tether, destined to become somebody's UFO.

This year, Heather knew, would be the greatest Halloween yet. She wouldn't bother joining the other kids in their annual trespassing of the haunted old Manor on the corner of Bloch and Lieber. She had something better now—a haunted house of her own to gaze upon and marvel about 'till her heart's utmost content.

Arriving home, she parked her bike in the garage, then hauled the House upstairs. Count, her beloved cat, meowed from the stair landing, although she was too excitedly occupied to pay him any mind. Inside her room, she placed the House on her large pink bed— the bed belonged to her mother, but after she'd passed away, Dad had purchased a new bed, letting Heather have the old one.

Mr. Burgess had showed her how the house worked. She decided to test it on her own, nabbing a nickel from her dresser and placing it on the doorstep. She drew back her hand and waited ….

A terrible grinding noise reverberated throughout the House. The windows illuminated white – so bright it hurt her eyes! – and inside her head was a deep and sonorous voice:

Hello there! How very nice to meet you, Child.

Heather's pulse quickened. She clamped shut her eyes, as if that would somehow banish the voice, then opened them again. It'd only been her imagination, she knew, but for a moment she could've *sworn* the House had spoken. She studied it now, and what a marvelous thing it was to behold:

The tin and plastic walls vibrating. The little weathervane atop the shingle-checkered roof spinning slowly, creaking, as if a wind turned it. The lights in the windows flashing staccato-like, and was that a breeze Heather felt? Blowing across her face like a cold draft as the door swung inward? Out of the pitch-blackness of the house—for she stooped and peered inside it, attempting to glimpse the mechanics of the thing—emerged the hand.

The Horror Hand, Mr. Burgess had called it.

A silhouette, at first, then it occupied the entirety of the door frame. Nasty, dirty thing. Its nails were like daggers, the fingers long, tapering, wrinkled.

How detailed! Heather's mouth opened in astonishment, her eyes roving every fold and crevice of the hand. Almost as if it were composed of *flesh*, not plastic. There was dirt between the pruned folds, filth and grime from many years gone, and even ... could it be? A dark red stain down the lines of its palm, like dried blood.

The hand slammed down on the silver nickel, then dragged it swiftly into the blackness. The door clicked shut and the wind that'd tickled Heather's face and stirred her hair now fell flat. All noises within the House silenced.

Heather's heart galloped. Everything was still, and quiet. Too quiet. She watched the House.

The House watched her.

Fat grey moths fluttered inside her stomach. A sense of awe and terror filled her soul. Cautiously, Heather scooped the house off her bed and set it atop her dresser.

She admired it still more: the twisted black rain gutter, cockeyed grey shutters, xylophone porch boards with missing keys, an eroding paint-chipped railing, perfect darkness stirring behind the windows, and lurking somewhere inside, at the farthest back of the house, the *Horror Hand* ....

A thing too realistic for its own good, too much like a human hand, all shrunken and withered like one of those infamous shrunken heads from the Amazon.

Heather shuddered, rubbing her arms to stir heat back into her bones. Was it the House that made her cold all over, or from being outside on a chilly autumn evening? She didn't know, nor did she care, for now her belly was rumbling. She felt a bit like the Horror Hand, eager to clasp onto any morsel and devour it immediately.

To her delight, her dad called from the bottom of the stairs, "Heather! Come down for dinner, sweet pea!"

Soon, she sat down at the table across from Dad. Two steaming bowls of tomato soup were laid out upon the table, along with an open package of saltines and a plate heaped with grilled cheese sandwiches—her favorite.

It was almost Halloween, two delicious grilled cheeses were piled on her plate, Dad's handsome face smiled, and best of all, she owned a haunted house of her very own.

A thought arrived in the grave-deep tones of the house, the voice she'd earlier dismissed as her imagination. Now, she knew it was real, and her face went sheet white. The house whispered: *No, my dear! We, the Things of the House, are most fortunate to have ... you.*

"Dad?" Heather looked up at his face, cast golden in the glow of her bedside lamp. He was tucking her into bed. She studied his warm chestnut eyes and the auburn hair that badly needed cutting; for it nearly reached his collar.

"Yes?" he asked.

"You like my house?"

He looked across the room, where it squatted on the dresser. "Uh-huh. I suppose you spent all your chore money?"

"Nope! I came across it in Mr. Burgess' shop. He let me have it for *free*."

"That's kind of old Burgess. Suppose he probably wanted to be rid of it." Heather perceived a twitch in his shoulders, and after a moment, realized he'd shivered.

"Are you cold, Dad?"

"Yes, I guess I am," he replied, rubbing his palms together. "Aren't you?"

She shook her head.

"That's all that matters, then. And I like your house fine, sweet pea. A bit ghoulish, but I know how fond you are of such things."

"Because I'm weird." Heather grinned.

"Yes," he laughed and kissed her forehead. "Because you're very, very *weird*, and because I love you."

"Love you too, Daddy. G'night."

Dad shut the door softly behind him. Heather listened as his footsteps descended the stairs into the kitchen, like she always did. His movements had become so ritualized, she could anticipate what happened next: the sound of the refrigerator opening, closing. The cracking open of a beer can. Then, a moment later, the switching on of the living room TV.

The house was old, and the walls were thin. It was a nice home all the same. Plenty of spare rooms for guests, two bathrooms (one with a big clawfoot tub), a dusty attic, and a dingy old basement with an earthen floor. It was a large home, built around the turn of the century, and because it was painted a bold daisy yellow, it caught everyone's attention. A rumor among neighbors was that the house was haunted. Heather found that silly.

The house creaked and groaned, but only from the wind pressing against the outside. And there were no ghostly moans. No rattling of chains. No screams in the night.

The only thing haunting her old two-story home was her mother— her enduring memory, her obvious absence. Dad missed her. That's why he drank several cans of beer every night, to wash away the pain of missing her. "How I pine for that woman," Dad had remarked, once or twice. It broke Heather's heart to hear it.

Heather missed her, too. Had missed her every single day since the accident last year, when Mom hadn't seen the oncoming Peterbilt truck before it was too late. Sometimes, Heather dreamed of seeing her again, only they were in heaven, a land of rolling white-cotton hills and crystal streams. Mom's freckled cheeks and cerulean eyes and blonde hair blowing in the warm, lily-scented wind, and her astonished exclamations: "Heather, my love, you've grown into such a beautiful young lady!"

It made Heather sad to think such things. She reached over and turned off the lamp. Darkness shrouded the room. Then her door nudged open an inch, then two, letting in a small stream of light from the hallway.

Heather knew who it was and reached down to pet him.

Count, her lovely black cat with a white underbelly and sweet disposition. Count bobbed his head up against her hand, then hopped into bed and curled up beside her, purring.

Heather sleepily eyed the House.

There it sat on her dresser, cold and silent like a tombstone.

A lovely little tombstone gleaming in the moonlight that shone through the window blinds; a pattern of ivory, horizontal stripes. Heather heard the House whisper: *Goodnight, dear Child. Don't let the bed bugs* ... bite!

Heather closed her eyes, unafraid of the voice which was surely only the edge of a dream she was about to drift into. Count purred beside her, warm and cozy. There sounded only the dull murmur of the downstairs TV and the groaning wind that pushed and rustled the leaves outside the house.

The week fluttered by swift as a leaf on the wind. Now, it was early morning of All Hallows' Eve. Heather readied herself for school. It was a Friday, for which she was grateful. It meant she could stay up late this Halloween. She smiled, looking forward to a weekend of eating candy and watching old horror films with Dad. It was their tradition, to watch spooky black and white movies together on Halloween. Heather's favorites were *The Bride of Frankenstein* and *The Old Dark House*.

Instead of blue jeans and a long-sleeve flannel like she wore nearly everyday, Heather put on tights, a ratty old dress, and a black pointy hat atop her head. Sweet Hollow Middle School had a costume party scheduled during Homeroom today, which Heather was greatly looking forward to.

She stood before the full-length mirror upon her door, admiring her ghastly transformation. Indeed, Heather Beauregard had become a witch! She contorted her face, bared her teeth, then let out a bone-chilling cackle.

Count mewled somewhere behind her. She expected to feel him brush against her legs. When he didn't, she turned around. Count wasn't anywhere in sight — yet she heard him again. A cry of distress.

"Oh, no!" Heather turned all about the room. She checked under her bed, wondering if Count had somehow gotten hurt. Nothing under there but dust and a random sock. Her closet was empty too, like some sad lonesome belfry.

"Count?" she called, setting her hands on her hips in frustration. "Where the heck *are* you?"

The cat let out a high, plaintive cry. Heather's heart shuddered inside her chest as slowly, cautiously, she approached the creepy little house on her dresser and stooped to investigate its windows.

Count was there—*inside*. Pawing at the glass with the tiniest paws. Heather trembled. "Count? Is that ... *you?*"

Count released a terrible yowl, his breath fogging up the plastic window, his paws raking against the glass, desperately wanting out. A lump formed in Heather's throat. She felt awful for Count. Guilty too, because she suddenly remembered Mr. Burgess' words: *You must feed the house one coin every night of your life. If you do not, well ... there will be dire consequences.*

"Oh, Count, I'm so, so sorry!"

Meow ... meow ....

Heather sniffed, beginning to cry. How could she have forgotten to place a coin on the doorstep last night? Such a simple, stupid thing, and now her precious Count — *trapped!*

"Heather?" Dad knocked, then opened the door and stuck his face into the room. "You're going to miss the bus, sweet pea."

"Be out in just a sec."

He frowned. "You okay? You look flustered."

"Fine, Dad, honest! I just need to finish getting dressed."

"If you say so ..." Dad closed the door. Heather turned back to the House, about to console Count, let him know not to worry, that she'd figure how to get him out of there—

The windows were empty, full of shadow. Count must've wandered away, perhaps into another room, the attic, maybe even the basement.

Is it safe for him in the basement? Heather wondered. What if that's where the hand lives? What if the hand grabs him, and hurts him? What if Count began caterwauling with pain this very moment? I couldn't live with myself if he got hurt!

Heather clutched the house in both hands, as if to crush it.

"Let him out this instant!" She glared into its dark windows, expecting nothing less than the door to fly open and for her cat to clamber down the porch steps before growing back into full size.

The house remained still.

Silent as a grave.

Heather found herself grinding her teeth. "Damn you," she cursed, in a burst of rage, "give me back my *cat!*"

The voice returned, a rich rumbling tone that flittered through her mind fast as a candy wrapper on the wind: *Dear Girl, the Things and I become hungry when you do not provide the simple sustenance we ask you for. Even a penny could have saved your cat. Alas, you neglected us. Now, we take a soul for sustenance. This is the house of Trick or Treat, my dear, and you have forced us into tricks.*

"Well, I don't find your tricks very amusing!"

Ah, but they are to us, dear Child. They are to us ....

"Heather, the bus is here!" Dad shouted urgently from the stairs. She had to go now, otherwise he'd become angry, and that was something she couldn't handle. Not today on Halloween, with her cat shrunken down to penny-size and lost in that evil House, and certainly not with that ghostly voice nesting itself a home inside her head.

She snatched up her backpack, rushed downstairs, and out the door. Dad spun toward her in confusion, without a chance of saying goodbye.

"Don't worry, Count," she muttered, claiming one of the empty seats farthest back in the bus. "I won't let that bad little house eat you. *Promise.*"

Mathematics, Language Arts, and American History swept by; all numbers, adverbs, and dead presidents swirling away into the void. Heather hardly noticed. Stooped over her textbooks she pretended to follow along, deliberating about the House.

When Ms. Blackmore called on her with some question or other about adjectives, Heather's cheeks blushed deep red. Tight-lipped as ever, Ms. Blackmore sighed with disappointment. Her black cat earrings wobbled as she straightened her posture and peered down her nose. "*Please* pay closer attention from now on, Miss Beauregard," she hissed.

But Heather could think only of Count, lost and wandering the narrow hallways of the House, and that dreaded voice croaking after it: *Here, kitty, kitty ... come now, I only want to pet you! Heh-heh-heh ...*

Her classmates ate candy and danced about homeroom to the *Monster Mash*, blasting through Mr. Applebaum's bluetooth speakers. Normally, Heather would've been laughing, having a good time with the rest of her fellow demons, devils, witches, and warlocks. She managed a false smile at best. The hands on the clock ticked tediously until the 3:15 bell rang.

Heather was first out the door, backpack slung over her shoulder, the brim of her witch's hat jittering in the autumn wind that prickled the hair on her arms. Kids swarmed the sidewalk, clambering onto the buses. Skeletons, princesses, superheroes, and goblins noisily filling the brown leather seats. Heather sat in back, anxiously tapping her foot. As soon as she arrived home, she knew what she had to do.

It'd be dangerous. She'd be taking a risk, undoubtedly, but she'd do anything to save Count. It was the hand she must face. *The horror hand.* Her deepest instincts told her the hand and the voice were one, that the hand was truly the malignant spirit of the house, the one that'd been speaking to her telepathically.

Reaching inside her backpack's outer pouch, she pulled out a bright shiny quarter—something the house couldn't resist. She'd use it like a magic trick, a token of deception. All she had to do was place it on the front step, wait for the hand to shoot out, and when it did ... well, she dearly hoped what she did next would work like a charm.

The moment the bus doors flew open, Heather sprinted up the driveway, burst into her house, then up the stairs. Flinging open the door to her bedroom, she gasped.

The house—*gone!*

Her dresser top was barren, save for her music box and a few trinkets. The dresser's pink paint was beginning to flake away, revealing old gray wood beneath. She looked about the room, half-expecting the house to be squatting on the floor, or her bed.

It simply wasn't anywhere.

Heather began to cry. Slinging her backpack into the corner, she ran downstairs. Upon hearing a clattering din to her right, she entered the door that led from the kitchen into the garage. The mechanical door was rolled all the way up now, and her eyes widened. Dad carried the House in his hands, now setting it on the concrete floor. Crossing his arms, he frowned down at it, as if contemplating smashing it beneath his boots.

Heather shivered at the thought. *Poor Count, he'd be squashed!*

"Dad?" she asked, reminding herself to steady the tremor in her voice. She didn't want him to ask what was wrong, because, well, what would she tell him? That Count had shrunk down to the size of a coin and was lost inside the truly haunted house? He'd think she was crazy.

"Oh." His head darted up from the house, startled. "Good to see you home, honey. How was school?"

"Fine. Dad, what are you doing with the House?"

"Well, I heard some noises coming from your room a while ago. Kinda sounded like Count, at first, before I realized it was coming from *this* thing." He regarded the House distastefully, as if staring at a slimy, skittering millipede. "I think you've got a mouse or something in here, Heather. I'm hoping to get whatever's inside to come out. More than likely, I can just smoke it out."

"*Smoke* it out?" Heather frowned deeply.

"You just use one of these." Grabbing something that looked like a stick of dynamite from his workbench, he held it up for her to see. "A smoke bomb! Good for chasing out gophers, woodchucks, groundhogs—heck, pretty much anything. I'll light it, put it inside the house, and whatever's inside is bound to come scampering out."

Heather's eyes widened. She thought of Count, choking to death on fumes, dying inside the house, and the hand grasping it and dragging it into the basement where there was bound to be something cruel and dark and full of teeth ....

Before she even realized what she was doing, she rushed forward, scooping the house off the garage floor.

"Heather, what are you—"

"You can't smoke it out!" Heather shouted, placing it into the wagon which they kept stowed in the corner. "Gotta go, Dad."

"Why? Hold on a minute! We've got trick-or-treating to do in an hour—"

"No time to explain!" She hitched the wagon to the back of her bike and pedaled fast down the drive onto Maple Street, zipping down the leafy sidewalk. The House rattled in the wagon. She looked over her shoulder. Dad stood before the open garage, hands on his hips, gazing after her with his mouth half-open.

Poor Dad. She'd really thrown him for a loop. But she'd had to do it—he was going to kill her cat! And Dad loved count almost as much as she did. After Mom died, Count had been there for them both, always willing to settle down between them, purring cozily, rubbing his head against their knees, eager to be pet.

The more Heather remembered these things, the sadder she became.

She peddled fiercely until turning off the main roads and heading up a gravel drive into Sweet Hollow Cemetery. She leaned her bike against a shaded willow tree, then lifted the house off the wagon and set it on the ground. The cemetery smelled woodsy of chestnuts and tattered foliage. The sun had been pleasantly warm on her skin, but now, beneath the willow's canopy, her arms and legs pimpled with goosebumps.

Her dress didn't have any pockets, so she'd stored the quarter inside her left tennis shoe. She plucked it out, kneeled on the ground, then placed it within the indentation before the front door.

She waited. Held her breath.

Why wasn't anything happening?

The House knew she was up to something. Wouldn't cooperate. It was reading her thoughts maybe, and now its door wouldn't open—

Yet suddenly, angrily, the door *did* swing open. The yellow hand emerged from the shadows and clamped down on the quarter just as Heather's own hand clamped down on *it*.

She grunted, yanking sharply on the hand. It couldn't be attached to anything more than old mechanical gears and electrical wiring. But the cold-as-ice hand did not give. In fact, its long, spider-leg fingers wrapped around her wrist with wild strength, tugging *back*.

Heather screamed in terror, finding her own hand *inside the house*, being drawn deeper into its dark shadowy belly. Her heart hammered, her temples throbbed. Tears splashed her cheeks, the hand's nails digging hard into her flesh and pulling her in up to the elbow.

Her dress collected leaves, dirt, and grass as she cried and fought and yanked, not trying to rip the hand out from its house any longer— merely trying to save herself.

Her feet kicked against the overhanging willow as she pulled and sobbed, thinking, *I'm going to die here in the cemetery. I'm going to die and become the stuff of Sweet Hollow legend and all the kids will talk about me, oh, help me, God, help me!*

She sucked air into her lungs. Its fingernails dug further into her flesh, drawing blood, and her hand stung with excruciating pain. Now, balling her free hand into a fist, she desperately struck the roof of the House— *Thwack! Thwack! Thwack* —the hand's grip on her own loosened just enough for her to yank her arm back and, suddenly, she was clambering backwards through the leaves, free of the house's awful grasp.

Staring back at it, eyes bloodshot with terror, chest hitching, she watched as the yellow hand held up its grimy index finger, wagging it to and fro. The voice spoke inside her head, indignant with rage: *Naughty, naughty child!*

The hand disappeared into shadow.

The door clicked shut.

Heather sat beneath the willow's swaying canopy, attempting to steady her nerves. The hand had shaken her, both literally and emotionally. She felt cold inside and her palm was bleeding from where the hand's nails had dug in. Tearing off a black strip from the fringe of her dress, she wrapped her hand with the fabric. At least now the wind would not blow over her stinging palm.

Beyond the graveyard, light brown hills rolled like an autumnal sea and a pumpkin sun melted into the horizon. Cotton candy clouds drifted across the sky, pushed by a wood damp wind reminiscent of fresh graves.

Soon, it would be dark.

Soon, it would be Halloween night.

Gazing at the House, Heather caught a glimpse of Count rubbing against one of the upstairs windows. He looked at her with yellow eyes. Blinked.

"Don't worry, Count. I won't give up!"

She said this as much to the House as to her cat; a statement of obstinate will. She *would* rescue Count. The house didn't deserve him! It wasn't *right!*

Swishing through the leaves, Heather scooped up the House and set it into the wagon. Then something glimmering on the ground caught her attention. She stooped low, picking it up.

The quarter. The one she'd placed on the doorstep to lure out the hand. In all that ruckus, she hadn't noticed it roll down the steps into the leaves. So, the house was yet unfed for the day. If it wasn't fed sometime tonight, it would take another soul. Perhaps hers this time, or her father's. Heather shuddered at the dreadful thought of seeing her Dad's face in a twisted scream, his fists pounding against the windowpanes...

Before midnight, she'd be sure to make an offering to the house. She wouldn't now, however, not this very moment. She was badly shaken by the altercation with the hand and could hardly bear watching it emerge from the darkness again.

Heather stuffed the coin back into her sock, then climbed onto her bike and rode out from beneath the willow, down the road, and beyond the cemetery.

CLOSED, read the sign in the display window of Mr. Burgess' Curio Shop. Heather gazed past her witchy reflection in the window, peering into the dim corners of the store. The old man didn't appear to be in, but she knew where he lived. In a town as small as Sweet Hollow, it was common knowledge where *everyone* lived.

Biking two blocks over into a suburb on the outskirts of town, Heather parked her bike beside Mr. Burgess' front door, then knocked. His one-story house was shabby brown. The lawn and front path were blanketed in auburn leaves. It took nearly three minutes of wrapping her knuckles against the door and calling his name before, finally, she heard a shuffling from inside.

The door creaked opened.

Mr. Burgess was pale as a sheet. His lips, purple as a bruise, and his eyebrows, once grey, were snow white. His brown eyes were glazed, as if he didn't recognize who she was. Heather opened her mouth when—

"Why!" Mr. Burgess' eyes blinked multiple times, his voice

trembling. "If it isn't little Heather Beauregard. Out for a bit of trick or treat, I presume?"

She shook her head. "No, Mr. Burgess. I'm here to talk about *that*."

Burgess looked where she was pointing and frowned. "Hope there hasn't been *too* much trouble?"

"There's been some."

"In that case, come inside." He opened wide the door, then shuffled slowly toward a couch in back of the living room. "You'll have to excuse me. I'm weak these days, my dear, for I fear my time has come."

Heather carried the House inside, then shut the door with a gentle back-kick. "Your time?" She set the house on the coffee table before a roaring fireplace.

"Death." Mr. Burgess nodded. "Eventually, everyone must endure a dance with death. I fear I'm rather waltzing with it now."

Mr. Burgess reposed on the couch, propping his back against an overstuffed pillow. How pale he was, like a ghost! For a moment, Heather trembled, quite frightened by Mr. Burgess. She'd never seen a dying person before. What if he was … a ghost already?

She took a deep breath. She was tired. Being silly. Mr. Burgess had been nothing but kind to her. Now, she must return the favor.

"Is there anything I can get you?" Heather asked. "Water? Or tea?"

"No, thank you. Nothing I need now, but for an eternity of sleep." His weary eyes turned in their yellowed sockets, now fixing on the Haunted House Mystery Bank. "I suppose, m'dear, you forgot to feed it its nightly coin?"

Reluctantly, she nodded.

"And whom did it take, in absence of the coin?"

"Can't you see?" Heather replied, and now Burgess's ivory brow furrowed, spotting the black cat rubbing whiskers against the glass.

"Poor little kitty-kat." Mr. Burgess clucked his tongue.

"Can you get him out of there, Mr. Burgess? You can, can't you? If there's anyone who can rescue Count from that nasty old house, it's you."

Then the voice arose from the House, resounding inside both Heather and Mr. Burgess' minds in a bold, icy tone: *Don't I have a say in this, friends? I am, after all, the spirit of this 'nasty old house', as the child so rudely asserts.*

Heather's wide eyes fixed upon Mr. Burgess' calm ones. "You hear it too, right?"

"Dear girl, I've heard it ever since I was ten years old."

"Didn't it ever frighten you?"

"It positively *terrified* me. But after a while, you become accustomed to the house's manners. Enough years, you grow fond of it. It broke my heart to give it away. But I knew you were a girl who loved dark and spooky things, someone who would treasure a haunted house of her very own. Isn't that so?

"At first … yes. But then it stole my Count! Now, I hate it."

"You love Count very much, so I can see. But that's no reason to hate the house. After all, it is merely trying to survive. It devours coins not out of sheer greed, my dear, but to remain in use, to have a purpose, don't you see? Everyone must have a purpose, or else they die."

"Don't *you* have a purpose, Mr. Burgess?"

Mr. Burgess smiled. Despite his gaunt, ghostly face, for a moment he appeared a charming old man again. "I used to," he replied. "Now, my purpose is to give my atoms back to the earth … and, I suppose, to make one Heather Beauregard happy."

Behind the eyes of the old man and little girl, the voice drifted like a curtain of black cloud: *How about a proposition? What say I give the child back her cat – Count, as she calls him. In return, I shall take – and keep – a soul. Mr. Burgess' soul, for instance. Surely, old man Burgess here is worth ten black cats!*

"No way!" Heather scowled at the House's audacity.

"Oh, come now." Burgess chuckled, then coughed roughly into his fist. "Don't be rash, dear. The house suggests a fair bargain."

"I want my cat back, Mr. Burgess, but not if it means *you'll* be trapped forever. It's cruel!"

"No, my dear, it's *heaven*. I've always longed to live in a haunted house. Inside that very one, in fact."

"But, *why?*"

Mr. Burgess pointed a trembling finger. There, behind the window on the opposite side from Count, a teenage boy with shaggy brown hair and spectacles and a red Sweet Hollow High jacket. Heather squinted, peering in at the handsome young man behind the glass.

"He looks sad," Heather reflected.

"Yes, although he'll be less sad with me in there with him. We've not embraced in years, you see. And although he has not aged a day inside that house, he remains my big brother. Besides, I'm quite afraid of oblivion. Inside the house, I shall never die. So long as the walls of that old thing stand, then I, too, shall stand."

"You wish to be immortal, Mr. Burgess?"

"Doesn't everyone?"

Heather considered. What would she do with the House once Mr. Burgess' spirit was locked inside it? She no longer wanted to keep it in her room. What if she forgot to feed it its nightly coin again? She informed the dying man of her concerns.

Burgess licked his lips, then spoke: "You must hide the house in a discrete location. Somewhere far from your home, and away from where people dwell. Bury it, perhaps? Despite whatever method you choose to obscure the house, you ought to do it tonight."

"Mr. Burgess, why is the house haunted? *Who's* haunting it? To whom does that voice in our heads belong to?"

"Ah, my dear! Those are mysteries I've longed to know the answers to since I was but a boy. Such as it is with mysteries, answers remain elusive. Often, it just so happens a person comes upon queer items. As the owner of a curio shop, perhaps I know better than most. Strange objects, material goods stuffed with age and curses ... came upon a typewriter once. I'm positive it was haunted. It nearly possessed me, that machine, but I managed to give it away, rid myself of it forever. Alas, I feel faint ..."

Heather dashed across the room, placing her hand on Burgess' arm. His eyes fluttered closed. His chest hitched, unable to draw in air.

Heather cried, until, at last, the old man opened his eyes. Faintly, he spoke: "I bid you goodbye, Heather Beauregard. You're an intelligent girl, and quite brave. You'll do well in the world."

"Oh, Mr. Burgess, please don't go. Not yet!" As the words left her lips, Mr. Burgess' head sunk back onto the pillow. He breathed no more, and snaking between his lips, a long tendril of mist.

Heather jerked back in terror, afraid the mist was death itself; that it would wrap around her like a boa constrictor, squeezing her to death. The thin smoky veil merely drifted across the room, toward the House.

The door swung open, and the smoke slithered inside. The little windows lit up white, starkly defining the silhouettes of Count and Mr. Burgess' brother.

When the door clicked shut, the lights flickered, then died.

Now, it was the House's turn to make good on their bargain. Any moment now, it would give back her cat as promised. Heather's breath caught in her throat. Her heart thumped rapidly. Something dripped into her eye and stung. Wiping her forehead, she realized she was covered in sweat.

"Please," she whispered through gritted teeth. "You *promised*."

Darkness and silence exuded from the tin-plastic walls and windows.

The House, at long last, seemed perfectly dead.

Heather stood tall. Her fists clenched in anger and defiance.

"Give me back my cat, you wicked old house!" She raised her foot high, about to bring it crashing down on the House's ramshackle roof.

She paused, thinking of the quarter in her sock, and remembered the House still required feeding. If Mr. Burgess was merely a trade-in for Count, the House was technically missing an offering.

Maybe if I give it the coin ... she reached into her sock. Placed the quarter heads-up before the door. Then waited, waited, waited.

Nothing happened. Her heart flooded with sorrow.

Creeaaaaak.

The door opened. Heather expected the horror hand to eject out of the darkness and wag its finger in mockery. It was only Mr. Burgess in the doorway, shrunk down to the size of one of those plastic toy army men. His cheeks were rosy. Smiling. Count purred in his arms, rubbing his head against Burgess' old hands.

"As promised, my dear." He set Count down on the front steps.

"Oh, Mr. Burgess, thank you!" Heather cheered, her eyes glistening.

"Adieu." Burgess bowed, picked up the coin that appeared enormous in his hands, then shut the door.

Count trotted down the steps. The moment he set paw onto the coffee table, his little body inflated like a balloon. Heather gasped, covering her ears, for there was a terrible crackling and snapping of bones as her cat's body reassembled into normal size. Beneath Count's fur coat, bone and ligament twitched like large, livid bugs. Upon returning to his rightful mass, Count leapt off the floor. Heather caught him in her arms and hugged tight.

Count licked her chin with his abrasive tongue.

"I thought the house had taken you away forever, Count!"

She took a final look at the House. It'd be the last time she appraised it, studying its every morbid crook and cranny, its each gothic detail. Behind an upstairs window, Mr. Burgess and his long-lost brother, Tom, hugged each other and cried.

She arrived at the old Sweet Hollow Bridge in the dark of night. A black ribbon of water glimmered beneath the bridge; its onyx undulation shimmering with moonlight. Count lay in the wagon hitched to the bike, blinking tawny eyes.

Scooping up the House, she lifted it high above her head, then stared down over the railing. The current flowed languidly, the reflected moon like an old painting she'd seen in a museum once. She remembered the advice Mr. Burgess had given her: "Despite whatever method you choose to obscure the house, you ought to do it tonight."

The Voice arose inside her head once more, shouting ferociously: *Stop there, Child. Don't even think of it. You wouldn't dare!*

"Oh, I dare," Heather retorted, then tossed the House and the souls trapped inside it into Sweet Hollow's main tributary. The river swallowed it up immediately. The House, despite its light tin and plastic walls, was far too heavy to float. Weighted, perhaps, by the souls it'd harbored over many years.

Fat bubbles arose at the surface, the rooms inside the House immediately flooded. Heather imagined the hand scrabbling across the floors, desperate to escape. Mr. Burgess and his brother, however, she imagined floating peaceably, or swimming from room to room, content with each other's company. The bubbles soon ceased rising, the river flowing unabated over the spot she'd dropped it.

"Time to go, home, Count. What do you say?"

Count was fast asleep in the wagon. A light snore exuded from his nostrils. His whiskers twitched with feline dreams. Mounting her bike, Heather rode on the sidewalks, gracefully zipping around a few remaining trick-or-treaters—a witch, a quarterback, an alien. The night was pitch-black, save for the luminous crescent moon and the orange halo of jack-o'-lanterns.

Arriving home after eight, she carried Count inside the house and set him at her feet. Dad arose from the kitchen table and embraced her.

"Good heavens, girl, where've you been? I've looked and called *everywhere!*"

"I'm really sorry, Dad," Heather replied, timidly. "I thought I'd be home much sooner."

He sighed, both relieved and disappointed. "I was worried to death, seeing you run off like that. What did you have to do that was so important?"

"It's, uhm, difficult to explain. But I'm fine now, Dad. Promise."

He stepped back to look at her. Crossed his arms. His brow was furrowed, about to ground her, but at last he cracked a smile. "Well, so long as you promise *never* to run off without saying where you're going, I suppose we're OK. Now, still on for trick-or-treating?"

"You bet!" Heather grinned.

"Go on and grab your bucket then. We haven't much time, nearly eight-thirty!"

With a squeal of excitement, she rushed to snatch her plastic Jack-O'-Lantern bucket from the kitchen pantry. "Tonight's the best Halloween yet," she cheered, meeting Dad outside the front door.

"It is now that you're home, kiddo." They stepped out onto the leaf-strewn front lawn, already shivering in that chill, damp, final night of October. Just before sliding on his skull mask, Dad bent low and gave Heather a peck on the cheek. "It is now that you're home."

OLD DANCE HALL

"There's an old dance hall on the outskirts of town," Marilyn said, her slender fingers nestling between mine. "Wanna go?"

An absurd question. No man in his right mind would say no to Marilyn. Gleaming brunette curls. High cheekbones. Deep, azure eyes swept with long lashes. Ruby lips. Petite breasts. Immaculate curves that switched as she walked.

"I'd be delighted," I replied. "Except, well, I can't dance."

Marilyn placed her thumb on the dimple of my chin and lightly pressed.

"We'll see about that, Mister."

We strolled hand-in-hand out of Emerald Park (where we'd met only an hour before) over to my Ford Explorer parked in the adjacent lot. I opened her door.

"A gentleman, I see," she said, climbing inside. "You're a rare breed, Paul Morrison."

I grinned, ashamed of the rouge creeping into my cheeks.

Sunshine streamed through the windshield. Her white blouse blazed. A breeze rippled her knee-length indigo skirt before I shut the door. I got in behind the wheel.

"So, where's this dance hall?" I asked.

"You know Harlequin road?"

I looked up and to the left, searching my memory files. "The old saloon is on that road, right? And a bunch of old buildings?"

She nodded. "Get us on Harlequin and I'll show you the rest of the way."

We cruised down Main Street, passing Ellie's Cafe, Leo's Ice Cream Parlor, a few bars, a library, some old houses—just a few of the locales native to Sweet Hollow. Wind blew through our open windows. It was a hot summer day. My face was sore from hours of sun exposure, but I couldn't have been happier. Marilyn's wavy brown locks fluttered and flapped in the wind.

I glanced at her, ordering myself to stop looking and not being able to. *She's stunning,* I thought. *Her beauty seems to surpass life itself ... God, what has this woman turned me into? A poet? I can hardly concentrate on the road!*

We didn't talk or listen to the radio. The drive was silent. Normally, on a date, I would've felt uncomfortable. I would've made up something to say to fill the space. Instead, I relaxed in my seat.

Marilyn smiled, her blue eyes cast to the passing scenery. I took it as a sign our date was going well.

"This is it," she said, as we pulled into the gravel lot.

I climbed out of the Ford, stretched and yawned in the sun, then realized I was alone. Marilyn sat in the car with a wry smile on her face.

"Oh!" I jotted over to her door and opened it.

"A gentleman, I see," she said for the second time that evening, then stood on her toes and kissed me. The brief touch of her lips was enough to put me into a coma. She studied my smitten expression and giggled, then turned toward the dance hall.

After passing through the old section of town with its tired, brick buildings and boarded-up windows, the dance hall was a shock. Its white siding was as unblemished as Marilyn's skin. The roof lacked not one shingle. The cement stairs leading up to the door had not a crack in it. Even the bronze hinges on the door gleamed.

"I thought you said this was the old dance hall?" I asked.

She smiled askew. "Do you know of any other dance hall in this town?"

"Well ... no. But this place looks in better shape than most of the buildings in the *new* part of town."

"I'm glad you see it that way," she said. "Some folks take one look at this place and want it torn down."

I studied the dance hall with its solid roof, walls, and bright red door.

"You're kidding," I said. "This building seems pristine!"

"Shall we go in?"

"After you." I winked, then bowed for comic effect.

Gravel dust coated my sneakers. A tissue soft breeze blew Marilyn's skirt, making it wave like a flag. *A gentleman, I see,* she had said, and kissed me. I longed to feel her lips on mine again.

An awning above the front stoop, covering half the bright red door with shadow. I scrutinized the back-and-forth rock of her perfect hips, until smacking my head on the awning frame.

"Oof!" I palmed my forehead.

Marilyn turned with a concerned expression, then her lips puckered with stifled laughter.

"Oh, hon! I'm sorry."

"I'm fine." I rubbed my forehead. "I should've been looking where I was going."

"I guess so," she replied, and now it was her turn to wink.

A prickly flush crept into my cheeks again.

"This time, Paul, *I'll* be the gentleman. How 'bout it?"

She swung open the door.

"Thanks," I said, stepping into the cool shadows of the spacious hall. A refurbished, cherry wood floor gleamed in shafts of sunshine through the tall windows. A three-foot-high stage occupied the end of the hall. To my left, a half-wall bordered a staircase leading into a basement. Above the landing, a sign: *Beer, Soda, and Snacks Are Served at the Bar, Downstairs!*

My date's melodious voice seemed as much a part of the old hall as the walls themselves. I drifted out of dazed astonishment.

"... Before there were discotheques and nightclubs," she said, "there were dance halls. Places where people came for a good time." Fraction by fraction, her mouth slid into a frown, slow as a spider descending silk. Her eyes welled.

"I've tried to leave this place, you know," she said, gazing upon the band stage. "Something called me back. Something *always* calls me back. This dance hall has been with me since I was a little girl. It'll probably be with me forever."

She shook her head and sniffed.

"Hey now ..." I said, touching her elbow.

She sighed. "I get nostalgic sometimes, I guess."

"It's all right," I told her. "I understand."

But I didn't. I racked my brain, trying to think how to cheer her up.

"Marilyn," I said, touching her sleeve. "Would you, uhhm—"

She grabbed my hand, pulling me to the center of the room.

"Thought you'd never ask." She placed her arms upon my shoulders. I chuckled mindlessly.

"Don't be nervous." Her dazzling blue gems gazed up into mine. "Hands on my hips, please."

I did so. It felt so right my heart melted inside my chest. Perhaps that's cliché, but all clichés are founded in truth. And the truth was, I nearly wanted to propose, right there and then. We danced a standard box-step, the only dance I knew. The clicking of our shoes upon hardwood echoed within the otherwise silent hall.

I counted in my head, so I wouldn't mess up.

One, two, three, four,

One, two, three, four.

At some point, I ceased counting. Our bodies instinctively merged in a graceful dance. I managed to twirl her twice, thrice, four times. We smiled from ear to ear, laughing. We were dancing to our own music. A harmonious series of notes only the two of us could hear.

The clicking of our shoes … faded. Rearing up out of a hollow silence, my ears prickling as I held the beautiful Marilyn in my arms, were the low notes of a bass intermingling with drums. The beat matched our dance; a moderately fast waltz. Piano and guitar flooded the room. Keys and strings coalesced, splashing chords into my ears.

It wasn't until a baritone voice began crooning when my hands fell from Marilyn's hips.

I gazed over at the stage, where a five-piece band performed. Each member wore a black tuxedo and bowtie. A young man with slicked-back blonde hair stood center stage, beaming with a microphone in his hand. He sang about true love. How easily it can be lost.

"Paul? What's the matter?"

"Hmm?" I said, turning toward her.

"You look like you've seen a ghost," Marilyn said, shouting over the music. An icy shiver twitched my shoulders.

"Th-that band," I stammered.

"Don't you like them? It's the Glen Miller Five." She nudged my arm. "They're the 'Best in the Midwest', you know."

I shook my head. "First I've heard of them."

"Hey," she smiled. "You need a cocktail."

"I do?"

"And so do I," she nodded. "Follow me."

We waded through a room packed with dancing couples. There

were women in long, flowing dresses and men dressed as handsomely as the Glen Miller Five. Gooseflesh covered my arms. My teeth chattered. Something was wrong, but I couldn't put my finger on what.

Hadn't we come here alone? Where did these people come from?

Marilyn's high heels tapped the floor. I followed her past the sign above the stairs advertising beer, pop, and snacks. As we descended into the basement, the music muffled. Marilyn no longer had to shout.

The basement was smoky. Four men played a game of pool and drank. Their wives chain-smoked, playing cards at a corner table. Children ran around the basement, making a ruckus. No one minded. Marilyn and I sat at the bar. Other than a lady in a red dress with a mink scarf over her shoulders, sitting four stools away, we were the only patrons.

"Two brandy cocktails, please, George," said Marilyn.

George was broad-shouldered. Strong jaw. Cleft chin. The glasses were small in his hands. Balls clapped amidst the pool players' amiable smack-talk behind us.

"Be a dollar and five cents," said George.

"That's all?" I asked.

George nodded. I pulled three dollar bills out of my billfold and handed it over.

"Keep the change."

"Thanks, pal," George grinned, pocketing the tip and inserting the rest into the cash register.

"That's quite the antique," I said, nodding toward the register.

"Whaddya mean?" George straightened. "Thing's brand new."

Marilyn pinched my arm.

"Hmm?" I asked.

"To us?" She raised her glass.

"To us." Our glasses clinked. We drank.

A light, euphoric buzz made my brain hum. I sighed.

"Seems like you're finally enjoying yourself," she smiled.

"I am. Felt dizzy earlier, and kinda confused."

I bit the inside of my cheek, trying to remember what had come over me. Trying to recall why I'd shivered as if caught shirtless in the Antarctic. But the bubbly cocktail was refreshing.

"Ahh, well." I shrugged. "Must've been nothing."

"That's the spirit." Marilyn patted me on the back. "Have a good time. The dance hall is where good times are had. Always."

"It's a nice place," I agreed.

Marilyn set her drink upon the bar.

"Anytime you want to visit, Paul," she said, "you can find me here."

There was a catch of sadness in her voice, although I admit I did not ponder the cause. My addled mind busied itself roaming a host of impure thoughts about Marilyn. When I looked up from the bar, she was studying me. Her teeth bit her bottom lip, forming a sly smile.

"You're cute."

"So are you," I replied.

Oooh boy, I thought. *Drink half a cocktail and suddenly you're Casanova.*

Marilyn laughed. "Hey, what do you say about another cocktail, then we dance?"

"Yes and yes," I replied.

We finished our drink, ordered another. I slapped down four Washingtons. The drinks were cheap. I was in a generous mood. George took a shine to me, calling me 'buddy'. The woman in the red dress ordered another glass of Moscato. Her green, inquisitive eyes caught me, like a fly on sticky paper. I forced myself to look away.

Tilting back my glass, I polished off the beverage and said, "What say about that dance, Marilyn?"

"Thought you'd never ask. Let's go!"

We hopped off our stools, rushed past the pool players, their wives, the rambunctious children, and climbed the stairs.

The Glen Miller Five played a slow dance tune, a Sinatra standard called *All the Way*. Maybe it was the cocktails providing liquid courage, but I was no longer nervous to dance. My hands guided Marilyn's svelte body, twirling her, even swooping her low to the floor to cradle her in my arms, all without giving it thought.

"You're a wonderful dancer," she whispered in my ear. Her breath was like ice upon my neck, sending not unpleasant shivers down my spine.

"Thanks. Dancing comes easy with you."

"You're awfully nice, Paul."

This time our kiss was long and deep. Our tongues danced, giving our feet time to rest. When she gazed up at me, there was love in her eyes. A light, airy sensation fluttered in my stomach.

Just as the singer crooned *All the Way's* romantic final note, someone tapped my shoulder. Marilyn's smile faltered. I turned.

The lady in red stood with the lifeless mink cloaking her slender shoulders.

"Mind if I have a turn?" Her voice was raspy, dry as a desert, yet her green eyes were luscious as a rain forest.

"Yes, Susan," Marilyn frowned. "We mind. Why don't you dance with somebody else?"

The mink bobbed with her shrug. "I've danced with every guy in this place for more years than I can count. They're boring. I need somebody new."

Marilyn exhaled. "Fine. But I want him back after this song."

"One song is all I need." Susan placed her hands upon my shoulders.

I watched her walk away, then faced Susan and tried to smile. She did not return the smile. 'The Best in the Midwest' played another slow one. Our bodies moved in time, very close together. Gazing over my shoulder, I spotted Marilyn in the corner, sipping a fresh cocktail. She caught my glance and winked reassuringly. The tension in my chest lessened.

"Do you like my pearls?" Susan asked.

"What?"

"On my necklace," she said. "Do you like them?"

I looked down at the gleaming pearl necklace upon her chest. My eyes wandered briefly to her robust décolletage before returning to the necklace, then her eyes.

"You can look," she smiled. "I don't mind."

"Uhhm, no. I wasn't—"

"Hush, darling. You've no idea how long it's been since a fresh pair of eyes appreciated me."

"Nonsense," I replied. "The guys around here must be crazy about you."

"Disinterested is more like it."

I chuckled lightly. "How do you figure?"

"Put it this way," she replied. "When you're stuck with the same boring people for eternity, things get boring. I can feel the *dust* settle on my cranium every second of everyday."

She wasn't making sense. Maybe I'd drank too many cocktails.

"Eternity?" I asked.

She laughed. "Oh, you poor, dumb thing."

"Hey …" I said, breaking from our dance.

"Haven't you figured it out?"

"What?" I asked.

"We're all dead, *silly,*" she grinned.

My head throbbed. The room spun. The music slowed to a heavy droll, as if someone had set a vinyl record on lowest speed. Baritone vocals swirled about the room, as if underwater.

An abrupt rattling. My attention was drawn to the cherry wood floor, now grey and rotten. Susan's pearls lay there, free from the lace. The last of the pearls vibrated into stillness. Then I noticed Susan's fleshless legs. Ivory bone filled her dusty high heels. My eyes trailed up her faded red dress, covered with mothballs. Her breasts had withered away. Attached to a yellowed sternum, her grimacing skull. I leapt back and screamed.

Black hollow sockets stared. A millipede crawled out the left nostril before disappearing behind the upper jaw. My heart galloped. Her skull leaned back upon its vertebrae as she laughed. I backed away, turning all about the room in horror.

The dead were everywhere, pirouetting and draining cocktails into their mouths to splash through their ribcages and soak their shirts and dresses. The Glen Miller Five looked like a band hired for a Halloween show, only the cobwebs that stretched from their mouths to their instruments were genuine, not store-bought cotton. Black spiders crawled inside the singer's mouth. A small bat fluttered behind the cello player's hollow sockets.

I collided into a couple behind me.

"HEY!" The dead man in the tuxedo said, though he didn't have lips, tongue, nor larynx with which to speak. He held his undead partner close to his clavicle.

I shrieked, running for the front door. Just as I touched the handle, someone snatched the back of my shirt. One of the dead.

"Wait! Wait!"

Marilyn's voice. I was afraid to turn around. Afraid she would not have flesh on her bones. I pulled away, scrambling through the door. Bright moonlight illuminated the land. Jumping down the steps, I once again smacked my forehead against the alcove's frame. I collapsed onto the gravel.

"Paul!" Marilyn yelled.

She turned me onto my back. Her flesh was beautiful and white under the moonlight. I sighed, relieved.

"Th-those p-people," I stammered. "They-they're all—"

"Shhhhh," she said. "Calm down. You're okay."

She pulled me to my feet and hooked her arm with mine. I glanced back at the dance hall, seeing it for what it was: A dump.

Over half its shingles were stripped, complimented by a cavernous rent in the roof. Bats flew out to flap wings across the moon. Spider-cracked windows gleamed in moonlight. The siding had weathered into a dull black. Flakes of old paint stood upon the front door as straight as the hairs on my arms. Various words were carved into its wood, presumably by teenagers with nothing better to do on Friday nights than trespass.

"Let's have a chat in your car," she suggested.

I nodded, too frightened to form words. We climbed inside. I locked the doors, for fear one of the undead would emerge from the darkened dance hall and attempt to get inside.

After many deep breaths, I said, "Tell me what the hell is going on, please."

"I'm sorry, Paul." Marilyn cried. "I thought you knew …"

Her youthful, ivory skin contrasted with impossibly wise, old eyes. Her fifty-year-old clothes and fifty-year-old mannerisms.

She wiped her tears. "I love you, Paul. Love doesn't just stop when you're dead, you know."

"I can't believe I'm having this conversation." I shook my head. "I can't believe what I've just seen."

"Well, believe it," she said, her tone somewhat testy. "It's the truth."

Shadows passed behind the dance hall's moonlit windows.

"If you're really a ghost," I said, "How come you don't look like the others? All bones and horror?"

"Because," she replied, measuring her words. "You don't see me through the eyes of fear and death, Paul. You see me through the eyes of love."

A few tears fell into the groove between her nose and cheek, then dripped down her lips. I tenderly wiped them away, then brought her lips to mine.

Our hands became lightning, flashing and racing along each

other's bodies; grasping, pushing, kneading. We tumbled into the backseat, stripping our clothes. Our breath came hot and heavy. Condensation fogged the windows. Marilyn straddled me. Her breasts were lily white, with nipples like buds of perfect flowers. A low groan escaped her as she slid me inside. Fresh goosebumps rose on my arms and legs. Her hips gyrated back and forth with the tempo and force of a locomotive gradually increasing speed. The back of my scalp tingled as she pulled my hair.

Yet again, we were dancing; rocking each other to the rhythm of our own song.

With the generous thrusts of her hips, all thoughts of death sloughed away. We came together, then stretched out on the backseat, exhausted. Our chests rose and fell like a tide. She held my head against her soft bosom and I did not hear a heartbeat. It didn't bother me in the least.

I fell into a sleep so blissful it was like a temporary death.

We sat in a plush booth beside the front window of Ellie's Cafe. Marilyn's blue eyes blinked above her ceramic cup as she sipped. We talked of life, death, and everything in between. I'd never witnessed a woman so alive, so animated and curious about everything as Marilyn.

She'd been apprehensive about sitting in the cafe, for fear of people staring at me (few people, she'd explained, could ever see her, and I was one of the few). There were two other people in the cafe that early dawn. Their gaze continually wandered to our booth. An old man fumbling the pages of a newspaper peered up at me every few minutes, scrunching his wiry eyebrows. He shook his head.

Cambria, the barista, stared from behind the counter. It made me laugh.

She was undoubtedly observing a middle-aged man (me) sitting in a booth, laughing and carrying on a one-sided conversation. He'd ordered coffee for two and she'd expected a friend to join him, but none did. The second coffee remained untouched upon the table. The crazed man nodded at the empty seat across from him, saying, "Not a bad roast, eh?"

Cambria shook her head, then went about wiping tables and tending register.

"They think I'm insane, don't they?"

"I'd imagine so," Marilyn said. "I hope this doesn't ruin your reputation."

"I hardly have one," I chuckled. "Even if I did, I wouldn't mind ruining it."

"No?"

"No," I affirmed. "I only relocated here for a job at a credit union in Emerald, about fifteen minutes away. Emerald means nothing to me. I can pick up and move anytime."

"Wish I could say the same." She gazed despondently into her coffee.

"Sorry." I reached across the table to touch her hand. "I didn't mean to be insensitive."

"No." She shook her head. "You're not insensitive. It's just ... I've been stuck in Sweet Hollow all my life. The dance hall is home to my earliest memories. It's a party there, at nights, with the others. A party that's never ended yet has become achingly tiresome. I just wish ..." She waved a dismissive hand.

"What?" I prompted. "You wish what?"

"I wish I could disappear," she blurted. "I wish I could float up to heaven if there's such a place. Either that or die. I mean, *really* die. Just go to sleep and never wake up."

"Don't say that," I said, tucking a stray curl behind her ear. The old man across the way was staring again, but I hardly cared. "You've got me now, don't you? You've something to live for."

"Until you leave me."

"I won't leave you." I frowned, sipping my coffee. "I think you're wonderful."

"You're very sweet. And while I might be wonderful, this old town is not. You'll want to move. See new things. New people. I'm *stuck* here, Paul. Maybe forever. You don't want to end up like me. You don't want to live the remainder of your life, perhaps even your afterlife, caught here in this stupid town like a fly in a web."

"I don't care where I am," I replied, squeezing her hand, "as long as I'm with you."

Ellie's Cafe was a full house by eight a.m. Voices chattered. Silverware and porcelain clinked. Cambria zig-zagged from table to table, far too busy serving the influx of patrons to worry about my sanity. I left a tip and we boogied. Marilyn and I drove down Main Street. The day was already hot, even with the windows rolled down.

Suddenly, Marilyn began to shriek.

"What is it?" I shouted, ears ringing.

She had one hand on her stomach, the other over her face.

"*Oh god it hurts!*" she cried.

She doubled over, resting her head against the dashboard, sobbing.

"What can I do, hon?" My voice quivered, panicky. "Should I pull over?"

She screamed again, like a high-pitch whistle, and writhed in her seat.

"Take me home," she pleaded, voice weakening. "*Please.*"

I took one hand off the wheel, reaching over to stroke her. My fingers touched something hard, not Marilyn's face. I flinched, inadvertently yanking the wheel, driving us into the opposite lane. Oncoming cars zoomed by, blaring horns. I swerved back into my lane.

"Marilyn!" I cried. "Y-your *face!*"

Her head lifted from the dashboard. Impossible tears fell from hollow sockets, splashing upon her ivory jaw. Silk brown hair lay all about her seat, most of it flying out the passenger window. The flesh around her neck began to dissolve too; blood, veins, larynx and all, eroding from top to bottom, as if an invisible acid poured from the top of her head to cascade down her body. Grey smoke plumes arose from her searing flesh. An acrid stench burned my nostrils. I leaned my head out the window, choking on smoke and weeping.

The gas pedal was smashed beneath my shoe. We charged down the streets, whipping around corners, horns honking, people shouting. I did not look at Marilyn. I couldn't. A dreadful instinct ravaged my brain as we barreled down Harlequin Road. I had to bring her home … before it was too late.

Gravel scattered into the air as the car bounced and rocked over potholes. The dance hall was coming up fast. Big, yellow machines with *Caterpillar* written in black letters along their sides crowded the area.

Steel claws. Gleaming metal buckets. Sunburned men squinting in the morning sun with yellow hardhats. A large iron ball swung on a crane, obliterating one side of the hall. The roof caved, collapsing inward.

I slammed the brakes hard enough to ram my face against the steering wheel. My forehead split open. Blood dripped down the bridge of my nose, into my mouth, bringing a taste of copper to my tongue.

Marilyn had long ceased screaming. She lay in the seat, mouth ajar, her skeleton now dissolving into grey talcum.

Throwing open the door, I ran toward the demolition crew, waving my arms. A fat man with a patchy black beard and reflective hardhat grabbed hold of me and did not let go.

"Hey," he shouted. "Can't go over there! Not safe."

The destructive pendulum swung a second time. Dead faces in the cracked, grimy windows screamed before bursting into clouds of dust. The southward wall caved.

I pulled and yanked against the man's sweat-stained t-shirt. The wrecking ball decimated the remaining walls as the sky choked with dust.

The dance hall was now a pile of rubble. Crewmen pointed at me, nodding while muttering jokes and condemnations to one another:

"Guy's off his damn rocker, I tell you."

"One of those historical preservation protestors."

"Some people just can't let things go."

"Someone call 911! That man could hurt somebody, if not himself."

"Let me go!" I hollered. My arms flailed. The large, bearded man only held tighter.

I ceased struggling.

"Listen …" I said, lowering my voice. "Let me go. I just want to go home."

He unclutched my arms. I fell to my knees, pieces of gravel cutting into my shins. Crimson droplets ran from my face into the dirt.

"Hey, man. Are you all right?" His name tag read *Ronny.*

Ronny offered me his hand. I pushed it away.

"Leave me the hell alone," I told him. "Do you have any idea what you've *done?*"

Ronny scratched his chin, glanced back at the obliterated hall, then faced me again. "Just doing my job." He shrugged. "After all, ain't like that building was home to anyone."

I glared at him with contempt, then returned to the front seat of my car. A gentle breeze cooled my hot, bloodied face. Crewmen carried the debris into the back of a tow truck, to be taken to a nearby landfill. Marilyn lay in the passenger seat, no more than a pile of dust.

I scooped up a handful. Tears, golden in the sun, mingled with blood and fell into the dust upon my palm.

"Isn't this what you wanted, Marilyn?" I asked the dust. "To be free of this place? To be gone from that lame, never-ending party? I'll never forget you. Ever. And perhaps ... we'll meet again someday. At a far better party."

I scooped as much of what remained of Marilyn as I could into my hands, then held my hands out the window.

The wind took the dust and made it free.

OUT BENEATH THE
JACK-O-LANTERN SKY

Halloween, 1959.

Johnny took a sip from the bottle, then passed it to the skeleton sitting in the passenger seat. The skeleton took the whiskey into his pudgy hand. Crammed the bottleneck under the plastic chin, tilted back his head and gulped.

Johnny smiled, stepping on the gas. The Ford F-100 purred like a satisfied pussycat.

"Hell with this, man." Bill tore the visage of death from his face, chucked it onto the cab's floor, and drank uninhibited. Bill's right boot stepped on the skull mask. A crack spread from the tip of the cranium down to the chin. "Shit." Bill wiped his lips on the arm of his leather jacket, handing back the bottle.

"Thanks," Johnny said, pleased to see the bottle half gone. He raised it to his lips and took only a sip, then offered it to his brother. Bill snatched it harshly in his thick pink paws. He drew deeply, Adam's apple bobbing like an arrhythmic metronome, then placed the diminishing whiskey between his thighs, letting it rest against the crotch of his dungarees. "Think I'll keep the booze on my side, little bro," he snarled, running stubby fingers through his greasy hair. "You're too muchuva puss to drink like a man."

Johnny kept silent at the wheel. Rolling hills dipped and lifted like waves upon an autumn sea. The honey golden sky deepened to tangerine, then bloomed pumpkin orange. Gravel dust clouded in the rearview mirror, dancing and pluming beneath the jack o' lantern sky.

"The hell you got that smile on your face for?" Bill growled.

Johnny glanced at him and liked what he saw. Bill's glassy orbs shimmered. Something vague floated in his sclera—an awareness beginning to wane and flicker like a candle flame in the wind. With any luck, that flame would soon gutter at the stub until dead.

Johnny thought of smoke, and of the dark night ahead of them.

"You think you're a man, do you?" Johnny countered, his smile stretching into a grimace. Sorrow and hatred addled his mind, an intoxication exceeding Bill's in intensity.

Bill leered. "I *know* I'm a man, Sally."

"Prove it." Johnny nodded toward Bill's crotch, where the bottleneck stuck up like an erection. "Bet you can't put that bottle away before fallin' dead as a doornail. I had a whole bottle of J.D. to myself last week and wasn't nearly as drunk as you are now. You think you're tough stuff, big brother, but you ain't."

Bill's hazy eyes sharpened into switchblades. "Why, you mouthy little fugger! I oughtta take this bottle and break your face with it. Talkin' to me like dat …" Bill shook his head and snorted. "Shit. You deserve what's comin' to ya."

"And what, pray tell, is comin' for me?" Johnny chuckled at the irony. Though he didn't know it yet, Bill was like a gazelle telling off a lion.

"I was gonna keep it from ya," Bill replied with a belch. "Cause what a person don't know don't hurt 'em, but since you's playin' nasty, I'll tell."

Johnny gripped the wheel until his knuckles paled. He knew what Bill was going to say. Knew, and didn't want to hear it. Didn't want to stoke the sorrow, pain, and hatred already roiling in his stomach and wringing his heart like a wet sponge. Johnny's grimace resembled the cracked skeleton mask lying face-up on the floor.

"She didn't want it at first, but after I got it in 'er, she did all right." Bill's fat stomach bounced with laughter, recounting a tale Johnny knew all too well. "Hell, she even moaned a little, right after she was done screamin'."

Johnny exhaled through flared nostrils, turned and looked Bill in the eyes and laughed along with him, as if he'd just heard a good ol' knee-slapper. His innards curdled, now on the cusp of vomiting.

Bill's mouth hung open, his blubbery lips lubricated with stupidity just as much as whiskey. Thus, the brothers laughed—one of them convulsing with drunken hysterics, the other performing giggling theatrics with fastidious eyes sharp and steadfast as a razor's edge.

When the outburst settled, Johnny said, "Whatever you say, big brother. Now shut that fuckin' mouth of yours and stuff it with that bottle. Walk your talk, or prove to me what I already know."

"Wuss that?" Bill guffawed. "What you know?"

"That your little brother can drink you under the table."

"Sheee-it." Bill wrapped his lips round the bottle, squeezed his eyes shut, and tilted back his head.

Johnny listened to the wet gulping inside Bill's throat, sucking down 80 proof liquor. The sun was a giant orange sinking into the horizon. The shadows of an occasional barn and farmhouse stretched long and dark and Johnny dreamed with those shadows.

He had told Bill they were going to a Halloween party. That part was true, but it wouldn't be held at the old dance hall on the outskirts of Sweet Hollow, like he'd claimed. Nor would their usual gang of Ronnie Harding, Jasper Clemens, or Don Wasserman be accompanying them. Tonight, he and Bill would be attending a small party of three, and the only dancing they'd be doing was with Death.

Bill belched. His head lolled left and right, eyes fluttering, speaking in some abstract Drunkanese: "Heyafugger! Justa wakemeup when weh gedder ..."

The bottle fell from his hands and thudded to the cab floor. It rolled around, occasionally scraping against the skull mask. Bill groaned, his head rolling all loosey-goosey on his neck. Then his eyes rolled too, into the back of his head. Like a grotesque volcano, vomit exploded out of Bill's throat, cascading over his lips and chin like lava and slopping all over his shirt, legs, and floor.

Johnny stared out the windshield, jaw clenched tight. The rancid odor of Bill's stomach expulsion filled the cab. He rolled down his window. Crisp cool wind ruffled his blonde hair— lost in the contemplative shadows of his loathing, he hardly felt it.

The jack o' lantern sky, gorgeous as it was, hardly existed.

All he saw before him was that pitch-dark night about a week back. He'd listened to Susan sob on the telephone, her voice choked with tears, attempting to relate the monstrosity. Johnny had told her to stay put, he'd be right over, and hung up the phone.

Susan owned a small cottage, bordered on all sides by rolling ocher fields that appeared golden in sunlight. But it was night when he arrived. There was not a star in the sky and the hills were waves upon a dark sea frozen in time. He lit the hearth when he came in, finding the cottage utterly cold and dark and Susan crying there in the gloom.

She was soaked from the rain, her clothes in tatters. The polka dot blouse hung open. White buttons dangled cockeyed like broken wrists. A rip had ruptured one side of her indigo skirt, exposing a pale hip which panties used to cover, before they'd been savagely ripped away.

Johnny helped remove the sopping wet clothes and dressed her in a bathrobe. He fashioned her a mug of hot sun tea, then sat beside her. Her voice was hoarse, relating the incident in a zombified tone. Her fingers picked idly at the tag dangling cup-side.

She'd been at the Starman Drive-In, she explained, with her girlfriends. Vanessa's new boyfriend, Ronnie, had drove them there in his spacious Cadillac. It was a creature-feature playing that night: *The Giant Gila Monster* and *The Killer Shrews*. The movies were silly, she said, hardly scary at all. She told her friends she'd be right back, was going to buy popcorn from the rickety concessions stand on the east side of the field.

She bought the popcorn. On the way back, walking through the dark field that flickered in bright flashes beneath the enormous screen, hands grabbed her and pulled her far, far away from the cars, down into the dip of the hills where the grass was wet with midnight dew.

She couldn't see his face, but smelled whiskey-laden breath and knew it was Bill Evans, that lousy *creep*. She hauled off, slapping him across the face.

When he punched her in the stomach, she dropped the popcorn and doubled over. Bill laughed while she gulped at the air. Finally reclaiming her breath, she used it to scream. No one heard and no one came and she was screaming, screaming, screaming.

The breath rushed out of her again when Bill slammed his size-thirteen boot between her shoulder blades, forcing her down where grass tickled her cheeks and damp earth flooded her nostrils. Then his coarse hands, ruthless and dreadful, ripped off her underwear. His heavy bulk pinned her with oppressive gravity, then he forced his way inside, pumping away like a rabid piston while she gasped, writhed, and clutched the grass with her fists, ripping out the roots.

Tears blurred her sight into grim watercolors. Her mind slowly dissolved into a dream-state where all she could think about was the popcorn she'd paid for and never ate because it'd spilled into the

TYLOR JAMES

grass, the bag crunched beneath Bill's feet just like she was now being crunched beneath the brute slab that pushed upon her, violating her body and soul, making her *bleed* down there, and the sounds he made, *oh God*, that grunting pig making those awful noises in between the rhythmic slapping of flesh and she dropped the popcorn she paid for all over the ground, only got a few kernels of buttery goodness on the tip of her tongue before, before, before ....

Johnny screamed, his face flushed red, his knuckles white. That rage in his heart bloomed into an explosion. He couldn't stop screaming, stomping down on that accelerator and tearing ass down the dirt road, gravel spraying up into that lovely, hallowed sky.

He threw back his right fist into Bill's slobbery, drunken face, while keeping his left firmly upon the wheel. He launched his knuckles into Bill's nose, cracking the bridge. Blood flowed thick down his lips to pool with the vomit dribbling out of Bill's slack mouth. Johnny kept throwing back his fist, relishing the feel of warm blood on his knuckles, and the sound of bones and teeth cracking so loud it overpowered the roar of the engine.

The sun melted into the horizon, now drenching the sky deep crimson. Johnny stared at his hands, then reverently held them up to the sky. He could not tell where his hands ended and the sky began.

Then he and Susan kissed, and her mouth was soft and warm. A memory from childhood suddenly flashed through his mind. Something he hadn't thought about in ages came rushing in like a wild river through a broken dam.

Mother on the floor—her eyes alabaster orbs, foaming at the mouth, shrieking demonic incantations. Father standing over her with his precious bottle of Johnny Walker (he liked it so much he'd named his youngest son after it), his lips launching spittle as he shouted, "You crazy *bitch*, I can't stand it no more! We're done. We're fucking *done!*" Johnny thought Daddy was going to lop his Momma upside the head with the bottle like he'd done a few times before. Instead, Daddy scooped her up, loaded her into the back of his jalopy and drove her to the insane asylum where she would remain the rest of her life. Meanwhile, Johnny was left at the house that evening with his big brother Bill, who laughed and punched Johnny's arm for crying about Momma being sick, being *real* sick, and was Daddy finally taking her to the doctor?

Bill stole one of Daddy's lucky strikes, smoked most of it, then stubbed out the butt directly beneath Johnny's left eye. He'd shrieked as embers ground and burned into his upper cheek, and he smelled the sour, acrid redolence of his own skin burning. Johnny ran crying to the kitchen sink. Splashed cold water on his face. It burned even more. Bill convulsed with laughter, amused by his little brother's agony. When Johnny settled onto the couch with a wet cloth beneath his eye, silent and brimming with tears, Bill sat at the table, smoking another Lucky, taking nips from various liquor bottles hanging around the house. He looks just like Daddy, Johnny thought, he looks just like Daddy and I hate him, hate him, hate him.

"Darling?" Susan asked. "Are you all right?"

Johnny gazed into Susan's broken eyes, where flecks of blood sun gleamed like burning embers, and he smiled because he saw a bit of himself inside her. "Yes," Johnny nodded. "For the first time in my life, I think I am."

Susan kissed him on the small, crescent-shaped scar beneath his left eye.

An autumn breeze ruffled their hair and clothes and skittered dead leaves across the lawn. They lounged in rocking chairs upon the front porch of Susan's cottage. They smiled at one another. It had been hard work, and the hours they'd spent on the task had devoured the waning sunlight. Still, they couldn't have been happier.

It was the first time in many days Johnny saw Susan smile. For this, he was grateful. There was a light and vibrancy in her gaze, and this was welcome change from the numb glaucoma that had settled like grey mist into her eyes on the night she'd sobbed and told him.

With glasses of Moscato in hand, they toasted to love and life eternal. Dusky blue twilight deepened into the sacred dark of Halloween. A full moon arose over the undulating sea of dead crops, gently sweeping the harvest with its ivory satin shadow.

Crickets began to sing. Stars twinkled in their snow-white luminescence, reminding Johnny of the long, cold winter to come. He didn't dread it, like most years. He was looking forward to cozy nights with Susan, snuggling and drinking hot cocoa, watching snow fall from within the comforts of the cottage.

"I love you," Susan whispered, squeezing his hand.

Johnny sipped from his glass, admiring her beauty in the moon-shadowed night with the Jack O' Lantern's red-orange glow flickering upon her face. He was surprised to see tears in her eyes, forming into transparent, jeweled beads to slip down her cheek.

"I love you too," he replied, feeling a bit like crying himself.

It'd been a trying evening. He'd have much work ahead of him tomorrow too: disposing of Bill's corpse, and cleaning all that foul blood and emesis from the cab of his pick-up. Susan might have work cut out for her too—answering perfunctory questions about Bill's disappearance to the police. She'd have to put on her best face of clueless nonchalance. A Halloween mask of its own, Johnny supposed.

Susan gazed into the Jack O' Lantern's glow. Johnny smiled, relishing in her obvious delight. They'd carved the lantern together, right there on the porch, covering the floorboards with a tarp so as not to get it messy and stained with gunk.

Most pumpkins were bright sherbet inside, filled with almond-shaped seeds. This was a different kind of gourd, however, and it served for a veritable Halloween masterpiece.

It sat upon the bottom step, facing them.

"There are few things I've seen," Susan said, squeezing Johnny's hand tight, "as beautiful as this."

Johnny grinned down at their handiwork. The scalp of blood-matted hair sat askew over the smashed-open cranium—a job done with chisel, hammer, and an abundance of determination. Ghastly pale cheeks glowed faintly with three tea candles they'd set down within the hollow of Bill's skull. Gouging out the eyeballs had been elementary, of course, as had been ripping out the tongue (it'd looked no more than a strip of raw meat from the butcher's shop, Johnny thought), but removing the brains had required formidable effort and time.

The brain, with all its folds and grooves, was a surprisingly dense organ. Susan had sliced it into sections with her largest kitchen knife, before Johnny could go about ripping out the contents. "Grey matter is no matter at all," Johnny had joked, stabbing, slicing and tearing—often ripping out chunks of slimy warm brain with his red slicked fingers.

They held hands across the space between chairs. The flickering glow emanating from Bill's sagging open eyes and mouth provided a romantic ambience. Once morning came, they would dutifully toss out the head with the rest of the body, burying it in the nearby Morton Woods. But at least Susan and Johnny would always have this special memory for the keeping—of the Halloween they had spent together beneath the Jack O' Lantern sky, and how when the sky died away, they re-lit the night with a Jack O' Lantern of their very own—a symbol of their love and dedication, and the fact they would do *anything* for each other, no matter what.

On that last chilly night of October, their hands fastened together with the bond of blood. They leaned in close, and within the lantern's red-orange glow, kissed deeply.

WALLS OF SHAME

Mother discovered my collection just three days shy of my fourteenth birthday. She was shocked, angry, saddened, and disappointed. I didn't like it when Mother was disappointed. I still don't, despite her being gone nearly a decade now.

It was an eighty-five-degree day and not a cloud in the wide blue sky. After hopping off the school bus, I strolled up our gravel driveway. Scents of summer drifted in the air along with the occasional dandelion fluff. The sun felt hot under my thick brown hair. My scalp itched.

Three whole months of sweet summer freedom lay before me like an infinite horizon. It was May 28th, 2008.

Yes, I remember the date. Yes, I remember what Mother said the moment I stepped foot in the house. I remember everything.

"Why don't you go upstairs?" Mother said, washing dishes with her back turned.

I smiled. Mother sometimes did nice things for me while I was away at school. She had left me an early birthday present on my bed, I was sure of it. Comic books, hopefully, even though she disapproved of them. I slung my backpack into the corner, then mounted the stairs two at a time. The old farmhouse steps creaked beneath my weight. Upon reaching the landing, I spun around the corridor, then burst into my room.

I stood there in the doorway, the doorknob (*cold, very cold*) in my hand. My mouth fell open, my eyes widened, and my heart pounded so fast, it was as if it weren't beating at all. Like when something goes by so quick, you hardly see it, or like those rapid-still wings of a hummingbird.

High upon my four walls, hanging in regions I could not reach— pictures of stark-naked women. Women much older than myself. Incredibly well endowed. Women on the beach, clutching their breasts with a gaze of seduction. Women in their twenties and thirties. Women frozen in time, mouths parted in expressions of passion. Women splayed on king-sized beds, their fingers touching … down there, opening that delicate crevice, jeweled with what I imagined must've been warm, velvety wetness.

Now, the women upon the walls took on a vastly different light. Their eyes communicated not sex, but sickness. Not seduction, but accusation. My ears prickled at the noise behind me. I turned. Mother stood just outside the door, her lips a thin taut line. Red fingernails tapping the burnished railing of the stairway.

"Mother," I began, clueless as to how to go on. "I-I …"

Sheer terror, hearing myself failing to form words. My face flushed red and I looked down at the floor, at the old planks which rewarded bare feet with splinters. The floor became an object of obsession. I couldn't stand Mother's eyes.

Blue, icy, piercing.

Arctic daggers that sheared with shame and sadness and stuck sharp into my heart. I went all frozen inside. Glancing up into those desolate winterland eyes, I wondered if it was snowing inside her brain.

I gulped down the lump in my throat, which settled in my stomach like a stone. The heaviness lay all over me, an iron cloak, a titanium blanket, a magnet that glued me to guilt — Mother had discovered *my collection*! I'd kept them hidden between books on my shelf. Now, all the women had been impaled on my walls with thick staples.

"Look at them, Raymond." Mother frowned, crossing her arms so tight it was as if she were giving herself a hug, one she needed.

Slow as a planet, I turned in the doorway, facing my walls of shame. Dozens of women gazed down, as if I were a sprawling insect. Their eyes penetrated me, but not in the way I had once wanted to penetrate them. All my prior fantasies were replaced with unbearable humiliation.

I'm bad, I realized. I'm the baddest kid I ever knew.

"Your eyes are closed, Raymond. I want you to open them and look, really *look* at what you've done."

I winced, eyes fluttering open at the walls. Sunshine beamed through the windows, landing on the industrial staples. They glimmered violently. I could almost hear the loud *thud* of the staple gun, launching sharp metal into the women, into the wood, into my wooly brain.

The women stared down with judgement, hurt, and anger, as if I were their murderer. As if I had killed all these women. Killed them and placed them under a microscope and reached down into my jeans.

"Please." I said, in a voice as small as a mouse. "Can't … you just take them down?"

"*Why?* So you wouldn't have to face up to what you've done?"

"I'm sorry, Mother," I quivered, stifling my cries. How disgraceful it felt, to be a full-grown teenager and crying in front of her like a baby. "I'll never do it again. I promise!"

She got down on her knees, her hands on my shoulders. In my periphery, I didn't see hands. I saw *talons*.

Her eyes leveled, glimmering with the same horror and accusation as the women on my walls. My chest swelled with rapid breaths. I was red all over, as if I were going to explode. I felt hot, yet frozen to my depths at the same time, my heart all fire and ice.

Sympathy filled Mother's dagger eyes, softening them to watery spheres. "You must pray daily and nightly. Confess your sins. And never, under any circumstances, will you take these pictures down.

If you do, I will send you far away, Raymond. I loathe to even think such a thing, but I won't hesitate to do it if you continue this path of sin. You're grounded for a month, understand? No leaving the property. You are also to write a seven-page essay on why, where, when, and how you got your hands on pornography, how you could possibly harbor any feeling for these, these …"

Her face twisted in a grimace, then she spat on the floor. "These *whores!* They're foul, unclean women. Now you too, Raymond, are unclean. I pray that God will have mercy on your soul."

She arose, kissed my forehead, then shut the door softly behind her. The kiss had felt strange. Not a mother's kiss, but the kiss of death. Her footsteps padded down the stairs. I was alone now, and yet I was not alone.

Out of the silence, voices of condemnation resounded. Forked tongues flickered in my ear, and I hated myself, because I knew those tongues and their spiteful words were telling the truth.

The women stared down from white plaster walls.

Stared down with Mother's eyes.

I sat in the center of my room, buried in an avalanche of dishonor, my world spinning, spinning. Everything had so suddenly changed.

Father left when I was a baby. A sinner in the house of the rising sun, Mother sometimes remarked of him, and when I turned fourteen in the solemn green garden behind the house, I wondered about him. Where did he live? Did he have sex a lot, or ever dream of the forbidden? Gazing at my reflection on the pond at the garden's edge, I wondered if I were seeing my father's face.

I didn't have any memories of Father, but I missed him.

I missed Mother, too. She was distant as a rain cloud on the horizon, looming deep and dark, threatening to break at any moment.

Before, we would stay up late playing board games and watching talk shows. All that was gone now, because even though I'd known Mother was growing darker and more somber every month, the day she'd discovered my collection something inside her snapped. Sundays, we used to go to church. Now, we didn't even do that. She stayed away from me, and I from her, unless she needed me to perform some chore or other. Inside the darkened house, curtains perpetually drawn, lingered an ominous sense of quiet and waiting. Quiet as a monastery; Mother waiting for me to make amends to God.

Which I knew I'd never do. I didn't know how. I'd written the seven-page essay she'd asked me to write, but we both knew that wasn't enough.

The pictures upon my walls collected dust. The thoughts inside my brain collected evil. I didn't want it to be this way, for God to hate me.

At night the women upon the walls chattered, making me dizzy with tears. Laying on my bed, I studied them up there in the dark—stars of pink flesh, gleaming sickly in the nothingness. Behind the pictures, a pitch-black void, as if God had cut out the walls with His merciless, omnipotent scissors. Those pictures belonged to my universe now, a universe of shame, and those pink stars orbited my head.

You're a bad boy, they'd say, clacking skeletal teeth. *You'll burn for eternity.*

Yes, I whispered. *Yes, yes, yes.*

Then I'd reach down into my pajamas. The Devil exists, and he lives in my brain, and he makes things hard. I stroked, the voices outraged and condemning. The louder the voices, the more I did it. Sticky white nectar of evil thoughts. Again and again, a pleasurable horror in each copulation. Hell's flames scorched my feet, making me sweat.

The voices never left.

You're the baddest boy who ever lived.

I groaned in despair. Why did God instill these perversions, derangements, evils in His own creation? Why does God blame me for my nature? I'm Frankenstein's Monster. A thing which is yet shouldn't be. I belong dead. I didn't *choose* this.

Watching my reflection ripple in the pond, the changes in my face became apparent. Pimples dotted the top of my forehead, the bridge of my nose. My jawline seemed defined. I was becoming a man. My soul was a stem, sprouting blossoms of evil, unfolding its petals of perversion, flaunting its fragrance of sweat, semen, and sickness.

The creepy-crawly sensation of someone watching me made me turn. She stood at the back door, smiling. Almost as if she were proud.

Mother's soul was a shoot of sacredness, the petals unfurling all bright daisy yellow and open to the sun. Mother's eyes were God's eyes—jewels of incredible condemnation and infinite mercy, a fence-line I continually straddled.

Mother was changing, too. She'd forget everything, walking into a room, eyes blinking rapidly, not knowing why she'd gone in there. Her wild, unbrushed hair formed a staticky mane, and the lines beneath her eyes tripled. The fragrance of her soul was sour and bitter, but I didn't hold this against her. God works in mysterious ways, Mother said, and I figured Mother for another of His mysteries.

Mother crossed herself, then disappeared back inside the house.

I would not see her the rest of the night. She kept her door shut, preferring to pray in solitude and drink strange ointments from tiny glass bottles. She was a holy woman, Mother.

"Raymond! Raymond, come out, will ya?!"

I surveyed the garden. Flowers swayed in the lazy June breeze, tickling the corners of the old house. My name drifted in the wind. Peering around the corner of the house's facade, I spied Chad, Andy, and his little brother, James, standing beside their bicycles in the gravel drive.

"We know somebody's in there!" Chad shouted, hands cupped around his mouth.

"Look," said little James, pointing a pudgy finger. "The curtain in the upstairs window moved! Raymond's Mom, I think."

"Correction," Chad grinned. "Raymond's *Mother*. Way he speaks about her, you'd think she was a saint or somethin'."

Andy, red-haired, freckled, and short for his age, piped up in his trademark squeak, "C'mon, Raymond, it's been *weeks!* It's summer vacation, so come outside already!"

I opened my mouth to shout, then happened to look up. A dark silhouette in my bedroom window. Mother stood before the sill, hair unkempt, her face ivory as a marble casket and lined with new wrinkles. Mother's piercing eyes peered down with the power of the walls, and I shrunk back. My heart withered into a rotten brown lump, like a weed exposed to chemical poisons. My buddies called once more, then cursed and left.

Silence reigned, save for the voices of the women echoing in my head. Gazing up at the window again, Mother was absent. Absent, yet somehow always there—omnipresent, omniscient, an all-powerful force unseen yet felt as intimately as the beat of one's heart, like the Holy Spirit.

I wondered, could the heart know if one's soul was impure, or evil? Does the heart ever tattletale on the soul? Does it ever refuse to beat once it knows too much?

Andy, Chad, and James came around the next week, and the week after that, begging me to come out and play. They spotted me one morning, while I wallowed in the garden, bored. I shouldn't spend an entire golden summer like this, they hollered from the drive. I'm too pasty-pale, like a vampire, and why don't I accompany them to Martin's beach for a swim?

Terrible temptations. Little hooks that pierced my flesh. Hooks attached to strings, pulling me toward them with an agonizing ache. But the slightest disobedience of Mother's wishes would've been sin—God knew, I'd done enough of that. The wall of women knew, too, and told me so night after night.

June flowed like a slow, languid river. My friends ceased their visitations. Their silence was devastating.

Then, one day, the sun arose, gleaming brilliant sherbet rays through my bedroom window. My blood surged with renewed energy. An inkling stirred in my heart. Could it be? Could it, really? I checked the calendar on my door for confirmation. Grinning, I flipped over to July.

"One month!" I exclaimed, and the women upon the walls, for once, had nothing to say. "A month grounded, and a month gone. I'm *free*."

Summer had only begun. I snagged a few dollars in quarters from my piggy bank—chocolate waffle cones from Leo's Ice Cream Parlor firmly in mind—then ran downstairs. Tripping on the second-to-last step, I tumbled onto the linoleum floor. My elbow stung where the skin had scraped, but I picked myself up without a hitch.

Maybe Chad and Andy, or even little James, would be out and about. I shoved my feet into my tennis shoes, never bothering with untying, then tying them again. Mother, hollow-eyed and scrawny as an alley cat, stood beside the kitchen counter.

"Where do you think *you're* going?" she rasped, her slender hands thin as hooks, sharpening themselves.

"Outside, Mother," I replied.

"You're grounded, remember?"

I shook my head. "No, Mother. Today's the first of July. See?"

I pointed to the calendar above the stove, but she didn't look.

"I don't care what month it is." She frowned. "I don't even care what *year* it is. Have you made amends with God, Raymond?"

She folded her arms then, and my spirit folded with them. I

desired freedom desperately. Desired a day with my friends, playing ball, or sitting up in Chad's treehouse, or catching a movie in the cool and darkened cinema. I looked straight up into the eyes of God, and I lied.

"Yes, Mother. I've made amends."

Her nose upturned, studying me intensely. I felt like an insect trapped under glass. Any moment now, my arms would shrivel off, replaced with raw, sprawling feelers. But Mother turned her back to me, attending to the counter where a dozen tiny bottles lay scattered. She picked one up, tilted back her head, and guzzled. Holy ointments made Mother holier every day; meanwhile I was always getting sicker, more depraved.

"Be back in a few hours, Mother ... love you."

Her jittery hands worked open the bottles, gulping them down. Sometimes a gloomy little man would arrive at the house, providing her ointments whenever she ran out. Someone from the church, I presumed, although his appearance left something to be desired. His ears were folded lumps, like boxer's ears, and his head was square, and his eyes were deep pits with beady buttons shining out of them. I called him the Hollow-Eyed Man.

But, at that moment, I didn't care about the Hollow-Eyed Man.

The doorknob was in my hand, and it turned freely.

Satan was an angel in Heaven before God cast him into Hell. Mother told me this once, while reading aloud Bible verses. That July first was like Heaven, and I was an angel yet to fall from its balmy paradise. I strolled along the sunny streets of Sweet Hollow, passing shops and cars and faces. It'd felt like ages since I'd seen people. Their easy, carefree smiles made me feel warm inside.

I was warm on the outside too, because there were only a few puffy white clouds in the sky. The sun was big, bright, and blessedly hot. A breeze washed over my sweaty skin like a refreshing ocean wave. *Ding!* The bell rung merrily as I stepped into Leo's Ice Cream Parlor.

A red and white tiled floor, cushion stools, and serving counter dominated the parlor. It was as if a giant candy cane had melted all over the place, coloring everything Christmas. An older kid named Billy Rosenthal sat at the end of the counter, chowing down on a banana split. He looked strange, though, with his hair cut. The guy used to have the longest hair I'd ever seen. Now, I could actually see his ears.

"Nice haircut, Billy."

"Thanks, man." He grinned up from his ice cream.

"So, how's it going?"

"Really great. It's my 18th birthday."

"Nice! Well, happy birthday. What're you gonna do now that you're a grown-up?"

He shrugged. "Hang out here for the summer, I guess. I'm attending college in the Fall."

Mr. Anderson strode out of the kitchen, slapped both hands on the counter, and smiled. "Why, if it isn't my dear boy, Raymond! How's your summer going, son?"

"It's splendid," I replied, finding I was getting better at lying all the time. The women in my head didn't like it, nor did God, and nor would Mother. Pushing these nagging reservations deep down, I forced a smile. "Could I have a chocolate waffle cone please, Mr. Anderson?"

"Bet your bottom dollar." Anderson pinched one end of his grey mustache, then went about preparing my cone. I liked Mr. Anderson. He was large, eccentric, and always friendly.

Ding! I turned to look. A grin spread over my face.

"Chad!" I exclaimed. "Andy!"

Both smiled, plopping down on the stools beside me.

"Where the heck you been, dude?" Chad slapped me on the back. My heart fluttered; it felt as if I were in a dream.

"Yeah," Andy reiterated, playfully punching my arm. "How come you never came out when we called? We saw you, you know, so no excuses!"

Mr. Anderson bellied up to the counter, holding out my towering cone.

"On the house." He winked.

"Geez, thanks, Mr. Anderson." I carefully took the cone into my hands. I licked the ice cream. It was cold and sweet. The most delicious thing I'd ever tasted.

"Most welcome." Mr. Anderson's head darted toward Chad and Andy. "Now, what the hell can I get *you* two troublemakers?"

All of us laughed, even Billy Rosenthal down at the end.

It would be the first laugh of many that bright, summer day. After finishing our ice creams, Chad, Andy, and I moseyed down to Martin's Beach. Blue waves shimmered like crystal and shattered against the bank. Seagulls screeched and swooped overhead. Families lay out in the sun on colorful towels. Adults drank beer and snacked on finger-sandwiches while their kids tossed and jumped and swam in the water, all laughing and crying and screaming. I hadn't brought any trunks, but Andy lived only a few blocks away, and he lent me a pair. They were a bit large, but I didn't care if I looked dorky in them.

We swam in the lake until the sun dipped into the horizon. We raced to the buoy line and back. Played Marco Polo. Waged splash-wars. Pretended we were battleships, and sharks and octopi.

The sun shone down from the heavens, and we were angels.

And when the sun came down to earth, all red and round and raw, I cried.

"What's wrong?" Chad asked, throwing his water-beaded arm over my shoulder. Andy threw his arm over me too, and I'd never felt so blessed with friends.

"It's over already." I shook my head. "The day went by so *quick!*"

"Dude, don't worry," Andy laughed. "There's always tomorrow, right?"

I nodded, yes. He was right. A stretch of summer months lay ahead of us, smooth and uniform as a field of golden wheat. The call of sweet freedom rung in our ears—sounding a lot like the welcome bell over the front door of Leo's Parlor.

I wish I could end my story here.

I wish this moment had been the end of my life.

It was only the beginning, and the sweet ringing of freedom's bell had yet to toll sonorous and deep as a grave, the tolling of Hell come to Earth, the tolling of the Fall.

But in that moment, I *was* an angel. I had wings and I soared.

We all did, us kids.

I slipped in through the front door, a yellow towel I'd borrowed from Andy cloaked over my shivering shoulders. My clothes lay in a bundle in my arms.

The house brooded in darkness. I shucked off my shoes, then padded upstairs to my room. To my surprise, my walls were barren. Mother had taken down the pictures, leaving only the silvery gleam of the staples.

Perhaps, I thought, this was the start of a new life. Maybe I could become a good person, and the voices will go away.

You're bad, they whispered still. *The baddest boy who ever lived.*

Ignoring them, I toweled off and put on my clothes, then tossed Andy's sopping wet swim trunks into the laundry hamper. I walked down the hallway. Mother's bedroom door stood wide open.

Strange. Mother's door was *never* open.

Peering into the dim room, it took some time before I realized

Mother was lying on the carpet, face-down. The hair on my arms straightened. My heart knocked like the industrial stapler. Flicking the wall switch, the overhead bulb's jaundiced glow shed a sickly pall over the room.

"Mother?" I asked, shakily, kneeling beside her. All around Mother's body lay all the other bodies—naked flesh, naked eyes, spread legs of sickness, my flowers of evil now become blossoms. I grunted, pushing Mother onto her back.

Glazed blue eyes stared emptily at the ceiling. A trail of spittle dribbled down her chin. Laying my head against her chest, there resounded that terrible thunder of silence which only a lifeless cavity can produce. At that moment, the yellow lightbulb overhead flickered.

I gasped, for the flickering was a sign. As if God were saying, *I have seen everything. You've murdered your mother, Raymond. Now you shall spend an eternity roasting in Hell-flame.*

I crumbled beneath the flickering yellow light, holding Mother in my arms, kissing her frigid, wrinkled face. Tears streamed off my chin and tasted salty on my lips. The women on the scattered pages opened their mouths, exposing deep yawning voids and sharp little teeth.

You're a bad boy, they shrieked, chanting it. *Bad boy, bad boy, baaaaad boy!!!*

The cops arrived soon afterward. The next-door neighbors had called 911, reporting a horrible, throat-raw wailing resounding from the house. I hadn't even known I'd been screaming. The only thing that existed for me was my dead mother in my arms, and the voices surrounding me, stuffing me into the blackest corner of life. How I ached for a life-sized cross, so that I could fix Mother upon it, where she belonged.

I never saw Chad or Andy, nor charming Mr. Anderson with his grey mustache, nor the now-grown-up Billy Rosenthal ever again. Nor even my hometown of Sweet Hollow. All of it was stripped away that gorgeous summer evening I murdered my mother.

Shuffled from one foster home after another, I spent my teen years eternally uprooted. My flowers of evil had blossomed, now taken to drift in a breathless, humid wind without rhyme or reason. Truly, all our lives are like that, though we may deny it. This universe is the breath of chaos. God hath made it so.

Those who are good are *born* good. Those who are bad are *born* bad.

Nature trumps nurture every time—I know because I tried.

Tried to be good. Tried to kill the voices in my head by pushing them deep down, drowning them in oblivion. I lost count of how many doctors, social workers, and therapists I've bared my soul to over the years. I've read every one of Freud's books. He's right about most things, except that he didn't believe in God.

God exists. I can feel him now, beating my heart.

My hellish, hateful heart.

Satan exists, too, sharpening our temptations into piercing blades to stick us with. Mostly, though, he just waits. Satan is the quiet waiting that forms the silence of lonely hotel rooms, sleeps coiled in the crevices and corners of one's psyche, looms in the forest-dark and lies in the shadowy bowels of one's necrotic nature.

You may disagree. Fine.

It's simply how I feel, and how I feel reflects who I am.

It's who I am tonight, tasting the devil on my breath as I guzzle from the bottle. The voices have not lessened over all these years. All those women from my walls still shriek and writhe with condemnation. All the while I'm nodding, telling them yes, *yes*, you're right, scream it again, and *again*.

I'm a twenty-seven-year-old child, sitting behind the wheel of my Grand Prix in my date's paved driveway. Through the windshield, I watch her approach—a curvy silhouette beneath the moonlight. Stuffing the rum bottle under my seat, I wipe my lips on the sleeve of my leather jacket. My date opens the passenger door, slides into the seat.

She's wearing a mid-thigh skirt—it's blue, blue like the heavens.

Her sweater is tight, accentuating her breasts—the fabric's red, red like Hell.

A blonde with an angular face and shimmering earrings.

"Good evening," I smile, very charmingly.

"Hi, Ray," she laughs nervously. "So, where we going?"

Her eyes shimmer, like distant blue worlds. Worlds that spin within the palm of my hand. A darkness thickens. Voices chatter.

Fingernails drum an old stair railing.

The Devil's in my brain and he makes things hard.

The voices, thousands of them now, ones I've heard moan within the pages of magazines and on X-rated movies, ones I've brought into my basement and have never let see the light of day, all agree: *You're the baddest boy that ever walked the Earth, Raymond.*

"Just wait and see," I grin, with a wink. "We're going someplace *very* special tonight."

Stephanie claps her hands, grits her teeth in bubbly excitement. I shift the car into drive, and we peal out onto the road, getting the hell out of Dodge. We've got a long night ahead of us.

A *very* long night.

The cool air is chilly through my open window, fluttering my hair and rippling Steph's sky-blue skirt. I reach over, placing my hand on her warm velvety thigh.

She fixes me with her eyes, *those eyes.*

Forked tongues flicker in my ear. Voices chatter, clatter, their dead, dirt-clogged throats urging me: *Take her home, Ray. Pamper her, flatter her, bring her down to the basement with the usual explanations. If she resists, push her down the stairs. Hopefully, her legs will break.*

I have grown to love this darkness. This filth. This immense peak of degradation.

These voices are my friends, and tonight is going to be a damned good night. I can feel it, feel it in the wind that ruffles my hair, feel it in my left hand as it grips the steering wheel, feel it in my right as it squeezes her thigh and she giggles, although she won't be giggling long.

There's immense evil in this universe—it courses in my blood, for I am its conduit.

And at long last, I can feel these walls of shame ... closing in.

THE MONSTER IN
H. PHILIP'S GROCERY

Rowen discovered the monster in H. Philip's Grocery Mart on a frigid evening in mid-December. His mom was sick at home on account of the stomach flu. Therefore, Rowen had been sent into town on an errand, even though he'd rather have played hockey on the town rink.

Little did he expect to discover the *thing* lumbering down the polished aisles, pretending to be a man.

Rowen carried a red basket with H. Philip's Grocery logo on the center: an uncut loaf of bread, an old-fashioned milk bottle, and stacks of cheese and crackers. Hovering above such wholesome food was Howard Philip and his wife, Margery—smiling in a jovial version of *American Gothic*.

Howard and Margery had managed the store for over fifty years. It remained the one place in Sweet Hollow where one could procure every necessity: food, cigarettes, alcohol—even a pharmacy to counteract the negative outcomes of all that food, cigarettes, and alcohol.

There was, as well, a photo development center stuffed into the far corner of the store.

Dropping a can of Campbell's Chicken Noodle soup into the basket, Rowen wrinkled his nose. He turned around to locate where the stench was coming from—an odor of spoiled meat, or dead animal. Like something lying on the side of a road, beneath the sun, scurried by flies.

A man in a wool black coat stood ten feet away, hunkered over the shelves as if studying the labels. Rowen wondered if it was *him* that smelled so awful, or perhaps a sewer pipe beneath the floor that'd broken?

The man swiped two large cans off the shelf and stuffed them into an inner pocket of his dirty, bulky coat.

Stealing! Rowen marveled, the tops of his ears tingling. The man staggered down the aisle before turning a corner. Rowen stood beside the soups, mouth half-open, riddled with questions. He'd noticed Howard stocking the newspaper racks when he'd first walked in. Should he inform the old man somebody's making off with inventory? But what if the foul-smelling thief was homeless, simply too poor to purchase groceries? Rowen hated the idea of getting the man arrested.

Sprinting down the aisle until reaching the main way, Rowen zipped past the aisle caps, scanning each alley for the man in the black coat. Neighborly faces inspected ingredient labels, weighed rye bread against wheat, considered, measured, argued with their children, *No, you can't have that cereal, it's nothing but sugar!* while married couples murmured and strolled, their lives easy as feathers floating the breeze.

Rowen scanned, searched, scoured the store for the soul who sought to steal. The thief was in the farthest aisle back, just beyond the row of refrigerators containing ice cream and frozen pizza.

The sign hanging above: *WINE/LIQUOR.*

This was no place for a boy his age. He would draw dark stares if noticed. Despite this risk, Rowen set his basket on the floor and slunk beside the shelves. The man loomed over a wine rack.

A deathstench lingered on the air, an odor too grisly for fluorescent lights, too ugly for the calming Muzak resounding from overhead speakers, too unseemly for a Grocery Mart that prided itself for being *the best family store in all Sweet Hollow.* Not that there were many stores to compete with. Sweet Hollow was about as small as a snow globe—that's how Rowen saw it, anyway.

Silent, secret, studying! Rowen watched the man sway on his feet, yank a bottle of Merlot off the rack, stuff it into his deep inner pocket, then button the coat.

The man turned, staring directly at Rowen.

The boy's face flushed red. Fear and humiliation made his heart thump wildly. At first, he'd mistaken the man's face as merely pale. As Rowen's eyes adjusted, he realized the man was completely covered in white bandages—like the Invisible Man.

Not a fraction of skin visible beneath the bandages.

Only the eyes; dark, hollow things.

Rowen knew immediately, irrevocably—this man *had no eyes.*

He stared out from empty caverns. Rowen thought, for the briefest moment, he could see into the man's raven-black brain. Rotting neurons dangled like dying roots. Pink mush of gyrus folds turned to blue-green mold. And deep, deep into those dark hollows, was there not something writhing? Twisting like grave worms?

Rowen froze with fear. He'd become a statue in the aisle, a boy gone from living-breathing to stuffed-dead. His heart balled in his chest as the man that was no man, but a monster, lumbered past and the fetor of decay swept over him once more, choking, suffocating him.

The monster disappeared around the corner.

A jittering heart, a glaze of sweat, a catch of breath—all symptoms of a sickness called Fear.

It took a moment to thaw, to break from the icy paralysis of terror, but the moment Rowen reached the end of the aisle, he dashed through the store, shouting, "A zombie! Monster! It's stealing, stealing!"

Lord, how heads turned! Eyes bulged!

Children pointed, giggled.

Fathers frowned, scolded.

Mothers rolled eyes, sighing.

Rowen tripped and slid across the gleaming linoleum just before the checkout aisles. Several clerks leaned over their casters, individual aisle numbers glowing above their heads. The pneumatic front doors whooshed open, letting in a cold draft as the monster stalked out into the snowy parking lot.

"It's escaping!" Rowen pointed, picking himself up off the floor. He'd bruised his knees, yet hardly noticed in all the excitement. Everyone stared at him, mouths ajar. He felt like a superhero in a movie.

Howard stumbled out of his office, white eyebrows twitching, scratching the top of his balding head.

"What the hell, son?" Howard scowled, clamping a liver-spotted hand on Rowen's left shoulder.

"That *thing*," Rowen gasped, out of breath. "It stole a bottle of wine, and beans, other stuff!"

"Where? *Who?*"

"It just walked out."

The pneumatic doors opened as Howard walked past. Rowen followed. The sun was out, glaring on the snow. The old man formed a hand-visor over his searching blue eyes.

"What'd he look like, kid?"

"It wore a wool black coat, Mr. Philip. Its face was all bandages, and it didn't have eyes."

"Come again?"

"No eyes, Sir. I could see up into its brain! It was a monster."

"Ah, shit." Howard turned, hands on his hips. "You think this is funny? I'm too busy for pranks, boy."

"Honest, Mr. Philip, no prank! The monster was stealing, and it looked at me and had *no eyes!*"

Howard frowned.

The boy stared up, eyes wide and credulous.

Stupid kid, Howard thought, then patted Rowen's head as if he were a dog.

"Good looking out, Rowen," he sighed. "But if all this monster's got is a bottle of wine and some Heinz beans, I ain't gonna fuss."

Howard made for the sliding doors.

"But, Mr. Philips, it wasn't alive! It was a—"

The doors swooshed closed.

"Zombie," Rowen mumbled, and trudged to the edge of the parking lot, and gazed out over the quiet town. Then, glancing behind him, he discovered cruel, judgmental faces staring through the Mart's glass doors.

"Oh, to hell with it!" Rowen tossed up his hands, then ambled into the street.

Birds chirped in barren trees. Chimney smoke curled up like phantom serpents, dissipating into the blue sky. Lamp posts glimmered with garland. Shop windows sported Christmas lights, nativity scenes, and miniature trains that puffed out smoke on a gleaming track.

Rowen wished he'd spent the afternoon playing hockey. Then he wouldn't have gone into the Mart, nor pursued the monster and been humiliated before half the town. To be sure, he'd hear about it at school on Monday—picked on, teased, mocked.

"Shit," Rowen grumbled, finding catharsis in the curse. He trekked through town, but upon turning onto Hodgson Street, halted in his tracks.

His breath puffed out, slow and steady like steam. The monster in the black coat walked stiltedly down the sidewalk, fading into the distance.

Just go home. A voice in Rowen's head commanded, yet he didn't obey.

Rowen followed the monster for blocks, observing the stiff, clumsy way Its legs moved—like a toddler that'd just learned to walk. But Rowen understood it wasn't clumsy, but *rotting* beneath that suit and coat, the ligaments and tendons in the legs decaying, the innards of the belly liquifying, the heart withering like an old branch and the lungs shrinking to leathery prunes.

Rowen followed It to the old house on the corner of Bloch and Leiber Street. Rowen knew the house well. His school bus passed it every weekday morning. Kids peered out the windows, and exclaimed, "The haunted Manor!"

The two-story Victorian jutted upward a high, steep roof. Its clapboards, once white, were grey and peeling. Its windows dark, staring, insane, like a catatonic crazy. The Manor, as the kids called it, had stood empty for as long as he could remember.

Rowen hid behind a snowman in someone's front yard. The monster looked about, his hollow sockets glistening like wet coal.

The street was silent. Empty.

Its breath did not fog the air like any living person's would. The monster mounted the creaking porch steps, then entered the old dark house.

There was a window, shoulder-high, at the back of the house.

Rowen peered in just as he'd done a dozen times before, messing around the 'haunted Manor' with friends. Someone recently hung up a burlap sack behind the window, forcing Rowen to peer into the narrow side-space between frame and burlap.

Within that space, the monster sat down at a kitchen table to drink.

The wine, stolen from old Howard's Grocery, was poured into a dusky glass.

The monster reached behind its skull, as if to scratch. Instead, it pulled at the edge of the bandage that enwrapped its head.

Round and round, like a spiderweb woven in reverse, the unbounding exposed the monster's forehead, eyes, nose, lips.

It stopped at the lips, letting the bandage hang from Its chin.

Rowen clamped a gloved hand over his mouth, stifling a scream. He kneeled in the snow, certain he'd be sick. The snowy ground became a whirl of white. His body swayed, as if on a floating dock.

Sucking in the icy air, he steadied himself, then stood and peered in.

The monster tilted back its head, guzzling glass after glass. Streaks of red dribbled down its rotting cheeks. Rowen squinted at the grotesque countenance, hardly believing his eyes.

For the man truly *was* a monster, a zombie, a paradox, the living-dead!

Lily-white maggots squirmed in the hollow sockets.

The nose was decomposed, leaving just two black orifices.

And the complexion of the face! A dirt-brown patchy thing, with wet, pale, withered flesh of cheek and forehead remaining. Black hair sprouted atop his head in sporadic strands.

Worse still, the monster was *familiar*—a face destroyed that was once handsome, a face everyone in town had known.

Rowen remembered, and his heart jabbered in his chest.

He clutched the paint-flaked sill with both hands, and the name echoed in Rowen's mind, over and over.

Robert "Bob" Aveeno, aka Bobby Aveeno—RIP!

Sure, everyone had known Bobby. A native son of Sweet Hollow, after all. He'd graduated from Sweet Hollow High, had worked the lumber mill, been a janitor for the motel, a construction worker, a mechanic, damned near everything before he'd moved away to Michigan. Word had it he went to college, got married, started a family.

Nobody much saw of Bobby again, except when he came into town during holidays. During his last return, about a year ago, his wife and son had accompanied. Only it wasn't a holiday. The three of them were dead from a car crash, their bones shipped in and laid to rest in Sweet Hollow Cemetery.

The raucous began the following summer, with endless police investigation and news reports about the grave-robbing. Some lunatic had dug up Bobby Aveeno's grave, leaving the coffin barren! Rowen heard all kinds of gossip from his friends, neighbors, his mother.

Hell, it'd been the talk of the town for an entire *year*.

But as all things do, the stealing of Bobby's corpse had faded in importance, becoming nothing more than small-town legend. Macabre trivia for the bored.

Now, the legend sat before him, drinking wine to console its resurrected soul.

Rowen watched as the dead man clumsily set aside the glass, pulled an ink pen out of its coat, and began writing in a yellow notebook.

What would a zombie write about? Rowen wondered, dreaming interminably at the sill. His mom would be angry at his tardiness. He was to gather the groceries and return before dinner. Now, the sun was setting in the red-orange sky.

After filling several notebook pages with neat cursive, the thing called Bobby Aveeno set the pen aside.

Is it a journal he's writing? An essay? But what business would the dead have with—

The monster brought out an envelope. Folded the written pages and stuffed it inside. Applied address and stamp. Sealed the envelope with a black snake of a tongue. Slid the envelope into his coat pocket, wrapped up Its face again, then stood and walked into another room.

Breathless, Rowen remained at the sill, awaiting the creature's return.

Instead, he heard the front door open and shut against the silent winter cold. He ducked low against the side of the house.

Its coat collar erect, the monster shambled down the sidewalk and vanished, the shuffling footsteps fading.

Bobby Aveeno, back from the dead, to mail a letter!

But to whom? Why?

Rowen found himself moving automatically. His boots made indentations in the snow, which he'd later have to obscure. All those tracks leading up to the porch, then up the creaking stairs—now Rowen's hands were on the doorknob! Initially, he'd been scared out of his wits. Curious, yes, but frightened. Now, all fear had vanished along with the Monster—replaced by pure exhilaration.

The boy looked around.

A car zipped by, and for a moment, Rowen considered himself discovered. But the car did not slow, and the street was empty again, and quiet, the sun loudest in the rosy sky.

The knob turned freely in his hand.

Rowen snuck inside.

Rowen and his buddies had messed *around* the house, sure. They'd even messed *under* it, devouring popsicles beneath the porch in the cobwebbed coolness during sweltering summers. No one, however, had ever been *inside.*

Because that was stupid.

Because that was suicide.

Because that's what people did in horror movies, and guess what happened to *them?*

Rowen knew all this yet did not care. The monster had provoked his curiosity from the very moment he had glimpsed Its dark, fetid presence in H. Philip's Grocery. With the monster gone to drop his letter into the P.O. Box, there was no better time than now to search the house.

Search for what, exactly?

Proof. Evidence. Material to bring back to his friends, the police, old man Howard. No one would believe that he'd seen Bobby Aveeno's corpse walking around, drinking wine, writing letters! Nobody would believe unless he brought something back.

Rowen hustled from room to room.

Fast—the light grew dimmer. His Mom would be worried and, most frightening of all, the monster might soon return.

The rooms were barren, grimy, the floorboards covered with dust bunnies. Rats scurried in the corners, little nostrils snuffing the line where the floor met the walls. Odd pieces of furniture scattered about the house. A ripped-up couch. A recliner with springs jutting out of the fabric. A grubby sink stopped up with oily black fluid. A room full of old, water-damaged textbooks.

There was an upstairs.

Rowen did not go upstairs.

It was, for some reason, a place he was afraid of. That, and the door that opened into darkness, with stairs leading down, down, down to who knew where ....

He would not go into the basement.

Only a fool would do that.

So, he went into the room that was most familiar. The kitchen.

And he snatched up the monster's ink pen, and the unopened can of Heinz beans, and stuffed them into the pocket of his winter coat. Then he flipped through the yellow notebook.

The pages were lined, blank, proffering nothing.

Rowen dropped the notebook onto the table, beside the stamps and envelopes and the empty glass and the bottle.

He'd never drank wine before. His best friend, Eddie, had though. Eddie said it'd given him the best time of his life.

Rowen reached for the bottle.

No. His hand withdrew. *Don't be stupid. You'll get into trouble.*

He reminded himself to focus. He was here for evidence, not for a good time. Upon turning around, he spied a small rectangular object upon the kitchen counter. A familiar, nostalgic item.

Picking it up, he peered through its tiny lens, and the dark kitchen world suddenly grew darker, more real, insane.

What was he *doing* here?

He withdrew the Fujifilm disposable camera from his face and noticed the picture counter was down to 23.

Had the monster been taking pictures? But of what?

Itself. A voice popped out of the void, into Rowen's brain, like a quantum particle. *It's taking pictures of itself, getting them developed, sometimes putting them into Its letters ....*

But who would want a picture of *It?* A face so gruesome and grotesque it made you sick!

Rowen pocketed the camera for evidence. He'd bring it to the photo center at H. Philip's Grocery, then bring whatever pictures were on it to the police. Rowen would tell them about the stealing. They'd search the Manor, discover the creature, then take It away.

This is how it should be. Rowen could not sleep with the knowledge of a monster residing in his hometown. The Manor had always been an empty old house. It did not need Bobby Aveeno, dead over a year, residing within it.

Maybe the police would help the monster return to where it belonged—beneath the earth in the Cemetery, where cold wind grazed over crosses and stones and none shivered, where mischievous teenagers sometimes hung out, trying to scare each other, yet none heard their giggling, where the seasons turned, turned, and none turned with them, but remained cold and straight and boxed and decayed, dribbled, drained away.

A part of Rowen felt sorry for the monster, the thing that had once been the living, breathing, handsome Bobby Aveeno. And maybe that's why It mailed letters—to do something only the living do, to feel alive, and not lonely.

Rowen blinked at the growing shadows. The window covered with burlap was lit about the corners with a rich pumpkin orange. The sun dipped into the horizon, nearly gone. He had to get out.

But his hand did not reach for the front door.

It reached for the wine.

Just a nip, Rowen told himself. Just to try. Just to see, to feel.

He uncorked it with a yank, raised the bottle to his lips, and gulped. Rowen grimaced. Coughed. The wine was red and raw and rough.

And it was *sweet.*

He studied the label in the dimness. A French name he couldn't pronounce, only knew it was cultivated from grapes somewhere far, far away.

Rowen took another gulp. He wanted to feel it. Wanted to know why Mom indulged in wine every night, why so many neighbors drank alcohol at summer baseball games and barbeques, why drunks were drunks.

It was rough on his throat, and bitter, but sweet, and he drank until the bottle was half-empty.

Then set it down onto the table with a thud.

Like eating potato chips, a single indulgence hadn't sufficed. He swooned and caught himself from falling by grabbing onto a chair, laughing loudly.

He shook his head, delightfully dizzy, and what little light there was in the room became a euphoric sight. What a wonderful world this was, even inside a damp, dark little hole such as this!

Still, he knew he had to leave. The monster would return shortly— the P.O. Box only a quarter mile away.

Rowen stumbled out of the kitchen, laughing all the way into the living room, and toward the front door. His vision twirled like a slow dance.

What an idiot! Mom's going to know, just from smelling your breath!

Even the voice inside Rowen's head sounded drunken. He laughed, laughed, and his hand reached the cold brass knob of the front door, and the knob turned, and the door swept open *without* him pulling it.

In the doorway, the monster's black silhouette.

Rowen leaped back, stumbled, and screamed. A woosh of air

rushed over him as he fell, smacking the back of his skull upon the knotty hardwood.

Darkness. Silence. Coldness.

The Monster closed the door, cutting off the frigid wind and all the remaining light. It picked the boy up in its arms. Brought him across the room to a door.

With one rotting hand, It opened the door wide, then carried the boy down the groaning steps into a black barren basement.

Click. Scratch-scratch.

Rowen groaned. Blinked dry, tired eyes. He shivered from head to toe, his body clammy as a grave. His head ached.

Oh, how the darkness swirled!

Click.

He gazed near the sound, his eyes centering upon the minimal light in the room. A tall candle, waxing its golden glow.

The candle brought light, yet no heat. Rowen watched his breath curl into the air. He tried to move, to sit up, and dug his fingers into the floor and discovered it was composed of hard packed dirt.

He knew where he was now, and gasped.

Panic fluttered ebony wings inside Rowen's head.

His heart thumped crazily, a jackrabbit with one foot nailed to the floor, desperate to escape. He sucked in the burning air to scream, yet it caught in his throat. He turned aside, vomited in the dirt.

Scratch-scratch. Click. Scratch-scratch.

Rowen gawked up into the candlelight. The monster's unbandage face leered beside it. Its putrefied eyes, nostrils, and mouth wriggled with wry worms, squirmed with small snakes, bustled with bulging bugs. It raised the camera to the upper half of its face. The mouth opened in a wide broken-bottle grin.

Click!

Bobby Aveeno, the lonely monster, the local legend, the living-dead—*laughed.* A broken pipe sound, an off-key organ with rats scurrying about the keys, accompanied by a breath so full of rot that it wafted over Rowen's face, promising suffocation.

Rowen shoved himself back against the stone wall. His chest hitched with jittering breath. The world churned. The monster set aside the camera, and laughing still more, reached out its frigid, broken hands and grasped Rowen's skull and yanked him forward, drawing Rowen toward its mouth of jagged-black teeth.

A sharp pain sliced into the flesh of Rowen's forehead, filling his eyes with warm, rushing redness.

The boy screamed.

But for a time, only for a time.

And the monster drank Rowen's blood, and was warmed inside, and felt truly *alive*—but for a time, only for a time.

IN THE TOWN OF SWEET HOLLOW

(A Novelette)

BY TIMOTHY WALLACE

1.

My agent, Walt Kaplan, gave me the impression I'd be writing my next book inside a haunted house.

God knows old Ravencourt should be perfect for a horror novelist ... Walt texted one night.

I'd thought about it over several glasses of scotch. Nothing like a stiff drink to put hairs on your chest and motivate you to make potentially disastrous life choices. After much brooding, lamentation, and gazing at the unfinished manuscript on my desk, I shrugged and texted back: *Okay, Walt. Make it happen.*

Walt made it happen. On the first of October, I packed a suitcase and locked up my house in St. Paul. After crossing the Minnesota-Wisconsin border, I drove two hundred miles east, arriving in the town of Sweet Hollow by sunset.

I'd been expecting a dumpy little town with nothing going, save a pub, a sun-dried park with rusty swings, and a dead-end street. The sort of town you stumble on while traveling through the Midwest.

Sweet Hollow, however, defied my prejudices.

Main Street was a smooth black ribbon, shimmering in the waning sun. I took it slow, gliding past quaint shops, pub-restaurants, a café, a bowling alley, a cinema, a bank. I lowered my head to gaze out the windshield, admiring the shop signs: Leo's Ice Cream Parlor. Mr. Burgess' Curio Shop. Ellie's Cafe. The Sweet Hollow Pub.

Residents strolled the streets, chatting amicably. Some locked-up shop and headed home. Others were just arriving. A group of men in greasy uniforms, hot and sweaty from a day's labor, entered the pub for a round of beers. Four children, hunched over the sidewalk, drew with chalk. A boy turned and waved an orange-colored hand. I smiled, catching a glimpse of his drawing—a grinning jack o' lantern.

The town was decorated festively. Black-orange streamers twirled about each lamp post. Fake cobwebs stretched across stair banisters, shop signs, and entryways. Every window showcased a paper skeleton, ghost, or black cat.

Reaching the end of Main, the GPS built into my dash informed me to take a right onto Hodgson Street. After a while, Hodgson gave way to gravel. Dust plumed in my rearview, fizzy orange in the light.

Beneath a jack o' lantern sky.

The phrase floated through my consciousness, a sherbet cloud across a tangerine expanse.

Golden corn fields, dark woods, and gently rolling hills swelled to the horizon. And I thought: *Hell, maybe Walt's right. This getaway into the country might be the best move I could've made.*

My creative inspiration, elusive as of this past year, seemed to be returning.

My last novel, *Doom Canyon*, hadn't sold well. Primarily because it wasn't any good. I knew it was a stinker every day I'd sat down to write it—still, I'd sent it off to Walt, then Walt passed it to the publisher. Come release day, an outpouring of negative reviews buried me in its avalanche of shame, lament, criticism, even attacks upon my character.

I'd taken it all in stride, telling myself the next book would be a Tim Wallace horror masterpiece, otherwise I wouldn't submit anything to the pencil-pushers of Putnam after all. When questioned by interviewers, friends, my agent, and my editor, I'd shrugged off every criticism with my best impression of *nonchalance*. On the inside, though, I was rattled.

Here I had three books under my belt, two highly acclaimed, and the last one a goose egg. Was my career finished at the ripe old age of twenty-nine?

I zipped past an old cemetery, its crosses and tombstones gathering shadows, a brief oasis amidst endless field and forest. The green line on my GPS took a sharp left. I stomped on the brake, skidding to a stop. On my left, a gravel driveway wound, serpent-like, into the woods. Beside the drive was a black mailbox with *RAVENCOURT* etched in white.

I'd arrived at my second home, purchased for a mere $300,000.

It was old. It was cheap. It was the historic Ravencourt House.

Languid, as if moving in a dream, I turned in.

2.

Parking beside Walt's shiny black Escalade, I stepped out into the crisp twilight. A narrow stone path cut through the leafy lawn, and I followed it to the stairs. Walt stood in his suit and tie upon the shaded porch, smiling.

"You made it, brother." He embraced me at the bottom step.

"Careful," I laughed, patting his back. "Or you'll crush me."

Walt Kaplan was a large man. Broad shoulders. Muscular arms.

Bear-like hands. Despite his gentle temperament, he resembled someone who could pop off your head with just his thumb, easy as a dandelion.

"So?" Walt waved his hand over the house's facade. "I know you've seen pictures, but whaddya think?"

In the gathering dusk, I studied the two stories of peeling clapboards, arched windows, gingerbread trim, and a brick chimney jutting out of the ramshackle roof.

"Looks haunted." I nodded approvingly.

"Nobody actually said it was *haunted*."

"What do they say then?"

"According to the locals, Ravencourt is cursed." Walt's eyes widened with recollection, adding, "The whole town is cursed, actually."

"Charming," I replied, and meant it.

Walt Kaplan covered half of his face with an arm, arched his eyebrows, bowed, and spoke in a Transylvanian accent, "I bid you welcome …"

I waved off Walt's goofiness, following him up the scuffed verdant steps, across the creaking porch, and inside the one-hundred-and-seventy-year-old house.

Walt took the role of tour guide, showing me upstairs and down. Four bedrooms, one bathroom sporting a marvelous clawfoot tub, several linen closets, a parlor, dining room, kitchen, even a library with a heavy oak table. Several antique sofas and chairs were shrouded in white sheets, lending them the appearance of oddly shaped ghosts. I sneezed occasionally, the house smelling of old wood and dust.

As darkness settled, Walt loaded the parlor's fireplace with kindling from a corner wood box, added lighter fluid, then tossed in a lit match. Flames licked upward, flickering red-orange tongues.

"Stay here until you finish the book if you'd like. I took the liberty of supplying you with coffee, groceries, and kitchenware." Walt shuffled toward the front door, preparing for his long drive home. "You've signed the papers, so the house is yours. Do whatever you want. However, the town Preservation Society *has* made one request. And I told them you'd obey it."

"And that is?" I smirked, wondering if the old vampires on the Preservation Board were worried I'd turn Ravencourt into a brothel.

For the first time that evening, Walt Kaplan didn't smile. His large brown eyes locked on me, as he said, "They ask that you decorate for Halloween."

I laughed, with a shrug.

"It sounds silly, I know," Walt held up his hands. "But Halloween is *huge* in this town, Tim. Matter of fact, decorating for the spooky season is official town ordinance."

"Say no more, Walt." I plopped down in an old rocking chair, resting my feet near the fire. "I'll pick up a pumpkin first thing tomorrow if it'll make you happy. Carve it up real nice."

"Excellent." A semblance of Walt's good cheer returned to his cheeks. "Enjoy your writing retreat, brother. Your next novel is going to be big. Just keep at it."

"Thanks," I said, "but it won't be a novel. It'll be a short story collection."

Walt froze, his hand on the doorknob. He turned.

"Uhm, Tim? I'm not so sure Putnam is interested in a collection. You know as well as anybody those don't sell."

"Too damn bad," I shrugged. "It's what I have in my heart to write. Putnam can take it or leave it."

"That's a hell of an attitude!"

Gazing up from the flickering flames, I said, "*Doom Canyon* was a novel, and look how well *that* sold. I'm going with my gut instincts on this. A book of short fiction is the way to go. Look, Walt, if you're worried I'm going to disappoint, I—"

"You artists and your instincts!" Walt chuckled with exasperation. "Listen, I know you won't disappoint. As your agent and your friend, I believe in you completely. Now, if you have any trouble up here, I'm just a call or text away."

"You always are, Walt," I said, but he didn't hear me. The front door shut solidly against the encroaching night. The flames danced, warming my bones. Walt's Escalade faded into the distance.

Quiet.

Warmth.

Aloneness.

I sighed deeply. Soon I rummaged the laptop out of my duffel bag and began to write.

The words trickled out of me, slow and languid like lava, steadily molting into paragraph after paragraph. I longed for an explosion, an outburst of fiery creativity, but I'd take this over nothing.

Hell, I'd take just about *anything* over a blank page.

After an hour of writing, I took a nip from my bottle of scotch, then went upstairs to the master bedroom and slept in a four-poster bed that smelled of dust. After the critical failure of *Doom Canyon*, I figured I should get used to the smell of dust—seeing as it's what my books will be coated with if I don't get my act together.

3.

In the morning I got my act together.

Even before the coffee had percolated, I sat at the table in the library to write. Towering bookshelves lined the walls, populated by dusty tomes—the *Encyclopedia Britannica* and Will Durant's *History of Civilization*, among many others. Although not exceedingly rare, the books were pleasing in their aesthetic.

My fingers danced over the keys. The pages zipped by, as did the voices and images inside my head. My book was finally taking shape, transforming into what I envisioned it to be.

Every story, before it's written, resembles a porous slab of clay. A writer must continuously shape and re-mold the tale, cutting away all excess until what is left is only the beautiful. Exactly what a sculptor does, except our material is composed of language.

That might sound lofty, or pretentious.

It isn't. It's just how stories get made.

By the time I'd returned to the kitchen, it was early afternoon. The coffee was lukewarm. I poured a cup anyway, and the moment my lips met the cup's ridge—

A knock at the front door.

"Damn." Abruptly, I set the cup on the counter and tightened my robe. *Who the hell could this be?* I passed into the parlor that smelled warmly of woodsmoke, then opened the front door.

"Good afternoon, Mr. Wallace." He was tall. Round in the belly. A toothpick clamped in his grin.

"A pleasure to meet you." I examined the silver badge pinned to his chest, adding, "Sheriff Bradley."

"Pleasure's all mine, believe me." Bradley's smile was too broad, too full of teeth. "Just thought I'd drop by and give you a proper welcome. Jim Chambers, your realtor and mine, informs me you've purchased Ravencourt for a writing retreat?"

"More or less," I shrugged.

"Well, I just *love* your books. Most folks in Sweet Hollow do."

"Thank you, Sheriff." I smiled politely.

"Although *Doom Canyon* was kind of a doozy, if ya ask me."

My smile strained.

"I don't mean any offense, 'accourse."

"None taken." I lied through my teeth.

"*Doom Canyon*, well, it just didn't have enough *horror* in it."

"Yes, so I'm told," I sighed. "Not enough blood, right?"

"Well, I'm not a blood fiend or anything, but your first books were just so…" The sheriff chuckled, shaking his head, "fucked up!"

"Right," I frowned. "Well, hopefully, my next book will meet everyone's grotesque specifications. Now if you'll excuse me, Sheriff."

I began pulling the door closed. Bradly reached out, grabbed it.

I studied his hand on the door as if I were an entomologist, examining a curious bug.

"Now, Tim, I didn't mean nothing by—"

"Mr. *Wallace,* if you please," I interjected, stifling a growl.

"My apologies! Guess I should've kept my mouth shut, Mr. Wallace. Writers, so I hear, are sensitive creatures."

I grumbled something, though I can't recall what.

"One thing I want to mention before I leave." Bradley's azure eyes roved the barren rafters of the porch, then over the empty windows. With pursed lips, he squared his shoulders, then looked steadfast. "You're planning on decorating, right?"

I cocked my head slightly. Never had an officer of the law asked me such a question. As if decorating for Halloween were just as important as keeping a building up to code, or parking on the correct side of a residential street.

"I plan on purchasing a pumpkin." I replied dryly.

"Or two?" Bradley smiled like a child.

"Maybe even *three,* Sheriff, if that'll get you off my doorstep."

Gently, I shut the door.

Gently, I returned to the kitchen and downed my lukewarm coffee in a gulp.

Not-so-gently, I threw the empty mug across the room. It shattered. I took deep breaths, reminding myself to be calm. My father used to get like this. All pent up, angry, defiant, stubborn. That was his dark side, but it didn't need to be mine as well. Upon returning to the library, I plopped down to pick up where I'd left off.

Yet the words proved elusive, invisible, absent. My mind just as blank as the pages ahead. I blamed the Sheriff's interruption, even began clenching my teeth with rage. After a futile twenty minutes, I closed the laptop. Then I slipped out of my robe and into some decent clothes.

I had pumpkins to buy—not per the Sheriff's request, but on behalf of my agent. Truthfully, I'd do just about anything for Walt Kaplan.

Sheriff Bradley, as far as I was concerned, could take a long walk off a short pier—preferably with weighty stones in his pockets.

4.

Initially, I'd been charmed by Sweet Hollow's quaint and festive spirit. Now, driving down Main Street, a vague unease replaced my affections; a dark cloud obscuring the sky.

Yesterday evening, the town had been modestly decorated.

Now, my eye roved and everywhere discovered an offense. Freshly carved Jack O' Lanterns lined the streets, steps, porches, and windowsills. Paper skeletons, witches, and ghosts adorned store windows in greater quantity, cluttering the view inside the shops. Festooned from two streetlights at the end of the main drag, an enormous black-orange banner: *IT'S A HAPPY HALLOWEEN IN SWEET HOLLOW!*

A groan escaped my throat. The town appeared cluttered, tacky, overwrought. Everywhere, the visage of death lingered with all the cheapness and superficiality of a novelty item.

Still, there was more here than met the eye. Blame it on the proverbial gut instinct, if you will, but I became convinced what ornamented these streets wasn't mere bad taste.

It was *obsession.*

Of all things one could obsess about, I wondered, why Halloween? I scratched my head, though the act itself proffered no answers.

I parked in the crowded lot of *H. Philip's Grocery Mart.* Fake cobwebs stretched across its neon-green sign. Wholesome pumpkins lined the plastic racks arranged outside. Upon the brick wall beside the entrance doors, a witch was comedically plastered, as if she'd been flying fast on her broom and smashed face-first into the bricks. Her black hat bent, her legs cockeyed over the broom.

I ambled inside.

After nabbing a red basket from the stack, I quickly acquired everything I needed: several cans of lentil soup, a box of *Count Chocula*, and a twelve-pack of Ramen. What can I say? I'm not sophisticated. The only luxury I'm particular about is my scotch—top shelf, or nothing.

H. Philip's Grocery was bustling. People maneuvered about the congested isles, many wearing orange t-shirts with black cats printed on them, or images of candy corn, or creepy clowns.

Standing in line at the check-out, I couldn't refrain from smiling. Placed beside the shelf of candy bars and flavored gums was a spinner of paperbacks—most of them mine.

Our Dreaded Earth.

Infinity's Hellscape.

And yes, even *Doom Canyon.*

"Good afternoon, Sir."

I gazed up at the cashier, blinking. The old woman ahead of me had already exited the store, and the line behind me had grown. Who knew how long I'd been standing there? I grinned like a fool, but what made everything impeccably worse was the fact the cashier was gorgeous. She smiled wryly, as if knowing I was none other than Tim Wallace, admiring his own books on the spinner.

"My apologies." I placed my basket on the roller.

"All is forgiven." She began scanning and bagging my items. As I dug out my wallet, a murmuring floated the air:

"That who I think it is?"

"That's Tim Wallace! I'd know that face anywhere. See 'em every day."

"You *do?*"

"Sure, on the dust jackets."

Maddy, her name tag read. She stroked a curl of raven black hair behind her ear, then adjusted her wire-rim glasses. "Total comes to seventeen dollars and sixty-eight cents."

I placed my debit card into the machine. While entering my pin, I attempted conversation.

"How's your day going?" I asked.

"Splendid," Maddy smiled. "Not every day I get to meet one of my favorite authors."

"You're a reader of my work?"

"*Our Dreaded Earth* is my favorite," she nodded. "Your characters are just so, I don't know. Authentic."

"Thank you." I felt like bowing, yet knew I'd never forgive myself if I did.

"You're welcome. And, uhm, your card …"

I'd left my Visa in the machine. It'd been beep-beep-beeping and I'd hardly noticed.

"Oops." I slid the card back into my wallet. Two children behind me were smirking, laughing. I winked at them good-naturedly. *Silly old Tim Wallace.*

"Receipt, Mr. Wallace?"

"Yeah, thanks." I stuffed it absentmindedly into my shirt pocket.

"Oh, one more thing," I shook my head, abashed at my forgetfulness. "One pumpkin from outside. I'll pay cash for that."

Maddy's full, luscious lips pursed over the screen as she tapped a few buttons. "That'll be four dollars even."

I handed her the money.

"Have a wonderful day, Mr. Wallace," she said, closing the register. "I can't wait to read your next book."

"Call me Tim," I smiled, "if you would."

"Tim, then." She winked, and it was all I could do to grab my bags and walk in a straight line out the door.

Distinctly, over my shoulder, a kid chimed teasingly, "*Ooh-la-la!*"

Swooping up the handsomest pumpkin, I carried it to my truck and set it in back. The bags of groceries I plopped down in the passenger seat.

On the drive home, I thought about Maddy. An autumn wind blew through the open cab, crackling the paper bags, ruffling my hair, stirring my dreams. What a fool I'd made of myself, behaving so absentmindedly!

Upon arriving at Ravencourt, I set my pumpkin on the porch step. I'd carve it later. For now, it was time to sit down and work on my book.

I tended the fire in the parlor, poured a glass of scotch, and started up the laptop.

Before I typed a single word, however, I fidgeted in the rocking chair. Rubbed my chin. Stared into the dark corners, searching for a way to begin the next scene.

Dreamily, my fingers dipped into my shirt pocket and pulled out the receipt from H. Philip's Grocery. I frowned, noticing a smooth black cursive just beneath the purchase total:

How about dinner, Mr. Wallace?
715-449-1229
—Maddy R.

5.

I'd wanted to call Maddy that very evening, let her know I was game for a pleasant night on the town. But I know the rules: call too soon, you're desperate. Call too late, you're apathetic.

I reminded myself I didn't come here to go on dates with cute grocery clerks.

I came here to write.

For the next three hours, I wrote my ass off. At last, my characters were taking shape. They'd started out two-dimensional, about as flat as my laptop screen. Now, they were transforming into human beings with real needs and drives.

Characters, if written correctly, are like jack o' lanterns.

They start out unconvincing and bland, but with suitable tools and a precise amount of aplomb, a skilled artist can hollow them out and carve a believable face.

I was on my third glass of scotch when I decided to carve the pumpkin. I carved it in the leaf-strewn front yard, using the biggest kitchen knife I could find. After scalping the gourd, I reached inside up to my elbows and scooped out its long, stringy guts, disposing of them in the woods.

Ravencourt House was surrounded by woods; maples and oaks bursting with blood-crimsons and sherbet oranges. Birds twittered, chirped, whistled in the branches.

Shadows gathered as the sun melted into a flamingo sky.

Triangle eyes, nose, teeth. I placed a tea candle inside, lit it with a match, then fitted the orange scalp on top.

"Just for you, Walt." After placing it on the bottom porch stair, I stepped back. Damned if I didn't feel a bit of pride. Its orange glow gleamed in the dark.

I snapped a photo with my phone and sent it to Walt.

A text notification *binged* thirty seconds later: *Well done! How's the novel coming?*

I went inside the house, fed the fire more kindling, then plopped down in the rocking chair and called up Walt.

It was comforting, hearing his deep, warm voice on a night that was brisk and chill. We talked novels, publishing with Putnam, and what I was spending my time doing, other than writing.

"Drove into town today," I said, sipping a fourth glass of scotch.

"You mentioned how the residents love decorating for Halloween, Walt, but I don't think you realize—"

A *thump*, followed by a scratching rattle.

Out on the porch.

"Tim?" Walt asked. "You still there, or the ghosts of Ravencourt get you?"

"There are no ghosts," I replied, frowning at the front door. "You said Ravencourt wasn't haunted, remember?"

"Correct," Walt chuckled. "Just cursed."

I drained my glass, then stood.

Thump! Scratch-scratch-thump.

I slowly approached the door, my heart pounding.

"How is it cursed, Walt?" I asked, hoping if I kept conversing my fear would lessen.

"According to the historical records," Walt explained, "a woman by the name of Elizabeth Ravencourt lived in that house. She was burned at the stake on the night of October 31st, 1851. The very last woman in America to be executed for witchcraft."

My hand rested lightly on the doorknob.

Thump. Scratch. Thump.

"That's fascinating, Walt," I whispered. "But I gotta go. Someone's making a hell of a lot of racket outside my door."

"*Really?*" asked Walt, and I imagined him leaning forward in his office chair.

"One of the residents, maybe," I suggested, "trying to one-up the horror novelist by scaring the shit out of him."

"It's probably just a critter, Tim. Plenty of those out in the woods."

"Well, it sounds *big*."

"Could be a bear." Walt offered.

"Nothing frightening about that." I hung up. After turning on my phone's flashlight app, I opened the door and stepped out onto the porch.

The moon was a white sliver in the cloudless sky.

I aimed my phone's white beam at the driveway, and the creature froze. Its eyes were big, round, glaring in the light. The raccoon blinked, then slowly withdrew its paws from the toppled jack o' lantern.

"Pssst! Get out of here!"

The raccoon hissed, exposing sharp little teeth. Then it scurried away into the woods, leaves crackling under its retreating paws.

I climbed down the stairs and examined the jack o' lantern. Its grinning face was busted inward. Claw and teeth marks marred the orange rind.

I laughed at myself, at the situation. My heart settled.

How frightened I'd been, and at something so *stupid.* I picked up the broken jack o' lantern, carried it to the wood's edge, then tossed it into the brush. The ground was dry yet icy cold beneath my bare feet.

"So much for decorating," I chuckled, sobered by the adrenaline. I went inside, poured a fresh glass, then phoned Walt.

"I was worried shitless, kid!" Walt laughed warmly. "Thought you might've had a real psycho on your hands."

"Just a critter, like you said," I grinned. "Now, you were telling me about this curse?"

"Ah, yes. Elizabeth, or 'Lizzy' Ravencourt was a first-class eccentric. She practiced witchcraft publicly, most of it benign. She's said to have mended a neighbor's fencepost with a few incantations and a wave of a hand. She was also known to heal the sick. And for a time, she kept more clients than the town doctor."

"Fucking wild." I sipped the scotch, feeling warm, breezy, almost excited.

"It is, isn't it?" Walt sounded pleased, happy to be telling a story instead of merely reading or listening to one of mine. "Anyway, there came a dry season. All the crops shriveled up and died. Times got tough, as they often did in those days. With not enough food to go round, people starved. Despite Elizabeth's good standing with neighbors, she was blamed for everything."

"So then," I said. "The patriarch reigns supreme, blames the woman for things beyond human control, then executes her?"

"Not before they tied her up, threw her in jail for one month. No trial, either."

"Why a month, exactly?"

"So that they could burn her on the night of All Hallow's Eve."

"And the significance of that was ...?"

"Her favorite holiday." Walt sounded amused. "Along with practicing magic about town, Elizabeth was known for proselytizing for Samhain. That's the Celtic word for 'Summer's End', which the Catholics then stole and transformed into All Hollow's Eve, aka, Halloween. The townspeople believed that torching the poor woman on the 'spookiest of nights' would serve as a warning for all other would-be witches."

"Brutal." My shoulders hitched with a shudder. While one woman deluded with magical thinking wasn't very frightening, an entire *town* of superstitious people most certainly were. I guess I've always harbored a fear of mob rule—the *tyranny of democracy*, in other words.

"Extremely brutal," Walt agreed, "but that's how people were back then. According to newspapers from that time, Elizabeth vowed that if every person in Sweet Hollow did not celebrate Halloween, a terrible curse would be visited upon them."

"What's the curse?" I stood from the chair and placed my glass upon the hearth. The fire warmed my legs, combatting the shivers that racked my spine.

"She claimed that Hell itself would rip open. More threatening than a dry season, more destructive than a tornado ripping through town, the evil of the world would swoop down from the sky and rip everyone apart. Unless ..."

"Stop pausing for effect. Just tell me," I said, grumpily.

"Well, there's a way to banish the curse, but I can't remember."

"Isn't that a bit anti-climactic?"

"Talk about the pot calling the kettle black!"

"Well, thanks for the bedtime story, Uncle Walt." I yawned.

"Talk to you soon, brother."

I drained my scotch, then climbed the creaking stairs up to the large bedroom. I lay in the dark, under the blankets, staring up at the cracked ceiling. Wind buffeted the house, groaning like a sad ghost.

This must've been Elizabeth's room. The very four-poster bed she'd fallen asleep in night after night. Perhaps she was lying right where I am now, when they snatched her up in the night, only to throw her in a dank cell, then burn her alive.

My eyes closed. I must've been exhausted, because I slept comfortably, dreaming not of cruel mobs or tortured witches, but of a romantic night out with *Maddy R.*

Maddy Ravencourt is her name, a voice told me, drifting through the fog of dreams, but I knew it was rubbish. The sort of the nonsensical things one thinks on that boundary-edge of sleep.

The darkness pressed in.

And the voice insisted: *her name is Maddy Ravencourt, heir of the last great American witch.*

6.

The blossom of mid-October gave way to barren branches and the decay of blazoned leaves. In the chill mornings, I saw my breath as I walked onto the porch. The last warmth of the year was gone.

The house became frigid. I found myself given to many days at the fireside, writing, reflecting, staring out the parlor windows. Walt called to check up on me sometimes. Deep down, I think he was afraid I'd pull a Hemingway stunt out here in the woods—drink too much, grab a shotgun, and blow my head off.

Immediately after the *Doom Canyon* debacle, I'd considered it. Now, having gone on several dates with Maddy, I wouldn't dare.

She was smart, funny, gorgeous.

And she loved my books.

We'd gone on dates to Summer's End Diner, Leo's Ice Cream Parlor, and the Sweet Hollow Pub. Once, she brought me to the highest hill on the outskirts of town, where we laid out a blanket in the dead October grass and made love at sunset, our naked sides kissed by a waning sun.

We drove through the countryside.

The Starman Drive-In was surrounded by rolling fields that resembled a billowing white sea in the moonlight. We snuggled in the cab of my truck, eating popcorn, watching black-and-white monster movies.

We read books together. In bed, after lovemaking.

We drank wine, sang songs, told stories about our childhoods.

Her last name really was Ravencourt, I'd discovered. The house I'd purchased from the city of Sweet Hollow had belonged to her great-great-grandmother.

We both knew there were no such things as witches—just powerful, eccentric women that made fearful men sick with superstition.

I loved Maddy.

Loved her wire-rimmed glasses, the ones I delicately removed. I loved her soft velvet skin, her arms around my neck, her legs around my hips. I loved our discussions about philosophy and politics. I loved her awful puns, the ones so stupid you *had* to laugh.

Smart, quirky, beautiful.

And she was a writer, too. She read aloud some of her work for me—prose poems, mainly. And they were almost as beautiful as her. *Almost.*

One morning, as the sun crept through her bedroom shades, she turned over and I saw it on her smiling face.

It.

Love.

And then she'd whispered the words—those sacred, time-stopping words that blurs the world and everything spins languidly, and you can feel the world orbiting beneath you.

I thought of these things over a glass of scotch, writing the next story in my collection. So far, I felt great about the book. Each story seemed fresh, original, unlike anything my readers have ever seen.

The words flowed fast from my fingertips.

I blamed Maddy for these past few weeks of incessant productivity. She inspired me. Lifted me up to the clouds, far from worry and suffering.

And the stories I wrote were stories of love.

Were they horror tales? Absolutely. Yet beneath them, underlying every paragraph, every sentence, every word—love.

Love amidst the blood and the wolves and the vampires—

I stood from the chair, interrupted by the knocking at the door. Could it be Maddy, arriving early for our date? I consulted my wristwatch—only one p.m.

Maybe it's Sheriff Bradley. My jaw clenched at the thought. *He's come to annoy me about the pumpkins again.*

After the raccoon had gotten to my jack o' lantern, I hadn't bothered heading into town for another pumpkin. At the parlor windows, I craned my neck to gaze through. I could see nobody at the door or on the porch. No one.

"Ah, hell." I pulled wide the door. Chill breeze ruffled my hair. The sweet odor of sundried leaves on the air. I looked around.

"Mr. Wallace?"

I flinched at the small voice, retreating a step.

A witch in a pointy black hat stood before me, so short I'd not seen her. A young zombie shuffled his feet beside her. The boy's face was round and white as the moon, a trickle of pinkish blood trailing from his lips.

They'd hauled a little red wagon up onto the porch, Halloween decorations packed neatly inside it.

"Isn't it a bit early for trick-or-treat?" I asked.

"It's October," the Witch grinned. "Halloween-time. We're raising funds to build a new park in Sweet Hollow, Mr. Wallace. Would you buy some decorations to help the cause?"

Her high tenor was adorable, and she certainly had her speech down pat. How could I refuse?

"Sure thing," I smiled. "Let me grab my wallet and I'll be right—"

I halted in the doorway and, peering down the driveway, squinted into the brush.

Sheriff Bradley's cruiser was parked out on the road, the rear doors visible from the break in the trees. A new flame trembled in my heart. That ridiculous *bastard!* He'd sent these two kids all the way out here—not to raise funds for a park, but to coerce me into decorating.

"Nice try, kids." I frowned as if I were their father, grounding them. "But I see your accomplice out there on the road. There is no park being built, is there?"

The Witch and the Zombie exchanged wary glances.

"*Please*, Mr. Wallace?" The Witch's lower lip stuck out.

"But look at these *nice* decorations, Sir," the Zombie moaned. "They're cheap, too!"

The zombie grabbed handfuls of decors from the wagon, holding them up for me to see: Silicone masks of Michael Myers. Black bats with fierce fangs. Window stickers of ghosts, goblins, and ghouls. Skeletons with screaming skulls. Deranged decorations of demons, dragons, and devils. A box of black-and-orange electric lights. Plastic bags puffed with fake cobwebs. Festive accordion banners that spelled out, "Happy Halloween!" when spread between your hands.

Zombie-boy showcased each item, with an accompanying sales pitch.

"Go home, kids," I said, flatly. "And tell the Sheriff he might coerce *other* people into doing what he wants, but not me."

I closed the door in their faces. Crossed my arms. Paced the parlor, then peered out the windows again. The Witch tugged something neon orange from beneath the brim of her hat, slapped it down on the porch. The two clanged their wagon down the steps, then rattled it down the gravel drive. Sheriff Bradley stepped out of his cruiser.

He hauled up the wagon, cramming it into the trunk.

The kids, heads hung low, piled into the backseat—a witch and zombie on their way to the clink. Bradley's tires spit up gravel. An angry plume of dust hovered in the air, dead leaves swirling in the kickback.

I stepped outside and picked up the orange thing the girl had left.

A ticket from the Sweet Hollow Police Department.

Printed in bold, black ink:

DECORATING VIOLATION.

Your property isn't decorated in accordance with town ordinance. Pay $200 to the Sweet Hollow Police Department at your immediate convenience and decorate properly, or further actions may be taken. These regulations are adopted under the general police powers authority granted pursuant to Wisconsin Statutes.

My first reaction was to laugh.

A lot.

I doubled over on the porch, wiping tears from my face. After stifling my giggles, I went inside and plunked down in my chair to study the ticket. Suddenly my stomach curdled with nausea.

The ticket was patently ridiculous, but what if it wasn't a joke?

Pay $200 to the Sweet Hollow Police Department at your immediate convenience, or further actions may be taken ....

I began to think Sheriff Bradley wasn't just stupid—he was fucking crazy.

And I thought: what if this entire town is fucking crazy?

I stuffed the orange paper into my wallet. I'd save it for evidence in court if necessary, or at least show it to Walt for a good laugh.

... or further actions may be taken.

I scoffed. What was the Sheriff going to do if I didn't hang up a few bats and skeletons? Arrest me?

Maybe.

If there's one thing I've learned over the years, whether it's from obsessive, unhinged fans begging for your autograph, or some stranger calling you at two a.m. claiming to be your lost twin, it's this: Don't underestimate crazy.

Crazy is just another word for *capable*.

7.

Glasses of Merlot. Firelight. An old quilt laid upon the floor. After the spaghetti dinner I'd prepared, Maddy and I sat beside the fireplace, listening to the crackle and pop of the wood.

I slid the ticket across to her. She glanced at it, then slid it back.

"Aren't you going to read what it says?" I raised an eyebrow.

"Lower the eyebrow," she smirked. "Makes you look deranged. And I already know what it says. Not that I've seen many of them."

"But it's a joke, right?"

"The ticket? Hell no."

I blinked, and asked, "*What?*"

"Decorating for Halloween is required by the municipal code," Maddy explained, adjusting her glasses. "Honest. You can look it up online, or in the archives at the library if you don't believe me."

"I believe you," I sighed. "It's just the silliest thing I've ever heard."

"You're telling *me*. I've had to put up with it all my life. Fairly sure the ordinance has remained untouched since the nineteenth century."

"Back when your great-grandmother was …"

"Burned at the stake?"

"I wasn't going to say it."

"I don't mind talking about it."

"You sure, babe?"

"What the hell do I care?" she laughed, as if I were being silly. "After all, that was *two hundred years ago*. I can't help my lineage."

"Well, in that case …"

I inquired about Sweet Hollow and its plethora of superstitions. Maddy, bless her heart, patiently provided answers.

She seemed not only comfortable but *relieved* to discuss the tragic fate of her great-great-grandmother. As if she'd been waiting her entire life for someone to ask.

"People here have never harbored hate towards me or my family," she replied after I'd asked if any stigmas had been attached to her, growing up in Sweet Hollow. "People here have always treated me with respect. Deference, even."

"Because of your relation to Elizabeth?"

She nodded. "They're a little afraid of me, I think. They suspect I harbor the powers of a witch, deep in my blood. It's that 'apple doesn't fall far' kind of thinking."

"Wait," I grinned. "They're … afraid? Of *you?*"

"Don't act so surprised, Tim Wallace. After all, I put a spell on *you*, didn't I?" She winked.

"Touché." I poured us more wine. We clinked glasses.

"Oh, yeah," I mumbled, recalling something Walt had mentioned. "My agent, who did some research before helping me purchase this house, said there's a way to undo the curse once it's in effect. Just for kicks, how do you do that?"

"Firstly, you don't *undo* a curse, silly," she giggled. "You *banish* a curse. Secondly, by 'just for kicks', do you mean you're looking for far-out ideas you can steal and put into your book?"

I clinked her glass.

"You're shameless," she teased. "Elizabeth left behind several articles in this house, one of which included a grimoire."

"Do you still have it?"

"Of course. It was handed down to me from my mother, from my grandmother before that, and so on. It's my most precious heirloom."

"Fascinating. Go on," I promoted, sipping more wine.

"Anyway, in her book, Elizabeth writes that to banish her curse, the one who activated it must sacrifice the thing they love most. And they must do so while reciting an incantation – the words I don't remember, they're Latin – and an heir of the Ravencourt bloodline must give of their blood, too. With the intermingling of blood, sacrificed love, and the incantation, the curse dissipates."

"Okay. I've another question, Professor."

"Mmhmm?" She sipped from her glass, the firelight bathing her face all light and shadow. Flames danced in her glasses.

"Do the residents *really* believe this stuff, or do they just follow tradition?" I asked. "Like the groundhog seeing its shadow, for instance. Nobody believes a groundhog gives a damn about his shadow, nor about predicting spring or winter—people just enjoy the tradition."

"No." Maddy shook her head. "People here aren't … oh, this is going to sound awful."

"Just say it."

"Okay. People here aren't *normal.* They believe wholeheartedly in the myths."

"Do *you* believe?" I asked.

A silence fell between us.

Before I could ask again, she placed her glass on the floor. I set mine aside, too.

She tugged my shirt collar, pulling me down on top of her. Her lips pressed hard onto mine, and we kissed, tearing our clothes off.

This time, I didn't ask questions.

8.

I awoke in the darkness of the bedroom. After our passionate row upon the floor, we'd transitioned upstairs to snuggle in bed.

I turned to wrap my arms around her. The bed was empty.

Slowly, I sat up and peered about the room. A waxing moon shone through the window, bathing the furniture in its lunatic glow.

On the wind, so soft it might've been a dream—voices.

From downstairs, perhaps. Or outside.

"Maddy?" I climbed out of bed. "You all right?"

The stairs creaked beneath me. Every room in the house was dark, save for the moon gleaming through the dusky windows. In the parlor, the fire had burned down to dim red embers. I turned about, squinting at the dark.

"Maddy?" I called again.

On the groaning autumn winds, subtle as dust motes floating in moonlight, the voices arose once more.

A *crowd* of voices—hushed, conspiratorial chattering.

I must be dreaming.

A man's voice, low and deep, rolling across the fields.

A woman's high, plaintive tenor.

Voices arose like waves on the air, cascading into a chorus, and then I knew I wasn't alone. I turned toward the front door, my heart racing. *Is Maddy in trouble? Has someone come here in the night to take her? Because she's with me?*

My fists clenched. I wished I'd had a knife or a gun.

All I had was my fists. An angry man in his pajamas.

So be it. I yanked back the door, stepping onto the porch.

The lawn was drenched in moonlight, and the gleam of my truck's hood caught my attention. Maddy hauled something out of the flatbed. She carried it in her arms, something fat and round.

She saw me and halted on the narrow path up to the porch. Gently, she placed the gourd on the ground.

"Tim." Her breath fogged the air. "I was going to surprise you."

"What are you *doing?*" I asked, and not in the friendly Q & A tone I had perfected earlier.

"I just thought since you didn't have any decorations, you might appreciate—"

"No." I held up my hands to ward her off. "No one's going to strong-arm me into doing anything I don't want to. No one tells me what to do. Not my publishers. Not the bat-shit residents of Sweet Hollow. Not even you, Maddy."

"Look, Tim, I just—"

An old man stepped out of the forest and into the moonlight. "C'mon, son," he grumbled, spitting a wad of tobacco on the ground. "Just accept the damned pumpkin! We ain't asking much."

"That's right, Mr. Wallace." Sheriff Bradley and two deputies stepped out of the brush, on the lawn's opposite side. "You don't want *another* ticket, do you?"

"Do ya, Mr. Wallace? Do ya?" The Witch and the Zombie chorused, emerging from the thickets, still dressed in Halloween garb.

"Please, allow me to introduce myself." A man in a wrinkled suit strolled out from behind a maple tree. "I'm Mayor Edmundson. Pleased to meet you, Mr. Wallace."

The man named Edmundson stuck out his hand. I did not shake it.

A rustling crunch of leaves. A whisper of dry reeds against pant legs. A crackle and snap of twigs. Many people stepped out of the forest.

A shiver ran down my arms.

"What the fuck *is this?*" I shouted, terrified by the idea that the entire town had come out to lynch me.

"Stand back!" Maddy commanded, and the men, women, and children of Sweet Hollow obeyed. She turned to me then, wringing her hands. "Tim, listen. I'm sorry, okay?"

"You're one of them," I observed, though I didn't want to believe it. "All this time! You've only been trying to convert me. Attempting to pressure me into following their bullshit superstitions!"

"Tim, that isn't true!" Her voice trembled.

"Just leave me the fuck alone, Maddy." I shook my head, disgusted with her lies.

She flinched, beginning to cry—or pretending to, at least.

"Listen up, everyone," I screamed at the crowd. "If you don't return to your homes *this* instant, then I'm going to get the police involved. *Real* police officers," I took a moment here to glare at Sheriff Bradley and his deputies with fiery accusation, "from elsewhere in the county, and you'll all be arrested. Got that? You'll be taken away from your children, your jobs, your lives—arrested! Keep in mind, as well, that I own a shotgun!"

I didn't own a shotgun. It was just better if they thought I did.

As I backed into the shadows, I took one last look at Maddy—fake-crying, morose, manipulative Maddy.

"Shame on you," I whispered, then slammed the door and locked it.

I went from room to room, locking every window.

From the upstairs bedroom, I guzzled scotch from the bottle, no glass, and watched the crazies vacate my yard. They ambled down the driveway onto the main road, where many vehicles were parked along the shoulder. Car doors slammed. Engines revved. Horns honked.

Maddy, wantonly staring up at me, was last to leave. Sheriff Bradley put his arm around her shoulders and walked her to the road. After every pair of taillights faded into the dark, I was alone—more than ever.

First thing tomorrow morning, I'd call up Walt Kaplan. Let him know staying in Sweet Hollow had been a terrible idea, that I was afraid for my safety, and was getting the hell out.

9.

I did not sleep that night. When dawn's orange light streamed through the trees, I reached for my phone.

I called Walt.

Walt didn't answer. Too goddamn early.

I paced the parlor, listening to the boards creak. Sadness and anger, like twin serpents, slithered around the nest of my heart. Like a fool, I thought I'd discovered love in this strange little town.

But I'd only discovered an imposter, a crazy person.

The world was full of them.

Everything was thrown wildly into question, like a stack of papers tossed into a tornado. What was I doing with a belly full of scotch at six in the morning, my duffel bag packed and waiting beside the front door? I had been so productive as of late, every day churning out the words and pushing my book toward the finish line.

I'd return to my apartment only to face what I always faced: *writer's block.*

Whether I love or loathe Sweet Hollow, it *had* opened something within me. A door. A portal. A cave entrance to my imagination.

Now, I was leaving. *Why?*

Because of a woman, I told myself. Lies. Betrayal. *Coercion*—that word stuck in my mind like a wrench lodged into a gear.

The primitive residents of Sweet Hollow desired that I tack up their stupid banners, their pathetic witches and devils, or else pay atrocious fines, or who knew what else? I shuddered at the possibilities.

Still, I grabbed my duffel bag beside the door. Hauled it upstairs. Unpacked everything. Shoved my clothes inside the antique dresser. Stuck my phone on a charger beside the bed. Then went downstairs to the parlor and fired up the laptop and began the day like I normally would—writing.

I wasn't going anywhere. *Why?*

Because nobody tells me what to do. I'd stay and write until my fucking book was finished.

No matter what.

10.

The sky was gloomy. Dust rose and sprinkled over the roads like cinnamon. I turned in at Derleth's Guns & Ammunition, located on Bradbury Avenue, just off Main Street. A man wearing a green fedora with a turkey feather sticking out of it sat on a stool behind a glass counter. His squinty eyes fixed on me the moment I walked in the door, as if zeroing in his sights.

Racks of rifles and shotguns. Walls of pistols and revolvers. Every inch of the store was occupied by weapons. Camouflage blanketed the ceiling, and the floor was cushioned by black matting. Spinner racks proffered neon orange hats, gloves, and sunglasses. Deer heads with black eyes and multi-pointed racks stuck out of the walls.

I've only fired a gun once—as a young boy, target shooting with my grandfather. I don't like guns, but I needed something to defend myself. Just in case.

I grabbed a 20-gauge shotgun from the back wall. A price tag of $300 hung from the trigger guard. I carried it to the counter.

"Are you Derleth?" I asked.

"No," the man grumbled, furrowing wiry eyebrows. "Derleth was my grandfather. Died in Salk City a long time ago."

"Okay," I said. "I'd like to purchase this shotgun."

The man with the feather cap squinted, questioned, then smiled and offered to sell me a nice compound bow instead—"at twenty percent off the original cost!"

"I don't want a bow," I replied, firmly. "I want a shotgun. *This* shotgun."

He asked for my driver's license and telephone number, then handed me forms to sign.

Fifteen minutes later, I walked out onto the street with a shotgun and three packs of shells and got into my truck and drove back to Ravencourt.

I'd passed Maddy's cottage on the way home. She lived in a field of rolling auburn hills. Her home appeared wasted and desolate out there beneath the grey sky.

To my shame, I missed her.

Her soft voice, her jokes, her educated opinions, her perfect touch.

Missed what had been a falsity all along.

I drove home. Loaded the shotgun. Stored it in the corner beside the armchair. I hoped I wouldn't have to use it, but if someone attempted to break in, threatening me with their barbarian traditions and juvenile curses and plebian superstitions, I would retaliate.

I'd show them the gun and promise to use it.

11.

I told Walt Kaplan everything.

"Jesus! I'm sorry, Tim." Walt sighed into the phone, and I could picture him rubbing his cheeks, like he always does when overwhelmed. "Those crazy sonsabitches. You're driving back here to Saint Paul tonight, I take it?"

"Nope." I stood at the window, gazing out at the lawn. Crickets chirruped. Owls hooted in the dark. "I'm staying here and finishing my book. I'm getting close, Walt. A few thousand words and I'll have a complete first draft."

"Uhm," said Walt Kaplan. "Believe or not, I value your safety over your writing, Tim. You should go home."

"Thank you, but no."

"Why are you so stubborn, boy?"

"Take after my father, I guess."

"Yeah, well, your mother was the better man."

"I can't disagree, but Mother isn't here to put me on the straight and narrow," I said.

"A shame, too. She was the only one who could."

"Don't I know it." I thought of mother. She'd died at home, in bed, her heart giving out the night before my first book was published. She never saw her son win literary awards or reach the bestseller list, but she'd loved me anyway, and had taken a shine to Walt whenever I'd invited him over for dinner.

"Well, if you need anything, gimme a call. I'll leave my phone off silent."

"I'll be fine." My eyes wandered over to the shotgun in the corner. "I can defend myself if need be."

"I'm regretting arranging this whole thing, Tim. Helping you purchase Ravencourt, I mean. I should've encouraged you to write this book at home."

"I wasn't able to write at home," I reminded him. "My apartment was stale, boring, and consequently invoked stale and boring prose. Here, though? Between this creepy old house and the town's crazy-ass residents, I've got nothing but excitement fueling my writing."

I thought Walt would laugh at that, but he didn't. He told me to be damned careful. I promised I would and hung up.

I fed the fire and wrote through the night. At one a.m., I stood, groaned, laughed at my numb, tingly legs. I was exhausted, yet happy to have written.

I told myself, at least, that I was happy, and tried not to think about defrocked love as I went upstairs, climbed into the empty bed, and lay in the dark.

Soft grumbles from the sky shortly gave way to raucous rumbles. Purple lightning flickered at the windows. Hail thudded upon the roof. Rain washed over the forest.

A drip from the ceiling, somewhere in the hall outside. Too lazy to get up, grab a bucket, and place it beneath the drip, I merely laid in bed, soothed by the sounds of thunder.

Within the next few days, I'd finish my book—a collection of tales about strange people living in a strange town. A locale of myth and legend, where monsters and murderers and fearful fates mingled and mixed.

If I worked hard, I'd complete it by Halloween and be out of Sweet Hollow by nightfall. There'd be no waiting around for the muse to get this done. The muse is a myth—a true writer rises in the morning and gets to work.

Thunder shook the house, and I meditated: *Nightfall. Halloween. Write until it's finished.*

Despite nature's sky-tantrum, I closed my eyes, and sleep settled swiftly, burying me like soft earth into a rainy grave.

12.

I groaned, stirred from bed by the mauve light beyond the windows. Cobweb clouds covered the sky. Rain drizzled from the gutters, splashing onto the soaked leaves and grass below. I checked my watch, then cursed myself for sleeping until noon.

I shambled downstairs, yawning, into the kitchen where the coffee had automatically brewed for seven a.m. I poured cold coffee into yesterday's mug and drank it.

By happenstance, I looked up at the window.

A face stared in.

Yellow eyes. Green, wrinkled features. A pointy black hat.

I flinched, sloshing coffee over the rim and all over my hand. I slammed down the mug, enraged. The face was a cardboard cutout.

"God *damn* you people!" I made for the front door, intent on tearing down the cheap decoration.

Stepping out onto the porch, my jaw dropped.

I gazed at the phantasmagoria that'd infiltrated my yard, windows, siding, roof. Only vaguely did my bare feet feel the chill roughness of the porch steps, then the lawn's slick wet grass. I turned about in awe.

Ghosts in trailing white gowns, strung from the nearby trees, stared with round black eyes.

Vampire bats, too, glared beady pupils and bared sharp fangs, hanging from the rain gutters.

Zombie arms stuck up out of the wet lawn, their plastic hands stained with blood.

Werewolves. Witches. Warlocks. Wild beasts.

Spiders the size of my head, weaving webbing over the windows.

Skeletons tied to the porch columns, their craniums just as cracked as the town residents.

And, of course, the jack o' lanterns. Not one, nor two, nor three. *Twelve*—I counted them—lining the stone path up to the porch. Six on each side, grinning grotesquely.

I shook my head at the madness.

I had to admit, the residents had done a number on me. Hundreds of decorations tacked, taped, and fastened to my house in the soggy morning rain, yet none of it had wakened me.

I wondered if Maddy hadn't carved the jack o' lanterns herself. Or if she hadn't taped the witch face to the window, knowing it would startle me. Perhaps the entire town had come in the night. Certainly, it required a great number of sickos to do a job like this.

I went inside, donned my tennis shoes, grabbed a garbage bag from the cupboard, then got to work filling it with the macabre artifacts.

I began to laugh, stuffing bats and ghosts and bloody zombie arms into the bag. This was all so strange and ridiculous.

At first, I'd felt threatened.

Now, it seemed none of this was any more serious than a high school prank. I considered saying to hell with it and leaving it all just as it was.

But then I would've lost.

And *they* would've won.

Maddy, who tricked me into believing she cared, would've gotten what she wanted all along. I wasn't about to do that.

Only two days until Halloween. Soon, this entire 'Ravencourt curse' debacle would end, and the people of Sweet Hollow would learn, finally, that nothing would happen if I, or anyone else, refused to decorate for their deranged holiday.

13.

October 30th.

A gray, melancholy day. I remained toasty beside the fire and wrote.

It wasn't love fueling the words anymore, but desperation. I'd made it my goal, my obsession, to finish the book by Halloween. I prepared for success.

I'd brought out the scotch, cleaned a glass, and ensured there was ice in the fridge. I'd packed my duffel bag for the long drive home, and dressed not in my customary robe, but in day clothes.

As soon as I typed 'the end', I'd be out of Sweet Hollow for good. I'd sell the house remotely, washing my hands of it all. No turning back.

And as much as I tried not to think of Maddy, I missed her deeply.

Maybe it was missing her that fueled my writing now, kept the prose sharp and desperate, each line jotted onto the page quick as a lightning bolt.

I wrote until exhausted, passing out in the chair. When I awoke, it was dawn again. The fire was but a bed of embers, and my laptop at zero charge.

Halloween morning.

I plugged in the laptop and got moving. Upon reaching for the scotch, I stopped myself from pouring a glass.

I wouldn't drink until the book was finished. If I needed a fire under my ass, then a lack of delicious, stomach-warming scotch was as good a motivator as any.

I settled for coffee. It was hot and black and jazzed my brain. Striding out onto the porch, I was pleased to find not one decoration in sight. The yard was sad and barren—exactly how I liked it.

Yesterday, I'd burned three garbage bags worth of novelty items. All those ghosts had gone up in smoke. All those bats had flapped their last rubber wing. All those skeletons had crumbled to ash. I'd driven over the jack o' lanterns with my truck, then smashed them to a carroty pulp beneath my shoes.

Once my laptop reached optimal charge, I sat down and began writing an ending.

I did not leave my chair beside the fire.

14.

The sky had cleared by sunset.

Glorious pink clouds drifted across the pumpkin sun. The horizon line was a dancing yellow flame, and the topmost portion of the sky was mauve as a dead man's lips.

I drove through town, where the shadows of trick-or-treaters stretched across sidewalks. Chattering, laughing, skipping, running amok: Devils and demons. Princes and pirates. Ghouls and goblins. Skeletons and sorcerers. Zombies and zany aliens.

And witches. More witches than anything.

I'd just returned from the Sweet Hollow Public Library, where I'd printed off the completed manuscript for *Beneath the Jack O' Lantern Sky*. It's what I always do once finishing a book—print it off so I can sit back with an ink pen and ruthlessly revise.

I was happy. An October breeze washed through the cab, smelling of dead leaves and rain.

Trick-or-treaters galloped through the evening with candy bags, smiling behind their snarling masks. Town shops kept their doors open and their lights on. Residential streets ran rampant with children. Even adults were dressed for trick-or-treating—though they didn't receive candy bars so much as nips of various liquors.

My manuscript, secured inside a manilla folder, lay on the passenger seat. I reached over to touch it, ensuring it hadn't magically vanquished.

While at the library, I had also consulted the town's historical archives.

Issues of *The Sweet Hollow Gazette*, stretching back over two hundred years, were available on microfilm. Most of these documents were amusing, yet innocuous. That is, until the microfilm dial led me to discover this peculiar headline—

SWEET HOLLOW NEARLY DESTROYED BY RAVENCOURT CURSE!

Dated November 3rd, 1852, the article reported an enormous storm ripping through Sweet Hollow on Halloween night, demolishing buildings, homes, barns, and nearly all Main Street. To quote one Mayor Edward Shelley, who'd gone so far as to write the article himself:

Due to our disobeying the curse Elizabeth Ravencourt set upon us last year, we find this Hallowe'en has wrought great vengeance upon us all. Many neighbors have died. Many loved ones' graves disturbed. Many hearts and businesses and homes broken. I assure you, fellow citizens, this will never happen again. From now on, it shall be a town ordinance that Hallowe'en be celebrated in Sweet Hollow, wholly and completely, every October for all time. May God have Mercy on our Souls!

Thus the legend, the myth, the asinine superstition of the Ravencourt Curse was set into motion. Strange—how one hysterical, persecuted, dying woman's last words, which so strongly influenced people two hundred years ago, continues to have an equal effect upon residents of today.

I was thinking on these things as I turned into my driveway and braked suddenly.

A thirty-foot line of trick-or-treaters snaked from my door, down the porch steps, and onto the path. The monsters rattled their jack o' lantern buckets, ruffled their pillowcases, wrinkled their black bags.

They turned and stared at me.

All those eyes. All those monsters.

Slowly, I got out of my car, manuscript clutched to my chest and strode past the line until standing atop the porch.

"TRICK OR TREAT!" They shouted in unison.

I looked at them.

They looked at me; hungry, expectant eyes staring behind make-up and masks of plastic and silicone.

"How long have you kids been out here?" I asked.

"A while," sang the little witch in front—the one that'd attempted selling me decorations along with the zombie boy.

"Well, I'm sorry to disappoint, but I don't have any candy. I came back for my belongings, then I'm heading out."

"Where to?" asked the Witch.

"Home," I said.

"But this *is* your home, Mr. Wallace."

Addressing the monstrous congregation, I straightened, and spoke loudly, "You kids head on back into town. You'll have better luck trick-or-treating there, trust me."

I was halfway inside the house when a little hand reached out and grabbed the door, preventing me from shutting it.

The Witch. She gazed up at me, blinking tears.

"But Mr. Wallace!" Her voice trembled. "We don't even need candy. We'll take anything. We just need you to *trick or treat.*"

I sighed deeply, then got down on my knees so I could be face to face with her.

"I pity all the brainwashing you kids go through," I said,

gently. "Honestly, I do. But that doesn't mean I'm going to cave to intimidation. Please. Go home, little girl." Then I stood, addressing the rest of them. "All of you. Just head on home. Okay?"

"No!" The witch shook her head, crying. "Mr. Wallace, *please!*"

Quietly, respectfully, I closed the door.

15.

Halloween night. Moonlight cloaked the land. Creatures of the surrounding forest hooted, howled, chirped, croaked.

I carried down my pre-packed duffel bag, setting it beside the front door. I had every intention to leave, yet it wasn't merely children at my door now.

Every resident of Sweet Hollow had arrived.

Mayor Edmundson, Sheriff Bradley and his deputies, town council members, parents, grandparents, even the sweet old librarian I'd met only hours ago.

All of them dressed as devils, demons, diabolical derangements of every denomination. They weren't carrying mere candy buckets, either—the adults waved pitchforks, shotguns, baseball bats, crowbars.

The mob had descended, demanding I give their children candy, or anything at all, to honor the custom of trick-or-treating.

I laid low. Stayed quiet. Listened to warning shots fired into the air.

Now, it was nearly midnight. I shivered beside the fire, despite its warmth. They shouted my name, demanding offerings. I figured they'd eventually grow exhausted and leave, yet their demands only grew louder.

I phoned Walt.

"Listen," I spoke rapidly, my heart racing a mile-a-minute. "I'm in big fucking trouble. I need you to call the police, get them down to Ravencourt. I'd call them myself, except every time I do I'm directed to the Sweet Hollow Police, and obviously *they* won't help me."

"Whoa, hold on a sec." Walt's warm, baritone voice insisted I relax. "Just tell me what's going on, Tim."

I told him.

"Jesus H. Christ in a Chevrolet," he said.

"I know," I said.

"Those people really *are* bat-shit crazy."

"You think?" I peeked behind the curtain, watching the residents mill about with jack o' lantern flashlights and old-fashioned candelabras.

"Just hang tight, buddy. I'll contact the police, let them know you're being threatened. I'll be down as soon as I can, too."

"No, Walt. Stay home. There's no reason for you to get involved in this mess."

"Damn if there isn't!" Walt sounded offended. "I'm the genius who helped you purchase that house, remember? If I sent you into that hell, then I'll help you out of it."

"That's a nice sentiment, Walt, but what you gonna do? Hug them all to death?"

"You underestimate my powers of intimidation," he replied. "*You* know I'm a gentle giant, but *they* don't. Besides, it sounds as if you could use some backup."

I considered that it was only myself against nearly four hundred people with guns and pitchforks and candy bags.

"You have a point, Walt."

"Keep inside, keep safe, the police should be there shortly."

"Okay," I said and hung up.

I grabbed the shotgun from the dark corner, clicked off the safety, then laid it upon my duffel bag. I went around the house closing each curtain and ensuring every window was locked.

An old woman with grey hair and bags beneath her eyes stared in through the study window. "I'm Miss Leslie," she shouted, breath fogging the glass. "Executive Director of the Sweet Hollow Heritage

Center. Just give us anything you've got! Doesn't have to be chocolate, dear. Anything!"

"Don't tell me what to do, Miss Leslie." I pulled the curtain between us.

In the kitchen window, where the witch decoration had been pasted days before, Sheriff Bradley peered in. We stared at each other.

"Fuck off, Sheriff," I said, finally.

"Tim, wait a minute!" He begged, his voice muffled behind the glass. "You're putting us all at risk—"

I closed the curtain and walked away.

"Crazy mother fuckers," I muttered. "Every single one."

I sat in the armchair beside the fire, sweating bullets. The clock above the mantel ticked, ticked, ticked, its bronze tongue wagging.

Three minutes to midnight—Maddy was at the door now, banging her fists against the wood. "Tim, for God's sake, the curse is real! Just give them what they want!"

"Jesus Christ," I whispered, trembling, and drank the last of the scotch.

Two minutes—shouts and screams outside.

Begging. Demanding. Cursing. Wailing.

One minute—I cradled the shotgun in my arms, for there came a violent pounding at the door. Multiple fists battered the wood. The door rattled in its frame. Somewhere in back of the house, a window shattered. The hysterical screaming of men, women, and children pierced the night, the entire town gone the way of a mad hatter.

Then: *Midnight. The Witching Hour.*

The bell tolled, and the clock ceased ticking. The hour and minute hand stood up, erect as the hairs on my arms.

An awful, ominous silence. Not one villager whispered, nor a cricket chirruped, or a wood owl hooted.

The fire, bright and flaming, settled into a bed of embers.

The parlor was dark.

A full moon lit the windows ghastly white.

I sat in the dark with the shotgun, sweaty hands clasping the stock and barrel. I rocked in the chair. Paranoid.

Finally, I stood up.

Merely standing produced an incredible creak from the floorboards, and the rocking chair squelched into settlement. I walked, creaked, groaned toward the windows. Peeling back the curtain with a sickening roil in my stomach (as if peeling back a flap of torn flesh), I gazed out at the moon-shadowed lawn.

Gone—every one of them. The area vacated.

In the distance, sirens. Unusually sharp and high in tone, but sirens, nonetheless.

The police. Thank God.

And yet, louder than the sirens—someone sobbing. Against my better judgement, I propped the shotgun against the wall, and opened the door.

Maddy leaned against the frame, her tears quicksilver in the moonlight. She clutched a book in her arms, an archaic brown tome.

She did not ask to come in. Merely cried, as if internally broken.

"For God's sake, Maddy." I spoke softly. "What do you want?"

"What do you love most?" she asked, wiping tears from beneath her glasses.

"It used to be you, up until a week ago," I replied. "Come in if you'd like, but you should know the cops will be here any minute."

"No, they won't."

"Don't you hear the sirens?"

"Those aren't sirens." She stepped into the house, into the darkness.

I closed the door behind us.

As the sirens grew close, I realized she was right. They weren't sirens, but an infernal *screeching*.

Thunder rippled in the distance, deep and looming, and the house shook. Windows rattled in their panes. I clutched the mantel's ledge to steady myself.

Maddy sat on the floor, opening the book.

She repeated assertively, "What's the thing you love most, Tim?"

"I don't know." My eyes roved the walls, the ceiling, waiting for everything to splinter and crack and explode. Something ripped the moonlit sky, loud as a fighter jet passing overhead. We gritted our teeth, palming our ears against that *shriek* which threatened to pierce our eardrums.

"Just fucking tell me!" Maddy shouted.

"I don't know! What the hell is happening?!" I shouted back.

The house trembled in its very foundations.

My empty bottle of scotch rolled off the mantle. *Shattered.* Cups and dishes in the kitchen fell out of the cupboards, cracking upon the linoleum. Furniture toppled. My duffel bag shifted and slid. I fell sideways, bruising my knee on the hardwood.

It's happening. The Curse.

A shiver scrabbled up my spine, fastidious as a spider. Gooseflesh prickled my arms and neck. Maddy shouted something—I couldn't make out what.

Everything rattling, cracking, splintering.

Then, something grabbed the outside walls and *squeezed.* Plaster crackled and wood beams snapped easily, as if Ravencourt House were composed of gingerbread.

The windows exploded inward, splaying glass upon the floor.

"We've got to get out!" Maddy scooped up her book and ran out the door. I followed at her heels, only to halt on the porch, spin around, and head back inside.

"Tim!" Maddy screamed.

The duffel bag and shotgun had slid across the room. I unzipped the bag, snatched out my manuscript, then ran out into the night. I didn't give a rip about the shotgun.

We sprinted down the moonlit drive, then piled into my truck. Only when I started the engine did I look up to see what was holding, grasping, clutching Ravencourt House.

An enormous grey claw, slimy with liquefying flesh, patched with sable fur, reached out of the starry sky and fastened Ravencourt within its grip.

Four fingers; long, bony, and tombstone grey. Sharp ebony nails glimmered in the moonlight, digging furrows into the earth.

I gawked out the windshield, at the ancient claw, and the thick slimy arm that snaked up, up, up, into the night and disappeared in the stratosphere.

I trembled behind the wheel, wondering, *what the hell is that arm attached to?*

"Jesus Christ, this is no time to meditate." Maddy yanked the hair on my head. "Put the truck in reverse and let's *go!*"

Gravel flew up as we backed out onto the road. I looked once more at the house, craning my neck to gaze past Maddy.

The claw rattled the house violently, like a dog jerking its head back and forth over a stuffed toy. There arose a terrible din and clatter and suddenly the house was high, high above the world. Dirt and dead leaves and glass and wood planks littered down from the sky like rain.

Then, silence.

Maddy and I gawked at the huge dark square on the ground where Ravencourt House had stood over two centuries.

The land looked so *big* without the House on it.

A cloudbank must've passed over the moon, as all light was suddenly eclipsed.

The road was full of shadow, except the shadow had a shape.

It was square, much like—

"The house!" Maddy shrieked, digging nails into my leg.

I stomped the gas, and for one terrifying moment, all the tires did was spin, spitting up gravel and dust and backroad talcum. But the treads caught, and we zipped down the road at seventy miles per hour, out from beneath the shadow.

In the rearview mirror, amidst the cloudy sky, I watched the claw unwrap its elongated fingers from around the house. The house dropped, smashing onto the road like a detonating bomb. Glass, nails, wood, plaster, and brick exploded everywhere.

Dust plumed outward in a radius of destruction.

As we sped down the road, I thought, *what would we look like now if we had stayed back there, beneath the shadow?*

I thought of cookie dough flattened by a rolling pin, the dough red and full of guts.

Maddy hugged Elizabeth Ravencourt's spell book to her chest. We sped down the road, the decimated house fading into the distance.

Behind us, the hideous claw multiplied into *four*, each belonging to an enormous leg or arm, and high above them—leathery pterodactyl wings that soared over the fields.

I could not see the creature's face, for which I was grateful. It flew far and away, an enormous hungry shadow blotting the horizon.

Then, with a ravenous *shriek*, it swooped down where the buildings and houses of Sweet Hollow stood in silhouette. In the distance, the screams of a hundred men, women, children—like little siren-shrieks of their own, a nest of babies being devoured by its starving mother.

Immense columns of smoke and dust arose, as if a thousand mummies had awakened, shaking out their ancient wrappings like filthy rugs.

The creature's wings whooshed the air, sending gusts to ripple across fields of wheat and corn. The truck was blown toward the shoulder. I let up on the gas and straightened our course, barely keeping us on the road.

A hot wind blew in from town, circulating through the cab. It carried screams and smelled of smoke, sulphur, and suffering—a draft straight out of Hell. Choking on the fumes, I rolled up the window.

Suddenly, Maddy squeezed my arm.

"Hit the brakes," she said.

I braked hard, and we skidded to a stop.

A woman wandered in the road. We'd nearly hit her, for her hands touched the truck's hood, as if to lean upon it.

"Oh, dear God, no ..." Maddy groaned, staring out her passenger window at the Sweet Hollow Cemetery. The graves had exploded open, its tenants breaking through frozen soil.

Coffins cracked and catapulted.

Crucifixes crooked and cockeyed.

Tombstones toppled.

The dead walked stiltedly about on broken legs. Some of them so long deceased, no flesh lingered upon their bones. Craniums shone in the moonlight. Jaws opened and closed, their tongueless mouths speaking words of dust.

"Dear God," Maddy repeated in a state of shock, but I paid no attention. My stare fixed upon the woman's face in the headlights. I recognized her. How could I not?

Mother shambled toward my window.

Brown eyes that used to gaze upon me lovingly, were now glassy, dark, and empty, like broken windows in an abandoned house.

Hands, soft and wrinkled (as a child, they used to tuck me into bed)—now grotesque and green. Ivory bone poked out of decayed flesh. Her breath was so cold, it frosted the window.

"Mother?" I whispered. I felt frozen with fright, as if an icy hand clutched my heart.

Its lipless mouth pressed against the glass, and in a voice of ragged earth and worms, it rasped, "A kiss for mommy? A kiss goodnight?"

Tears slid down my cheeks, into my open mouth.

"It isn't your mother, Tim," Maddy turned my head, so she could look into my eyes. I inhaled sharply, delivered only slightly from my terror. "Put your hands on the wheel, your foot on the gas, and let's keep going."

I knew Maddy was right. This desiccated *thing* wasn't my mother—I'd buried her in the Solemn Groves Cemetery back in Saint Paul.

Her rotting hands smeared the window with dirt as I stepped lightly on the gas and slid past her.

Rotting cadavers shambled onto the road, but I weaved skillfully around them.

Maddy placed an arm around my shoulders, stroked the back of my head.

"It's all right, Tim," she soothed. "Shh."

I was groaning yet hadn't realized it.

"The curse creates illusions," Maddy whispered, attempting comfort. "Horrible hallucinations that *everyone* can see. But the dead are Elizabeth's own creation. Soulless zombies. Not the people who'd once lived and breathed."

I glanced at the terrible flying thing darting and shrieking about the horizon, wondering if *that* were a hallucination too. Yet the panicked screams blowing on the wind, carried easy as smoke, were undoubtedly *real*.

"People are dying," I said.

"Yes." Maddy gazed sadly ahead. "Everyone is."

We didn't speak, although the din of terrified screams swallowed all potential silence. Then, Maddy said, "Turn left."

I turned onto Hodgson Street, which led us into town. The earth trembled beneath us. A horizon of smoke and desecration zoomed into view.

We arrived at the end of Main Street, its smooth black ribbon now frayed and ragged. Children hunkered beside the ruins of buildings, their Halloween makeup soiled with tears. Parents scrambled in circles, screaming their children's names. Dead bodies lay scattered upon the sidewalks in pools of blood, their faces white and scarred as the moon. A man lay half out of the shattered show window of Leo's Ice Cream parlor, the shards within the frame wet with blood.

Black scorches marred several buildings while others had burnt down entirely. A fire had spread rapidly yet had since died down to embers and charcoal.

Corpses littered the broken asphalt, most of them unrecognizable— save for the little boy and girl who'd once dragged a wagon loaded with decorations up to my door. They lay in the road, a deranged Romeo and Juliet holding each other in death.

The creature soared above, encircling its carrion. Then, in a sudden rush, it dived down into the street, crushing bodies beneath its enormous black talons.

Its ragged sides brushed against dilapidated buildings. The multi-veined wings flapped smoke and ash against my windshield, until they settled against its sides.

Voices, belonging to those few survivors, cried out somewhere.

From out behind a pile of rubble, Sheriff Bradly ran into the street. He gritted his large teeth, firing his service pistol at the monster.

The shots embedded into its black feathery chest—to no effect. The creature bent down and snatched up Bradley's flailing body with its massive beak, tossed him up into the air like a ragdoll, then swallowed him in one meaty *gulp*.

Bradley's screams abruptly ceased.

The creature rustled its naked ebony wings, glaring through the windshield of the truck—directly at *me*.

It possessed a face thick with hatred, each rugged line and wrinkle seemingly carved with Lucifer's chisel. Black saucer eyes—hungry staring voids that shimmered in the night.

Yet beneath its monstrous veneer, like a silhouette beneath a sheet—the face of none other than Elizabeth Ravencourt.

I don't know *how* I knew it was her, but I did, beyond any shadow of doubt. Beneath that blood-stained beak, and that hideous molten face, lingered the soul of the last American witch.

The Witch of the Ravencourt Curse.

She flapped her wings once more, sending up black smoke, wafting the odors of sulfur and death.

Then she waited.

Waited for me to make a move, for I was the ignorant fool who'd conjured her wrath.

"I'm going to ask one last time," Maddy placed her hand over my heart, as if longing to reach inside and touch it. "What is the thing you love the most in this world, Tim? If you don't tell me now, we'll both die."

I recalled the last night Maddy and I had spent together. Inside the house, beside the fire, over glasses of wine. How she'd said the curse could be banished with incantation, sacrifice, and with the blood of Ravencourt lineage.

"My book." My tongue clicked dryly in my mouth. I looked into her blue eyes and told her. "The one I've just written, the one that will give me my career back. That's the thing I love most, selfish as it may be."

Maddy followed my gaze to the floor of the truck. The manuscript pages had spilled out of the folder. She swept them up into her arms along with her spell book.

"Follow me," she spoke quietly, climbing out of the truck.

Knowing this was crazy, practically suicide, I followed her into the road. Simply driving away, at this point, wasn't an option. We approached the great witch—a towering cathedral of wings, claws, wrinkled flesh, and black eyes. Beneath the beak, a wide grin exposing dagger-sharp teeth, slick with blood.

And she laughed—a throaty, hell-clogged cackling.

I trembled staring up at her, hemmed in by ash and smoke, broken dreams, and demolished lives.

Before her Great-Great Grandmother, Maddy lay my manuscript upon the cracked asphalt. Then she opened wide the grimoire and read aloud the incantation:

"*His, venefica, magus, sanguiem meum, qui sanguis uss est, do, et hanc gemmem animae stulti, ut horrorem finiat. Miserer nobis.*

"*Miserere!*"

The Witch's black eyes narrowed. Wrinkles bunched. Veins in her face bulged. She cocked her head, observing us, and I felt like an insect caught between slides of glass beneath a microscope.

"*Miserere!*" Maddy repeated, then flipped to the back of the book, where she'd kept a razor blade between the pages.

"Here," she whispered, handing me the tome, and I felt the weight of ancient, desiccated flesh—the book, I realized, was bound in human skin.

Maddy placed the razor against the inside of her forearm and drew it down.

A line of blood followed the razor, trickling onto the manuscript. *Drip-drip-drip-drip.*

The Witch's salacious grin stretched impossibly wide. Her eyes closed, and her head lifted, basking in the scent of Maddy's blood.

A blood that was her own.

"*Sangues meus est sanguis uss,*" Maddy did not whisper now, but shouted, screaming the chant as her blood splashed across the pages, obscuring my words in red blotches.

The Witch-creature shuddered with pleasure, her talons curling, wings quivering. I shivered with disgust.

Walking over to a portion of remaining sidewalk, Maddy fetched a burning piece of lumber out from the smoldering ruins.

The lumber flamed like a torch, and Maddy carried it forthright.

She gazed at me with an apologetic expression yet did not pause in her work.

I kept silent, knowing I'd be a fool to utter one word of protest. Sweet Hollow was destroyed, its lives stolen, snatched, swallowed by the claws of the Witch.

And it was because of *me*.

Maddy touched the livid flames to my manuscript, and the fire and the blood conquered every page, paragraph, sentence, and word. The pages shriveled and shrunk and became ash. And when I gazed up from the pathetic heap, there remained only a sky of smoke and stars.

The Witch was gone.

Maddy and I held each other in the wasteland. There wasn't anything *sweet* about this town anymore, for it'd all become a black, smoking *hollow*.

Ashen ruins. Charcoaled flesh.

Even the brilliant stars seemed smudged by the desecration.

Main Street, the heart of Sweet Hollow, was leveled. Squinting and coughing through the smoke, Maddy and I glimpsed the rise and fall of the hills beyond.

My stomach churned with guilt and sorrow. I bent over, vomiting in the street.

"Let's go." Maddy grabbed my hand gently, leading me toward the truck.

We drove down what remained of Main Street—a long, dislocated spine.

Pre-dawn light tinged the sky indigo. We drove into the hills. Passing the Sweet Hollow Cemetery, the dead now stood perfectly still, like grotesque statues, only to crumble and fall back into their graves.

Mother stood beside the road. She did not speak nor gesture, merely stood there growing thinner, fainter, and like a cloud into mist, was gone.

We arrived at the Ravencourt House, a pile of wood and stone and glass. I swerved down into the ditch, going around it.

I parked in my driveway, beneath the shade of maple trees. My hands trembled, thinking about the children with their melted faces, and the countless lives lost.

Dead because of my obtuseness, my stubborn refusal to believe. Up until that point, I'd thought Sheriff Bradley and his ilk were idiots. Now, I realized, they were just people. People attempting to protect themselves and their families.

"It's over." Maddy placed her hands in mine.

"It doesn't feel over," I said.

"Watch," she nodded toward my barren property.

As the sun broke over the land, blooming the deepest oranges, crimsons, and violets, we watched the Ravencourt House reassemble itself.

Flying like a flock of bizarre birds, every wood plank, every fragment of plaster, every rouge brick, every sliver of glass glimmered and shadowed through the air, only to fall into place.

The House stood once more

"I can't believe it." I sat there, stunned.

"Not surprising, coming from you," Maddy laughed, her smile brighter than the dawning sun. "Don't you see, Tim? We did it! We banished the curse."

We leapt out of the truck and beheld the gothic glory of Ravencourt House.

Its every gingerbread trim, its every shingle, its every door and window fixed into place.

Better than new.

I laughed out of sheer amazement, saying, "If the House can reassemble, then shouldn't—"

I grabbed Maddy's hand and we ran into the road.

The smoldering ruins of the distant town straightened itself, rebuilding wall after wall, roof after roof, chimney after chimney, until we could hear cars and trucks driving out of the neighborhoods and into town.

Adults heading to work.

Children preparing for school.

Life in Sweet Hollow returned as if the curse had never existed, as if the witch named Elizabeth Ravencourt hadn't descended upon the earth with savage claws and bloody teeth.

The sky was an October field, every whisper of cloud an auburn leaf on the wind.

The sun blossomed into a vast pumpkin, fit for picking.

A lone car sped up the gravel road, pluming dust behind it. It skidded to a halt beside us.

"Oh, thank sweet Jesus!" Walt Kaplan leaned out the driver's side window, his face wrenched with worry. "You all right, Tim? Why didn't you answer my calls? I called you like fifty times!"

"Sorry, Walt," I muttered my reply. "I've been, uhm … kinda occupied."

Maddy and I exchanged a glance. Her lips lifted into a smile, and the next thing I knew we were bent over, hands-our-knees, laughing with nervous relief.

Walt frowned quizzically, leaning back into his seat.

"If this is a joke, kids, it isn't funny. I was worried sick."

"I'm sorry, man," I chuckled, regaining composure. "We're just exhausted, that's all."

"I tried calling the police," Walt sighed, "but couldn't get through. Thought it was my phone, at first. So I stopped at a gas station, used theirs, and same thing. Not even a dial tone. Weirdest fucking thing."

"Trust me, Walt. We've seen a lot of weird fucking things tonight."

"You guys are covered in dirt and sweat." Walt examined us like a disapproving parent. "Sure everything is okay?"

"We're sure," Maddy smiled, nodding. "Thanks for trying to help, but we're fine now."

I wrapped my arms around Maddy's waist, felt her warmth, and in the chill morning of All Soul's Day, I said, "*Everything* is fine now."

I leaned in.

And we kissed.

ON HALLOWEEN ~ ONE YEAR LATER

It took half a year of painstaking effort to rewrite *Beneath the Jack O' Lantern Sky*. I think, in the end, it turned out a better manuscript than the one Maddy torched last Halloween.

The book wasn't published by Putnam, but by a small press more suited to my style. And it not only topped the New York Times' Best Seller list (rare for a short story collection)—it also won a Stoker Award, which is a bit like the Pulitzer Prize for horror writers.

The publisher is happy.

Walt Kaplan is happy.

My readers are happy.

Most importantly, my wife and I are *very* happy.

We've just returned from our wedding at Sweet Hollow Park, facing an orange sunset on Ouspenskaya Lake. Walt said he'd smiled so much his jaw hurt. The wedding pictures, I'm sure, will reveal a proud 'best man'.

All the town's people were present.

Every single one.

Mayor Edmundson and the Town Council. Sheriff Bradley and the entire S.H. Police Department. The librarian, the shopkeepers, the children, their parents and grandparents and distant relatives—everyone.

Maddy's side of the family all attended, save for her parents, who have been dead a long time. As have mine.

Naturally, I wish my mother were still alive, as she would've been happiest for me. But I'm glad I have Walt, whom she loved almost as much as me. I'd mentioned as much in my toast that evening.

Now, carrying Maddy over the threshold, careful not to let her dress catch on the rough frame, I set her down and we kiss.

"You're very dashing, Mr. Ravencourt," Maddy winks, placing a finger beneath my tie, loosening it. "Why not accompany me upstairs, help me out of this dress?"

"Be right up," I reply. "Just one thing I have to do first."

"Don't make me wait." She bites down on her lip. "Or I'll get started without you."

Her white dress trails behind her.

I've changed my last name to Ravencourt, instead of Maddy changing hers. I don't know why. Perhaps to better respect Sweet Hollow's strange, yet wholly necessary, traditions.

Fetching a barbeque lighter from the kitchen drawer, I step out on the porch and light our Jack O' Lanterns. Two of them face the leaf-strewn lawn.

Despite the autumn breeze fighting the flames, the candles wax their glow, and the orange hollows beam with triangle eyes and nose and pointed teeth.

The sky and the jack o' lanterns match in hue and tone. I feel immense, as vast as the sky, as if I could do anything, become anyone.

But I know exactly who I am.

I'm Timothy Ravencourt, writer of the strange and macabre, and husband to the most beautiful woman in all Sweet Hollow.

I turn back into the house, shutting the door firmly against the jack o' lantern sky.

Upon hearing Maddy call my name, I do away with my tie, begin unbuttoning my shirt, and bound up the stairs.

STORY NOTES: DREAMS OF
SWEET HOLLOW

In an interview with Time Magazine, Bob Dylan told his baffled reporter, "I don't have anything to say about (my songs). I mean, I just write 'em!"

Sometimes, this is how I feel about my stories. And I wonder, how can that be? Any given tale requires several drafts to complete, hours of time, days' worth of energy, and a Zen-master's penchant for patience—yet the writer of the tale seems to find himself speechless as to what to say about them.

It's somewhat like a dreamer reciting his dream, only to be asked, "Why did you dream something like *that?*"

The answer is, "I didn't *choose* to dream it, my subconscious did."

I suppose, in a way, it's a bit like saying, "The Devil made me do it."

It's interesting to note, too, what Socrates observed about poets in Plato's Apology:

"I am ashamed to tell you the truth, gentlemen, but I must. Almost all the bystanders might have explained the poems better than their authors could. I soon realized that poets do not compose their poems with knowledge, but by some inborn talent and by inspiration, like seers and prophets who also say many fine things without any understanding of what they say."

We're led to conclude, then, that even the great poets of Athens were not wise—they were *inspired.*

The dreamer dreams because they're inspired by the subconscious.

The writer writes for the same reason (plus, perhaps, an urge for an ongoing 'immortality project', but that's for another day).

Our dreams are kaleidoscopic composites of emotions, sensations, identity, and our past. The difference between dreams in one's sleep and dreams on paper? The former merely requires a place to lay down, while the latter requires *craft.*

This is the only sense in which a writer or poet may claim to be wise—in craft only. It's a wisdom of how, as opposed to why. A pragmatic skill, not an understanding of life.

And that's okay.

Perhaps our dreams are merely trying to figure our lives out for us. Whether we dream in our sleep, or on paper, or by staring out the window to woolgather, does not matter.

What matters is we are creatures capable of dreams, and it's this ability which makes life worth living. Remember, dreams are the impetus for all ideas and art. Without them, human beings will cease to exist, leaving the pastures barren for far simpler beasts.

It'll be my attempt to place my dreams before the mirror and examine them for you. I'll tell you where I was when I dreamed them, and, if possible, what I was feeling. Let's see if we can make a little sense out of this book after all, shall we?

We'll begin at the top and descend from there ....

Billy's First Haircut

Of all the residents in Sweet Hollow, Billy Rosenthal is perhaps my favorite.

Some stories seem to galvanize the fingers, the words stabbing down fast as lightning. Other stories require much sitting back and meditating. *Billy's First Haircut* belongs to the former category.

I wrote it in January of 2021. It's one of the final tales I wrote at the 'haunted factory'—my affectionate term for my place of employment from September 2019 to February 2021. The building was old, musty, leaking, and perfect; a shutdown dairy factory located not far from Sweet Hollow, Wisconsin. As a security guard working the graveyard shift, it was my responsibility to ensure the boiler continued running, pipes didn't burst, and no vandals broke in. I performed these duties while writing two books (*Daydreams of the Damned* and *Matters Most Macabre*).

If life was fair, I'd still have the job and I'd have written this entire book on the clock! Alas, I was laid off when a new company purchased the building. Still, my memories of writing *Billy's First Haircut* are joyful. This was truly one of the most fun yarns I've ever spun. The entirety of it came out in a single night (very rarely does that ever happen).

As I place Billy before the mirror, meditating on which lock of hair to clip, it occurs to me that I *am* Billy Rosenthal. His reflection is my own. A great many of us, in particular outsiders and creative types, often feel marginalized and stigmatized growing up.

So, I wrote this story to console my younger self.

And I wrote it for Billy—while Billy might not be mortal, he *does* have feelings.

(*Originally published in Cosmic Horror Monthly, June 2022.*)

Mosquito Summer

I wrote Mosquito Summer on July 2nd of 2020, on my 26th birthday. My fiancé (now wife), daughter, and I were staying a few days at the family cabin. Despite it being our family getaway, I found myself in a melancholy mood. For whatever vain and mysterious reasons, I'm quite susceptible to depression on my birthdays.

While my wife did not appreciate my dour, withdrawn temperament, she understood that I needed to write. As my patient family splashed about in the lake below, I sat outside the cabin, writing what would become *Mosquito Summer*.

Well, I got quite bit up writing this tale.

Can't you tell?

(Originally published in *WEIRDSMITH: Number One*, from Too Much Weird Press, January of 2021, *NZZZZZRRRRRRRRRRRR*).

One More Night with Snow White

As my readers will no doubt notice, I tend to vacillate between cruelty and sentimentality. While *Mosquito Summer* and *If Fish Could Scream* tend to be horrid little tales of the grotesque, I do possess moments of affection.

One More Night with Snow White, though not without nervous tension, is a gentle and charming tale about an old man pining for love. And, in the end, he is rewarded.

A fellow writer-friend of mine, in his mid-70's, lost his wife at the time I'd written the tale. I molded my main character, Duncan, after him—a kind, generous, knowledgeable old man who, I hope, will live happily for many years to come.

I showed my friend this tale, without mentioning I'd had him in mind as the main character. He was delightfully surprised by the tone, as it was remarkably *not nasty*, and quite *sweet*, and he replied, "What's got into you?"

I've truthfully no idea what got into me—save that I care about my friends, and hoped Duncan might be happy.

If Fish Could Scream

After reading bioethicist Peter Singer's marvelous essay, "If Fish Could Scream", I knew that I had to steal the title for a story.

While many animals will shriek or scream upon being stuck with a blade, a fish does not possess this capability. If they *did*, however, I wonder if the fisherman's 'peace' and 'tranquility' out on the waters wouldn't be disturbed? Bad enough they flop about in agony in the boat, what if they informed us of their distress through a high-pitched *shriek*?

But, obviously, a lack of vocal cords will not produce such alarm.

Nor does Lawrence Chaney, our fisherman-reincarnated-into-a-fish, elicit the slightest vocal sign of agony—he experiences it, nonetheless.

And that's the point of this lake-tale, this strange dream of transformation and terror. So, next time I go out in my boat on Lake Ouspenskaya, won't you accompany me?

We'll drink a few beers and catch us some *big ones.*

(Originally published in *Forlorn, The Periodical,* in April 2021)

Night of the Child

Hallowe'en has always been my favorite holiday. As a boy, I relished decorating the house with skeletons, cobwebs, vampire bats, and animatronic ghouls.

And I still do. In this respect, devoted reader, I've not grown up in the slightest—worse still, I'm *proud* of it.

Night of the Child is my ode to the awe and wonder that Hallowe'en produces in the young. Once again, we glimpse my dark sentimentality creeping about the corners of the 'Old Manor' and, without warning, striking the grandfather clock MIDNIGHT.

What could be better than a "perfect pinnacle of gothic ghoulishness", as my prose in *Night* would have it?

To both the young and the old who still marvel at the strange, mysterious, *memento mori* qualities of Hallowe'en, I respectfully tip my hat.

As Ray Bradbury would've said, we are *the autumn people.*

This one is for Ray.

Bells are Ringing at the Transit Station

This was my first attempt at writing a traditional gothic tale. In my honest estimation (I can only hope my readers might agree), I have succeeded. Truly, I think *Bells* is among my finest.

There is plenty of horror in this narrative, yes, but it's mostly a tale of *terror.* All the elements of a great gothic dream are manifested in the prose. Elements handed down from Horace Walpole's *The Castle of Otranto (1764)* to Edgar Allan Poe's *The Fall of the House of Usher (1839)*, to Bram Stoker's *Dracula (1897)*.

The gothic air is easy to inhale, thought it be macabre, musky, and morose. Upon sitting down to pen this dream into a readable narrative, I found myself instinctively incorporating the necessary gothic tropes.

The discovery of a mysterious manuscript.

A crumbling building of death.

A grey, melancholy atmosphere.

While prose written in a 19th-century language isn't necessary for a gothic tale, I had great fun writing it. If I were to write another gothic (and I hope I will), it will likely be composed in the same vein.

I believe in crediting those dreamers who came before, who inspired us to pen our own.

That's why *Bells are Ringing at the Transit Station* is written for Edgar A. Poe—a sensitive and complicated genius whose works shall continue ringing throughout all time to come.

An Obsolete Art

Dear Reader,

Perhaps you've not received a letter in some time. If that's the case (or, even if it isn't) this one is for you.

The impetus for this tale came to me while lying in bed one snowy December night, discussing Christmas cards with my wife. She'd mentioned sending a card to her old high school teacher yet wasn't sure if this person lived at the same address, or even if they were still alive.

I thought, what if they were indeed located at the same address, yet not alive?

And, being dead, wouldn't it be chilling if they wrote *back?*

This was the idea, but the *story* arrived through the simple act of sitting down and writing it. I combined the premise with two all-important elements: narrative and theme.

Regarding narrative—as a person who is horrified by industrial slaughterhouses, I thought it'd be fascinating to write a tale from the perspective of a woman working inside of one.

Regarding theme—this tale is about *not letting things go*. It's about wanton desire and desperation in the human spirit. It's about wish fantasy. These things can save us, or they can vastly disappoint us—or worse. Sometimes, as Michelle learns in this tale, it's better to *let the dead be dead.*

Such a maxim excludes letter-writing, however. An obsolete art it ought not be.

Sincerely,

Tylor James.

PS: I'd gladly provide you my home address so that you might write back. Unfortunately, I do not entirely trust the public with such information. Send me an email however, and perhaps we can become pen pals.

The Haunted House Mystery Bank

I'm a seller of used books by day, a writer by night/early mornings. Because my day job exposes me to an endless deluge of printed materials, it's often I'll strike up an idea based upon a book title, a nostalgic magazine, a half-filled journal, forgotten scribbled notes, Polaroids stuck within pages, etc. The idea for *Haunted House Mystery* arrived in the form of a box.

Inside the box—a hundred 60's-era Archie comics, ripped, jaundiced, and falling apart.

The comics were not sellable. I tossed them into the recycling.

This would've been the end of the story, and, indeed, *Haunted House Mystery* wouldn't have been written … if I hadn't glimpsed it.

A *Haunted House Mystery Bank* advertisement on the back cover of one of the comics. Immediately, I fetched it from the bin, reveling in the idea of a unique, creepy bank which 'monster kids' must've been thrilled by in the 60's.

I still have the article in my possession—a tattered advertisement sealed in a zip-lock.

This is one of the few tales I've written that's suitable for young readers. Perhaps, if you have children of your own, you'll consider reading this tale aloud to them? Or perhaps you'll think the author unbalanced to suggest it.

I'm grateful to have dreamed up this story, and even more grateful for that charming advertisement on the back of a disintegrating comic book.

So, just put a coin before the door.

And wait for the *Horror Hand* ....

Old Dance Hall

I have a friend obsessed with hosting bonfires. On a cool spring day around the fire, the grass damp with melted snow, he pointed beyond the flames to a building at the back of his parent's property.

"It used to be an old dance hall," he'd said.

It was a dark and looming structure, paint-peeled, faded gray, crumbling. I hadn't let it out of my sight from the moment I arrived.

I went around the building, taking pictures with my phone. A low awning half-obscured the entrance, upon which I'd nearly smacked my head.

I opened wide the front door.

"Weird," my friend muttered. "It's supposed to be locked."

The place was a disaster. Heaps of papers. Suitcases half-emptied on the floor, spilling out old clothing, cheap jewelry, and women's shoes. Children's grimy, plastic toys from a decade ago.

To the left of the front door, a staircase descended into a basement.

The stairs had fallen apart halfway down, leaving one to leap over the pile of wood and nails if they chose to explore the basement (how they'd ever get back *out*, I don't know).

I did not explore the basement.

I did, however, appreciate at old sign above the stairs:

"BEER, SODA, & SNACKS!" with an arrow pointing *down*.

I explored the place for the next twenty minutes, rifling through piles of junk. I don't know why, save that I have an appreciation for mystery and decay.

"I'm going to write a story about this place," I told my friend.

"Do it," he said.

So, I did it.

(Originally published in *WEIRDSMITH: Number One*, from Too Much Weird Press, January of 2021).

Out Beneath the Jack O' Lantern Sky

This is a nasty, grisly little tale.

I almost feel guilty for writing it.

Almost.

The gory ending, I feel, saves it from being utterly 'bad taste', as it is about romantic love, one of the finer human emotions.

I wrote it on a Halloween evening at the old factory. The sun melted into the final night of October, its sheer beauty inspiring me to ugliness.

I typed angrily, madly, click-clacking on a 1940's mechanical typewriter. After writing half of it, I decided it was worth continuing, and, consequently, transformed it into the tale you've just read.

Its themes are of love, anger, and revenge. All three of which are pure to the human heart—for better or worse.

I should mention here the influence of midwestern landscape, which I utilized in the description of the setting. In rural Wisconsin, there are a great many rolling hills and fields of grass and corn. It looks beautiful in moonlight—an ivory sea with deer swimming in it.

I grew up in this land. It's in my blood.

Like almost anybody, I possess a deep fondness for sunrises and sunsets. This appreciation for aesthetic colors my tale, along with many others in this collection.

Note: I was paid $5 dollars for this story, which is almost the lowest I've been paid for my writing.

Almost.

(Originally published in *Madame Grey's Vault of Gore*, from Hellbound Books, Inc. in Fall of 2021).

Walls of Shame

Walls of Shame is the most personal of the bunch. In fact, I'm tempted to skip this story note altogether. But since I've brought you this far, I might as well send you right over the cliff with me.

My good Mother, I should make clear, isn't the crazy, drug-addled, religious fundamentalist featured in this tale. She's thankfully the opposite. However, when I was fourteen years old, she did discover my collection of naked lady pictures. Confused, angry, perhaps disgusted, she stapled them to the walls of my bedroom. Upon returning from school, I believe I was just as shocked as Raymond was in the tale.

The worst of it: an incredible sense of shame, the chore of writing a seven-page essay on why and how I came to possess such vulgar pictures, and a grounding for one week.

This moment in my young life, due to its sheer awkwardness and guilt, burned itself into my mind as an indelible memory.

Indelible memories, of course, are grist for stories. I thought to myself, what if I my shame turned inward and swallowed me? Turned me into something *other* than human?

From that point on, *Walls of Shame* transformed into something very, very dark.

Perhaps you, devoted reader, have felt the walls close in. If so, you may find this tale consoling.

After all, how rarely is anyone truly ever *alone* in their feelings?

The Monster in H. Philip's Grocery

The Monster is one of the last stories I penned for this collection, and it is a companion piece to *An Obsolete Art*. In this tale, we are shown an expanded portrait of Bobby Aveeno. He is a bit like the invisible man in appearance, although far more grotesque beneath the bandages than Griffin, the character in H.G. Wells' 1897 science-fiction novel.

Our main character, Rowen, is a curious youngster.

Curious, even virtuous—yet very foolish.

Edgar A. Poe wrote of the 'Imp of the Perverse', a demoniacal force within every human soul which encourages us to do bad for the *sake of doing bad*. To procrastinate and eternally put off something important, or to meditate a plunge over a high bridge into icy waters, or, perhaps, to devour an entire carton of Ben & Jerry's Ice Cream, despite its contrariness to our health.

Rowen is conquered by the Imp of the Perverse when he enters the old Manor, still more when he reaches for the wine bottle abandoned upon the table. He tells himself he ought to go home yet cannot help disobeying himself. Thus, curiosity and indulgence intermix with a deadly result.

The Monster isn't a morality tale, so much as an observational one commenting on the contrary forces within all of us. Sometimes those forces win over us. Sometimes they do not; if our soul is strong, and if our wisdom and will be ironclad.

Poor Rowen, so young and naive—hopeless from the start!

In the Town of Sweet Hollow (A Novelette)

I have little to say about this novelette for the simple fact that I did not write it. It was composed by Tim Ravencourt, a neighbor of mine.

Tim Wallace isn't his real name, of course—but he *is* a celebrated writer of horror novels (a Bram Stoker Award winner, in fact) and was exceedingly gracious in allowing me to include his novelette in my collection.

Tim tells me two things: First, that he'd come up with the title *Beneath the Jack O' Lantern Sky* many years before I did. Seeing as one can't copyright a title, Tim will simply have to live with my using it. Second, this tale is based upon true events which occurred in Sweet Hollow many years ago. Although I trust Tim's integrity, and have never known him to tell a lie, this is a claim I can neither confirm nor deny. Note: I've only been a resident here for a short while, and a seasonal residence, at that.

These things are beside the point.

The point is: Tim is one hell of a neighbor, a fine writer, and a good man. It's a pleasure to know him (and his darling wife) and an honor to include this tale which further expands the Sweet Hollow lore.

Lastly, I'd like to thank you for sticking it through to the end.

I hope you've found these tales to be stimulating, perhaps even frightening.

Until next time, I'll be here, hammering out the pages for your reading pleasure.

Thank you for dreaming with me.

Best,
Tylor James,
in his basement office, at sunset, home in Sweet Hollow.

ABOUT THE AUTHOR

TYLOR JAMES lives with his beloved wife and daughter in Sweet Hollow, Wisconsin. He's a writer of the strange and macabre, as well as a member of the Horror Writers Association (HWA).

A dreamer of dark things from an early age, he grew up in a century-old farmhouse and has always possessed an intrigue with horror tales. Each day he keeps his head up and heart open in search of new ideas—like a ravenous monster, he is hungry for them.

When not writing, you may find him reading a good book, stargazing, drinking copious amounts of coffee, and taking midnight strolls past the graveyard (however, he never whistles).

He is twenty-eight years old.

Please Visit: tylorjames.com